HID

We lofted in ha̶̶̶̶̶̶̶̶̶̶̶̶̶̶̶̶̶̶̶̶̶̶very of the humans came. We told each other that our lower mass would bring us to loot faster than vessels with full crew and armaments. We were in the fore-front, ahead of other Kzin ships our size, avoiding notice of the battleships, when Gutfoot's Horde plunged into Sol System.

It was great fun. The fusion reaction motors used by humans leave a hot ionized wake, a line that shouts in X-rays. We found such a line, aimed for the con-verging point of it, popped up next to a ship, and shot off the drive module. We took four cringing humans— the first we'd seen. Took what else we wanted most, and went off to do it again.

It worked once.

Then moving at a few hundred klicks per second, the ship ran through a stream of pebbles. Humans have been defending their turf with all manner of reaction motor. This was an electromagnetic accel-erator, part of the asteroid mining concern. The humans sprayed us with their slag. The ship was shredded. My companions fought the invaders and died. I hid, but in a pressure suit I was too bulky.

They found me. They found our human prizes, too, battered but safe in the shielded room we use for hiding. For sparing their lives I may have been given better treatment.

For a time they kept me in a small dome, in freefall. Later, here on a little moon of a gas giant planet. But they didn't know what I was!

I can read minds. . . .

— from "Choosing Names" by Larry Niven

CREATED BY
LARRY NIVEN
CHOOSING NAMES
MAN-KZIN WARS VIII

BAEN

CHOOSING NAMES: MAN-KZIN WARS VIII

Copyright © 1998 by Larry Niven

A Baen Books Original

Baen Publishing Enterprises
P.O. Box 1403
Riverdale, NY 10471

ISBN: 0-671-87888-3

Cover art by Stephen Hickman

First printing, September 1998

Distributed by Simon & Schuster
1230 Avenue of the Americas
New York, NY 10020

Printed in the United States of America

CONTENTS

CONTENTS

CHOOSING NAMES

•

Larry Niven

The light in this room was redder than Sol's, more like the light of his own world, or of the Kzin homeworld which he had never seen. Creditor's Telepath found it friendly. The room's other occupant was behind a wall of armor glass. He sat in darkness. The kzin could make out his posture a little, but not the set of his face. It didn't matter.

The kzin said, "I can read minds."

The previous dose of Sthondat gland extract was wearing off. Creditor's Telepath would retain traces of his peculiar talent for another few hours, no more. He could taste a bit of the other's thoughts. His interrogator was wary; distrustful.

Creditor's Telepath asked, "Do you see the implications? I have been among your enemies. I know their thoughts, their plans, hopes, fears, goals."

"That could be very valuable."

"My price is high. I want a name."

He sensed his interrogator's amusement. Rage rose in him; he quelled it. He was skilled at that. "Our lower ranks are named for what we do," he said, "but any

3

may aspire to gain a name, a rank. Our lowest are named for what we are. Cowards, mutants, cripples, or telepaths. I am Creditor's Telepath. I would be the first in living memory to have a name."

The other shifted his weight behind the protective glass. He had seen what an addiction could do to his kind. This kzin wasn't just scrawny and undersized, he was warped. Creditor's Telepath made him uneasy.

He asked, "Who have you been among? Did they know anything worth knowing? Do you?"

"You shall judge," Telepath said. "Our ship was *Creditor*, with a crew of eleven and space for sixteen, mountings for two plasma cannon but only one mounted. We lofted in haste when the news came. We told each other that our lower mass would bring us to loot faster than vessels with full crew and armaments. We were in the forefront, ahead of other ships our size, avoiding notice of the battleships, when Gutfoot's Horde plunged into Sol System.

"It was great fun. The fusion reaction motors used by humans leave a hot ionized wake, a line that shouts in X-rays. We found such a line, aimed for the converging point of it, popped up next to a ship, and shot off the drive module. We invaded the shell, took four cringing humans—the first we'd seen, much smaller than we'd supposed from the messages alone. Took what else we wanted most, marked the shell as our own property, and went off to do it again.

"It worked once.

"Then, moving at a few hundred klicks per second, *Creditor* ran through a stream of pebbles. Humans have been defending their turf with all manner of reaction motor. This was an electromagnetic accelerator, part of an asteroid mining concern. Humans take the metal and use the slag for reaction mass, and they sprayed us with that. *Creditor* was shredded. My companions fought the invaders and died. I hid, but in a pressure suit I was too bulky.

"They found me with our human prizes, all battered but safe in the shielded room we use for hiding and for a pantry. For sparing their lives I may have been given better treatment.

"For a time they kept me in a small dome, in free-fall. Later, here on a little moon of a gas giant planet. But they didn't know what I was!"

This burst forth in a shout, for the surprise had never left Creditor's Telepath. He sensed his listener's startlement. "I felt their fear. At first I didn't understand it. I was the last of my crew, and the first kzin they had ever seen. There were no other kzinti about. In this system-wide series of battles there have been other captive Heroes, but my own captors saw us only on screens. They did not see that I am stunted. I mass three or four times what they do, though I'm half the mass of a Hero.

"They did not understand my addiction, either. They did see that I was sick and growing sicker. They blamed it on my smashed ribs and a dietary imbalance. It concerned them. Humans come near being herd animals, and my pain distressed them. They tried to do something about it.

"Their doctor machines adjust for their own biochemical imbalances. They fiddled and adjusted until I was getting nourishment to keep me healthy, and if I never quite recovered they were sure they hadn't quite got it right.

"Though some nourishment reached me through tubes and some as food, I was still starving! They offered no live prey. I ate worse than I had aboard *Creditor*! But every telepath is addicted to Sthondat lymph, and my stock is lost. Of course I was sick.

"Without periodic injections I would have trouble reading even another kzin. I picked up almost nothing from the dozen humans who were my guards and doctors. But that little made all the difference. I survived because I could feel their fear. They perceived me as a return of terror and Old Night into what had been their paradise. I was a looming nightmare of fangs and claws." Again he felt his interrogator's amusement. He shouted, "I had their respect!"

More calmly, then, "Before they brought in more prisoners, something else was happening to me. One like myself loses his sense of self very easily. Can you understand this? The Keepers do not inject us until we are old enough to breed. We must not breed, but we must develop a sense of who we are, while we can, before the flow of others' thoughts us can drown us. Truly, for our own defense, telepaths should always have had names!"

His listener shrugged. He didn't care.

That galled Telepath. He said, "I have told you nothing yet that can help you. Will you give me a name?"

"Certainly."

So easy? But within his murky thoughts he seemed to mean it. Telepath said, "Well, then. Locked within my mind, somewhat protected from the physical horror of withdrawal, I came to know myself. To know that there is a self in here." The kzin thumped his ribs above the liver. It seemed his listener understood.

"The next attack on Sol System was by another bandit group on the Patriarchy's borders. I think Pareet's Pride learned nothing from Gutfoot's Horde, if any of us escaped to tell tales at all. Pareet's fleet plunged into Sol System just as we did. Like us they found industrial lasers and flying slag where their telepaths, and ours, had found slothful minds at peace with each other and themselves. To the moon came four Heroes, variously injured.

"Understand, to be captured and imprisoned alive

was the earmark of these four. I call them Heroes, but they were not. Neither were they telepaths nor users of Sthondat lymph. They outmassed me by nearly double.

"I was not to mingle with them. Our human captors feared we would share secrets. A double wall of iron bars set an eight-meter gap between us. We must gesticulate and shout at each other, so that our words and posture-language may be recorded against a time when our speech will be known.

"Of course I shouted greeting. For a quarter-year I was closed within my mind, knowing myself, doubting the reality of anything else. Now kzinti had come, but I couldn't penetrate their skulls! I shouted, and they didn't answer.

"One rarely moved and never spoke. The human doctors took better care of him than his companions did. In the end he died. One had lost most of his left leg, and he didn't move much even in the low gravity. One, big and burly and belligerent, had no ears at all. The last battle had flayed him: he was pink skin over half his body. He stood at the bars and glared hate at me. The fourth bore a broad slash of white fur around the eyes. He looked healthy, and he studied me, though our captors would not have noticed.

"A mealtime passed before he spoke. 'I am White Mask, rank of Strategist. I have what you need.'

"They knew me for what I was, of course. I need not ask what he meant. I asked, 'How?'

" 'I only had an instant,' he said. 'I took what was close at hand.' There was nothing in his hands except steel bars, and I wondered where he could have concealed any tool at all. 'We know too little of these prey-who-would-fight. One of your kind could tell us more of them, if he does not die! So, I have what will heal you, and be glad we came in time!'

"In time? Eleven years taking Sthondat extract, then a quarter-year without! I'd be dead without my captors' medical machines. Now my body was beginning to recover from eleven years of abuse!

"But I said only, 'We are observed,' and then, 'We are studied.'

"White Mask turned to the earless one and rasped a command.

"Earless screamed and lashed out. The one-legged one snatched at the dying one's ankle and scuttled backward on all threes while the others fought.

Those two were clumsy, unused to low gravity. They fought more in the air than on the ground, and every blow threw them apart. Earless was massive and powerful, but twice White Mask trapped him in the air and battered him like a slashball. A flurry of blow-and-kick put them between the windows and One Leg, and that was when One Leg threw something to me.

"It was what I expected, a small zip bag, half empty. We had no pouches, of course, so I hid it in my mouth, betting that it was watertight. I waited for feeding time.

"Food arrived in pouches; bowls were not suited for the moon's low gravity. The pouches came on a conveyer line. No human would come near any kzin without a good deal of care. I positioned my dinner pouch to hide the zip bag, looked in and found Sthondat lymph preparation. I swallowed less than a normal dose, then lay down. After so long I didn't know how it might affect me.

"The thoughts of the others flowed into me, intrusive, disorienting. No human was near me, not yet, but I shared my mind with four warriors. They were not of rank to be given names, and they had fallen away from using military designations. They had been humiliated in battle, and here in their presence was a smaller, weaker kzin.

"White Mask had learned strategy as a child, in role-playing games, and won adolescent fights by forethought more than strength. He saw that I was a tool they might use to free themselves, and he tried to force that view on the others. They had worked this out together, the fight to cover a thrown package. But Ear Eater kept forgetting.

"Ear Eater had made his reputation before a victim's father beat him and chewed off his ears. He wanted only to reach me. His claws would tear his lost pride out of my liver. He might have to kill White Mask first. And Stumpy.

"Stumpy outranked the rest. He had been Captain's Voice, but of course he couldn't fight with one leg gone. He thought Ear Eater might be more malleable if he could kill something that fought back. The humans served our meat dead.

"Toolmaster was dying. He had neither speech nor lucid thought. Vacuum had torn his throat and lungs. Toolmaster's mind felt my touch and welcomed the company. He didn't want to die without passing on a lifetime of knowledge . . . nothing of any great use, as it turned out. How a kood hides . . . a creature of a world I've never seen, imported to Shasht, another world I've never seen . . . how it is found, how it wriggles, how it dies, its taste. The ecstasy and terror of mating with a stronger male's kzinrett, the terror and ecstasy of outrunning him. Swimming. Not one in a thousand kzinti can swim, but Toolmaster could. The attack on Sol System. I sensed what was coming and tried to pull loose.

"The gravity generator is gone and everything is falling, falling. A rolling dive across the command room while breathing—air shrieks through a ripped wall. That wonderful instant when my arms and legs close around my pressure suit. Zippers open, legs in first, keep it graceful, arms, torso zip seal, I'm going to live! The helmet is suddenly a cloud of high-velocity splinters. My neck and head are wet and chill with boiling/freezing blood, and it all fades . . . and I was curled in a ball, sweating fear, while the others watched me through the bars.

"To them I was only Telepath.

"Telepaths can't hurt their tormentors without feeling the hurt. Every child knows what it is to win a fight, but we know only through another mind. A telepath will do anything for the Sthondat preparation. Knowing these things about me, they knew everything they cared to, just as if they could read my mind.

"White Mask didn't wonder if I had taken the stuff. A telepath would. When the doctors netted me and took me away bound, White Mask was trying so hard not to watch that his eyes hurt.

"The doctors hooked me to their machine doctor. I smelled the other kzinti's scent: they had been brought here before they reached the pen.

"I felt the doctors' complacent pleasure: I was healthy, strong. They couldn't know how my strength was growing as I recovered from Sthondat addiction. Another thing pleased them: my heart rate showed that the calming chemistry was working, too. Humans dose each other, sometimes, to keep each other docile, and they'd found similar stuff for me. It was the first time I had sensed this. For just that instant I would have killed them all."

"Why didn't you?"

An odd question; or was it? Telepath said, "I suppress such thoughts as a conditioned reflex. Do you think I *offered* to take my first dose of Sthondat lymph? I was born with a knack for reading minds, but others made me Telepath. What if I tried to kill each of them? I would have died over and over."

"Did you get a chance to talk to the other kzinti?"

"Yes. After they examined me, the doctors asked me to do that, to reassure the other prisoners. 'For you, the war is over,' they said, 'tell them that.' Magic words to make an enemy docile. For us, no war is over," Creditor's Telepath said. "I was told that I would not be let into their compound. That suited me well. I did not want to be in reach of Ear Eater.

"So, back in our cages, we shouted at each other. The first thing I shouted was, 'They don't know the Heroes' Tongue!' It was almost true. Humans had learned a dozen words, and I had learned many more.

"I tried to describe how we stood. The pen, the hospital, humans on site, humans visiting. Weapons: I'd seen almost nothing. Air, water, food supplies. The great bubble of greenhouse perched above us on the crater wall. A pinprick would burst it. They saw that and believed me when I told them that humans had put away war—told each other they had outgrown war— before we came.

"I told them what the doctors knew of the war, which was little. They told me of the second attack. They knew nothing of the first; but they had come in haste, with little preparation, because word of Sol system was already flowing at lightspeed toward the Patriarchy. Larger, stronger hordes would follow."

The interrogator asked, "Flowing from what point? Where was the ship when it sent these messages? We need their transit time. Can you show me on a star map?"

"Yes. Now?"

"No, go on."

"Near sunset White Mask told me, 'We need to break free. Have you given any thought to escape?'

"I said, 'Vacuum surrounds us. Stealing pressure suits wouldn't be useful. They've got some of ours, but those went off to be studied. Once free, I can't lead you to spacecraft or a spaceport. They had me in a windowless box when they brought me.'

" 'They must have pressurized vehicles,' White Mask said.

" 'I arrived in one,' I said, 'a box with rockets—'

" 'If we can take a ship and an alien pilot, can you read the pilot's mind? Well enough to fly the ship?'

"I said, 'I've seen their input keyboards. Our fingers aren't small enough.' I saw his thought, *Telepath will try to talk us into sloth and cowardice*. I said, 'Take two of their writing sticks, one in each fist, and you could punch commands on their keys. But you need a pilot, not just some random prey. I'll have to find one for you.'

" 'Await word,' White Mask said.

"That night I listened to them working up an escape plan. They needn't shout at me; I heard their thoughts. A working spacecraft would be ideal, but a damaged or empty ship might still send a message, and a mind-taster could tell them how to do that too. They had to integrate Creditor's Telepath into any plans at all.

"I saw their image of me every time my designation was spoken: *Remember he can't fight. He has to live until we're in free space, and that means we move fast. We must be loose before that evil goop he uses runs out, or else we're here for keeps. Why didn't you snatch a full pouch? Because our own crazy Telepath, shredded when a patch of hull turned to flying shards, let the flack shred his carry-pouch too!* White Mask's memory forced upon me a diminishing radio howl from within a globe of bloody froth, frozen at the surface, lobes of fluid breaking through as blood boiled and froze and expanded.

"In the morning White Mask called to me. 'Talk to them. Give them a reason to move us out of this box!

If we were inside together we could do something. Not you, Telepath, stay where you are. We'll free you after.'

"I had been thinking, too. I said, 'Toolmaster is dying. I can feel him disappearing into dreams, and even the dreams are fading. Tell the humans. They will try to save him.'

"I felt how that startled Stumpy. He shouted, 'They have four. Why strain to keep a damaged fifth?' I felt his fear that they would not keep a damaged fourth, either, on this airless moon where every breath must be made or imported.

"I tried to answer him. 'These are not quite single entities,' I said. 'To be complete they need a community. Isolated humans turn strange. Partly they live for each other. They imagine they feel each other's fear, lust, agony, rage.'

"I was speaking a truth that I could feel and taste, and in that instant I knew I was describing myself. I had to force myself to go on. 'Their instinct will be to care for any injured creature, a weakling human, an animal, even an enemy, even an alien. Tell them that Toolmaster needs his companions about him and they will believe. They will take you all inside. I can't guess what precautions they will take first.'

"White Mask's scream of triumph rang through his head and mine. In his throat it was only a strangled squeak. 'Tell them, then! Get us inside and we will do the rest!' He stooped over Toolmaster. 'Of course he's dying. Is he dead already?'

"I reached for Toolmaster's mind. 'He lives. Let me guide you now and I'll get you in. Huddle around Toolmaster. Ear Eater, imagine how his posture might be more comfortable, and move him. White Mask, talk to him.'

" 'Saying what?'

" 'Does it matter? Speak, listen, speak again.' I could

feel Toolmaster's remote agony lessen: he could just barely sense the attention, and he liked it. 'Now, White Mask, go to the window and shout. Wave your arms at the doctors. Stumpy, you join him. Ear Eater, you stay with Toolmaster. Lift his head a little and slide that flat rock under it for support. Gently! Good.'

Toolmaster felt the motion and was soothed.

Doctors massed on the other side of the window. The merest touch of their minds gave me their thrill of anthropomorphic empathy, as that scarred monster showed such tenderness to his fallen fellow. I called, 'Now, White Mask, shout at me! Your friend is sick and you don't speak human language, so tell me, instead! They don't know I can read minds—'

"He came to the bars and shook them and shouted, 'Did you think I'd forgotten, you fool?' Stumpy had got the idea: he was beside White Mask, shouting poetry we'd all learned from the Keepers as children. And the doctors came running to my window, the window to my pen, and listened as I shouted at them in their language. In the midst of all that I felt Toolmaster die.

"So here I am."

The interrogator nodded behind the glass. "So here you are. But you weren't saying what your companions thought you were saying. I take it you do not advise us to take them out of their cage."

"I do not," Telepath said. "You might bear in mind that they know what I told them of you. They should not run loose to shout their news. They should not even be brought near another telepath."

"Uh-huh."

Telepath said, "I caught something in your mind. A large ship, drive shredded, survivors—?"

"Yes, we believe we found females of your species."

"Dead, though. You found an Admiral's harem."

"If you want to mate—"

"Yes! But you don't have that to offer."

"There will be a next time, a chance to capture female warcats. We can bargain. But as for your name, take that as a gift. Would you like Selig? Or Aycharaych? Or Greenberg?"

Mind-readers out of humans' classic fiction, Telepath saw. "Better some ancient warrior's name," he said, and reached for what surfaced. "Ronreagan. Call me Ronreagan."

"So be it. Ronreagan, it's feeding time, and if you're not hungry, I am." I saw him for an instant as meat, prey, and he sensed that somehow, and it amused him. "But then I want you to tell me every last thing you know about, what did you call—"

"Patriarchy."

"About the Patriarchy. And gravity generators! Can you tell us how to build one of those?"

"When you capture a warcat female, find me an Engineer, too."

TELEPATH'S DANCE

•

Hal Colebatch

Easter Island

Arthur Guthlac, who could never hope to go further into Space than a cheap package holiday to the Moon, envied his sister Selina more than he could easily say.

Apart from the ramrobots and the few, incredibly expensive, colony-ships, journeys beyond the Solar System were rare, and the queue of scientists with projects for Space was always growing. It was a staggering accolade for the gravity-anomaly project to have been selected for funding.

But the museum attendant and his brilliant sister had always been close, and the separation would be long. They stayed together for the last few days before the *Happy Gatherer* left Earth. He produced the model the night before the research ship's departure.

"Take this," Arthur said. "A small gift for you."

It was an ancient sea-going ship, cast in metal, a little more than the length of her hand.

"An antique? You haven't stolen it from the museum, have you?"

She put a laugh in her voice. So did he.

"Antique, but not stolen. I was at a conference at Greenwich Museum in London on automated security for children's galleries, and they gave the delegates mementos. So I hand it on to you, setting out on a voyage, like those old pioneers of the sea. I got one for each of us. They were two sibling-ships, I gather: built to the same design."

"Nice of them to give you two."

"They were throwing them away to make space for dance-history exhibits. I saw hundreds in a trash-compactor . . . Perhaps," he added with seeming carelessness, "they were Military Fantasy cult objects."

"A depiction of a . . . military ship? You wouldn't have such things in a responsible museum, would you?"

"I don't know if there ever were real military ships. There have been Fant stories, of course. If they did exist, they would have been much earlier. This ship is from the iron-age. The steel-age in fact . . . No, it's not that.

"Anyway," he continued in the official voice of an ARM, "it's impossible that pirates or banditos could have had the resources to build a ship like this. It was very big engineering for its time. Only major companies or governments could have built such a thing. Besides, the Military Fantasy was about sociopathic ideas, and this doesn't look to me like the idea, however diseased, of a military ship. Where would the war-men fire their weapons from?

"I guess this was some sort of bulk cargo-carrier. These devices here would have been to pour grain or ore or something into hoppers. This is unless they are meant to be giant 'gun-barrel' weapons."

He gave a cautious, almost furtive smile and inflected his voice with mockery as if to show anyone monitoring the conversation that he was making a tasteless private joke.

He pointed to a model of a small boat attached to the main model. "That shows the scale—about 1,000:1. I'm not sure how they measured length in those days, but the real ship would have been about 35,000 tonnes. Police—the fore-runners of ARM—still carried guns then, but for these things to have been guns,"—he touched one of the three sets of triple tubes on turntables on the foc's'le—"they would have had to fire 'bullets' as big as a man! Also, see how wide the hull is. That's for weight and volume. In any real world, of course, races that made war with each other could never advance to build machines like this."

"That's a—what did they call it?—a lifeboat?"

"Yes. Analogous to the boats on a Spaceship. Used for going ashore when the water was not deep enough for the main ship to go right in. And for emergencies, I suppose. Not very nice to have to get into such a thing when your ship was sinking in a storm, though. I bet the sailors on"—he read the name and date on the model's stand—"the HMS *Nelson* of 1928 would envy your conveniences. The other was called the HMS *Rodney*. Of course civilization was long established then. I don't know what the names mean, but they were built the same. Perhaps a bit like us . . . It might matter, you know."

This last was their private cryptic, indicated by inflection. Satellites could detect key-words. "Quixotic" had gone from the unrestricted vocabulary, but she knew something of his mission that dared not speak its name.

A strange linkage between them. It had been suggested that she had some telepathic potential, but she refused to be tested. Her internal life was complex enough, and if she had any abilities, latent or otherwise, in that direction, she did not want to know it. Without proper shields and controls telepathy might be a fatal gift.

Modern research hinted that telepathy had killed the Neanderthals, making them too vulnerable, too able to empathize with the pain of prey, of competitors, and of one another. Modern telepaths—the very few there were—tended to be abnormal in a number of ways, and often desperately disturbed. She had met a few when the idea of testing her was raised and that had been more than enough.

Arthur and Selina were perhaps lucky to be brother and sister. Otherwise they would undoubtedly at their first meeting have become lovers, in an intense, consuming relationship probably ultimately doomed, for they were consort personalities, not complementary ones. As it was, there was much of closeness and comfort they could give each other which no lover or husband or wife could touch, in a relationship that had no sexual tension or jealousy about it.

A last night of delicate, careful talk. Then it was time for her to board the shuttle to the *Happy Gatherer* in its parking orbit. They had driven to the field together, under the gaze of the preserved monoliths.

Angel's Pencil

"We've lost the wreckage." Steve Weaver turned from the instrument console and stood up. The remnants of the alien enemy had dwindled and vanished on the last screen.

"And no more headaches." Sue Bhang's eyes beseeched him for reassurance.

"No more headaches. Maybe never again."

The nightmare still pressed against them, almost physically, as the *Angel's Pencil* drove on its fixed course behind its vast ramscoop field. Ship and crew had changed much since the colony expedition had left Earth. The console was a small cleared space. A colony ship is crowded with cargo at the best of times, but now what

had been the few free areas of the *Pencil* were piled
with alien machinery, weapons, and instruments, whole
and in pieces. And in the hastily-improvised cold-room
(cold, at least, tended to be easily available in Space)
were the corpses and salvaged fragments of the things
themselves, dissected, fragmented, burned, or—in a few
cases—as nearly whole as explosive decompression in
vacuum had left them. Jim Davis and Helen Boyd were
supervising the filming.

The cadavers were like a declaration of intent: huge,
far bigger than humans, with black razor claws, huge
slabs of muscle, cable-like sinews, bolt-cutter jaws with
tremendous gape and dagger fangs. All the eyes were
gone, but the huge sockets told of binocular and night-
vision, and the cast of the features was still plain.
Convergent evolution had produced something like
enough to the ancient sabre-tooth tiger of Earth for
them to name it *Pseudofelis*. But there was more: bigger
than human brain-cases. An upright stance. Hands. A
hideous contradiction in terms: *Pseudofelis Sapiens*.

The resemblance to that family of creatures which
made up nature's master-work among Earth's predators
was obvious. But that qualifier *Sapiens* overarched
all else. Not only knife-like teeth: some of the bodies
had equipment that included real knives of some
monomolecular-edged metal which cut through steel.
There were fusion-bomb missiles, weapon-lasers . . .
there had been the heat-induction ray. And there was
a drive immeasurably better than the *Angel's Pencil's*
hydrogen-fusion ramjet which was the best that human
brains could build.

The *Angel's Pencil* could flee from the wreckage of
the battle it had miraculously won, but the nightmare
was travelling with it. The humans aboard looked older
now, and more than one had a tendency to wake up
screaming. The doc remained busy.

Like so many of the best nightmares, it made no sense. There was no reason carnivores should not evolve intelligence—the dolphins had, and Steve knew something of the story of the sea-statue the dolphins had found—but intelligence like *this*? The evolution of humanity had surely shown that civilization and technology were interdependent.

Well, they weren't. There were plenty of mysteries among the things they had salvaged—the drive-motor that made no sense, the smashed bodies of a couple of things like giant starfish, weird tools and artifacts, an untranslatable script—but the overall picture was clear: the long search for intelligent extraterrestrial life was over, and humanity was in trouble.

"They won't believe it," Steve said. "I wouldn't believe it . . ." He stared into the humming, moving battery of camera lenses and shook his fist in confused, frustrated fury.

"They'll have to believe it . . ." Jim said. Hundreds of pictures had already been sent back to the Solar system.

"And we," said Helen, "have no business wondering whether they believe it or not. We've made our decision. All we can do for Earth is to keep sending.

"And for ourselves, we had better finish fitting those missiles and pray for time."

Gutting Claw

First Telepath taught me new uses of the Sthondat-drug, gave me new spoor to follow, thoughts to chew bitterly upon. When Telepath talks to Telepath, we are not always humble. Are we not also Kzin?

Long we spent in bases and in the great ship. My hunting began as First Telepath was dying. I was to succeed him.

We had been roused from hibernation by the help-call of *Tracker*, our lead scout, one thirty-second of a light-year ahead of us. Our ship replied in war-code. No messages returned save the ghost-cry.

Later First Telepath probed far down the tunnels of what some call the World of the Eleventh Sense. He thought at last that he touched strange minds at the extremity of his range. Feared Zraar-Admiral expended him. I felt his collapse, though I shielded as I could. First Telepath was old as we are counted but Feared Zraar-Admiral would not scrap him while any of his power remained: we are always used to the end. Though we may not shame the Heroes' Race by breeding our ability is rare.

When I probed in my turn I found no minds. If they had been, they were gone. To find *Tracker* I was not needed, and often I was left alone to sleep. Dreaming, I was, when Orderly kicked me awake, of Karan when I was her kitten, the warm, milky time of purring and kneading. Often I had that dream now.

Tracker, when we closed with her, was in two pieces, hull chopped rather than blast-damaged. I saw mirror-shine laser-cutting at myriad points in the gaping structure. Around it was debris, much wreckage of heavy fittings which should have been securely mounted in the hull and seemed to have been pumped out like gut by hind-claws from a prey after the disabling wound.

Damage Control and Alien Technologies Officers with crew had gathered the wreckage and investigated. Alien Technologies was on the bridge when I arrived.

"It was one slash. The laser was close. The ship was ransacked. The gravity-planer, weapons, stores, medical supplies and many computers and memory-bricks are gone."

"Pirates, Weeow-Captain?" Zraar-Admiral asked. His tail was twitching.

I caught Weeow-Captain's thought: *Pirates attack a Patriarch's warship?* And his polite answer.

"That was my first thought, Dominant One. But holes were cut to sealed compartments for bodies far smaller than ours. They did not know access points or service ducts or corridors. They did not disable the beacon. Some remaining memory-bricks are intact and the bridge recorder is in place. If the enemy recognized our equipment they would surely have taken these or destroyed them completely.

"The gravity motor was an Admiralty standard type. Indeed it was fitted here. I estimate from the slash in *Tracker* that it would have been too damaged to use again. Therefore the fact that it is gone suggests that it was a technology which the destroyers of *Tracker* did not possess and took to examine or copy."

"Urrr. What of the recorder?"

"The laser passed through it. We're working on it, Dominant One."

"Patriarch's priority!"

"It is so ordered, Sire. We have found small artifacts made of primitive alloys we don't use. We have rayed and otherwise examined them and I am sure they are not miniature mines. I think they are minor tools. But if hand-tools, not for our hands.

"Further, Feared Zraar-Admiral, some seals re-engaged. That preserved some atmosphere and what was left of the lifesystem recycled a little more. Some compartments were not completely sterile. In one we found this."

Alien Technologies Officer showed a computer-enhanced print of a space-gloved hand with five long digits. Like the hand of a *kz'eerkt*.

"This is the clearest but others are similar. No bodies, Zraar-Admiral, not of any kind. There were Jotok slaves aboard, but even their bodies are gone.

"We cannot tell if or how deeply *Tracker's* claws

slashed the enemy. It looks as if she was taken by surprise."

"She was a scout. It was her task not to be taken by surprise."

"Dominant One, perhaps the attackers used some alien warfare method. But from the absence of spreading we think the enemy laser was fired from close quarters. Perhaps close enough to have been in easy visual sight. I do not understand how such a thing happened."

Zraar-Admiral twitched his tail and his ears contracted. He merrowered thoughtfully. "Urrr. Her Captain did not have a name."

"He was of good record," Weeow-Captain said. "A brave and competent officer though he died nameless."

"Yes." Feared Zraar-Admiral still had only a partial name himself. Had name-desire betrayed the scout-cruiser's Captain into folly? Then Zraar-Admiral's mind was again an unscalable crag. But an alien Space-faring race that fought! Light-years from any star! No aliens had so far been discovered—at least by what we knew of the Eternal Hunt—with more than interplanetary flight and with vestigial weapons systems. By the time lower races got into interplanetary space they had become soft and weak, had lost honor and warrior skills.

But the Dream of the Day! *Those* thoughts were not new, nor strange, nor secret: *We need a worthy enemy!*

The minds and the odors of the bridge-staff were pouring out messages. Enemies now had the booty of Kzin weaponry and drive-technology to add to whatever demon-arts they already owned. If they eluded radar and Telepaths, they might be targeting *Gutting Claw* at this moment. Or, beyond reach of my mind or Zraar-Admiral's weapons, they might be assembling a Fleet.

A Tech spoke urgently.

"Sire, we've got something out of their bridge recorder. We're stitching it through now. It's only a few words."

A new voice spoke.

"*Keep all your weapons ready to fire but don't use them unless I give the order . . .*"

"That's the Captain."

Hissing interference, then the same ghost-voice.

"*What kind of weapons do they have?*"

Another ghost answered. A Telepath deep in the World of the Eleventh Sense, strained and bewildered. I caught no secret vibrations inserted for the benefit of a Brother Telepath, nothing of the code we had developed for our own war.

"*. . . a light-pressure drive powered by incomplete hydrogen fusion. They use an electromagnetic ramscoop to get their own hydrogen from space . . .*"

Zraar-Admiral stopped the record for a moment. All thought alike. That was no Kzin ship the ghosts spoke of. Such a drive was not even on the same path as Kzin technology. The ghosts spoke again.

There was a blur. Something in the Captain's voice that I could not make out, then the Telepath.

"*. . . not even a knife or a club. Wait, they've got cooking knives. But that's all they use them for. They don't fight.*"

"*They don't fight?*"

"*No, Sir, they don't expect us to fight either. The idea has occurred to three of them and each has dismissed it from his mind.*"

"*But why?*"

"*I don't know, Sir. It's a science they use, or a religion. I don't understand . . . I don't . . .*"

A scrambled shriek, then a voice identified as *Tracker's* Alien Technology's Officer: "*Sir, they couldn't have any big weapons. There isn't room . . .*"

There was more interference, then a spitting scream

in the Battle Imperative from the Captain: *"WEAPONS OFFICER! Burn . . ."*

There the recording ended, in mirror-surfaced fused metal.

Zraar-Admiral and his officers stood silent for a moment. Zraar-Admiral's testicles were still in the relaxed position and his tail and whiskers did not stir now. An old red-sandstone statue. His tongue flicked out for a moment across the tips of his fangs. Then Weeow-Captain spoke.

"But those first words. 'They don't fight.' No weapons. That was the Telepath."

"Then the Telepath was deceived."

"Urrr."

I shrank further into the submissive position, not meeting those stares. Telepaths, whatever else might be wrong with us, did not make factual mistakes in collecting data, any more than a hunter mistook a prey when it was plainly before his eyes.

Sometimes Telepaths could get things out of context, or be overwhelmed by the alienness of prey minds. Yet the Telepath in *Tracker* had spoken with absolute certainty. "No weapons" did not admit of context errors. All Telepaths searched, unceasingly, for allies in our own war. In any case, reading alien minds was part of our training and the Telepath in a lead scout was specialized in alien animal contact. Thoughts flowed about me, some tinged with disquiet. If we were despised, we were also taken for granted as an infallible weapon. *Can this enemy beat Telepaths?* It was the worst part of our lot to have our minds open to the secret fears of Heroes, but now those were my thoughts also. Urrr.

Five long fingers. On the cunning and trickery of wild *kz'eerkti* many tales and legends turned, from the admonitory to the obscene. Some *kz'eerkti* breeds used stones as missiles and sticks as tools. Some could ambush Heroes in forest hunts.

Bad, that hand-print in Space, as the wreckage of a destroyed Kzinti ship fell in endless darkness before us. Traps, deceptions. In any event, for better or worse, a Space-travelling enemy we knew nothing of.

"Dominant One, there is more. Later, another cell in the recorder was activated. Possibly by aliens sacking the ship."

Gibbering and gabbling. *Kz'eerkti* gibbered and gabbled, when they had played tricks on Heroes, or when they pelted Heroes with fruit or excrement from the branches of tall forest trees, ready to scamper away through the branches when the Heroes concerned began to slash the tree-trunks down or climb them.

"Record this for yourself, Telepath," Feared Zraar-Admiral said. "It may be useful when we meet this prey. AT, translate it. You will allow Telepath to assist you."

I know now what it said.

"Energy discharge now."

"It looks inert."

"Look at the meter: there's movement there. We should get out. We've done what we came to do."

"Yes, we should get out! I don't mean just back to the Pencil. You know that ship could not have been alone."

"I have thought of it. However I admit there were once a few seconds when I stopped thinking about it. That was quite a pleasant sensation, I recall."

"There may be more cats coming here. I mean *here*. We've picked up other emissions from the hull. Maybe calling them. They could be here . . . now. Those first headaches the cats may have caused—I had another not long ago. Milder, though, but there."

"I had one too. Jim said several people did. I put it down to strain.

"Or some cat probe. At extreme range now but coming closer? Some mind-weapon?"

"Tanj! Do you have to think of things like that? We've had nightmares enough since this all began . . . Anyway, we still have a job to do . . . There's a light flashing on that control surface."

"There's a Tanj light flashing in my mind. And it's the biggest warning light there is. Run! Run now!

"It doesn't look like a weapon . . ."

"I say run! Aren't we in a bad enough state already?"

"We've got to get every scrap of knowledge we can. We've got to keep transmitting to Earth. Keeping the transmission going is more important than our lives."

"Can we do that if another warship full of cats jumps us? They may not be so obliging as to leave themselves in the way of our drive next time. Or several ships? These things must be co-operative, with organization. We've got the motor, the weapons, the bodies. Enough to keep us busy for years. It's crazy to wait for them . . ."

Jabber.

"Weeow-Captain, you may fall the crew out from Battle-stations. Remain closed up at Defense-stations.

"We have the direction of *Tracker's* drift. We track it back. There must be spoor, and *Tracker* has given us a sign. They did not die in vain. Urrr . . . *a light-pressure drive powered by incomplete hydrogen fusion. They use an electromagnetic ramscoop to get their own hydrogen from space . . .*"

A sudden rush of understanding.

A trail of burnt hydrogen!

"You may howl for the dead, and you may howl vengeance for our companions in the Hunt. But no heroes are to die in the mourning. And no death-duels till further notice. No station is to be uncrewed."

Happy Gatherer

Paul van Barrow waited for the hubbub to die away, waving for quiet with a smile. His responsibilities as leader of the *Happy Gatherer* expedition tended to make him pompous and even stuffy at times, but he was as excited as any now. There were several projects running on the ship, and a score of impressively multi-skilled people on board. *Happy Gatherer* was a big ship, hired not purpose-built, but they made a crowd in the room.

"The gravity anomalies are still inexplicable. If they really are Outsiders, they may have some gravity control. There's another thing."—He pointed to a projected diagram, a wedge-ended ovoid—"that ship has a sort of streamlining, as if it can land and take off through an atmosphere from a planetary surface. And it's big. I think that's also evidence of gravity-control."

Signals to trustees? The thought crossed several minds. An instruction transmitted now would reach the stock-market in about eight years' time.

"We signed undertakings," Paul reminded them, "About windfall profits from new knowledge."

It had been one of the ways finance for the expedition had been raised.

"If we can understand this new knowledge," said Henry Nakamura. There was a note of caution in his voice.

"People that intelligent should be good teachers."

"Are you certain, Paul?" Rosalind Huang's voice had an odd edge to it. Her eyes seemed somehow unnaturally large under her red-black pattern of hair. *She needs reassurance*, Rick Chew realized. *What's wrong? This is a great moment*. He stepped in.

"If these are signals, we will translate them. It's difficult, certainly, but that's only to be expected."

"A new bunch of careers when we get back," said

Michael Patrick, "There will be a stream of PhDs rolling down conveyor belts."

"Not only with the language. We've probably just set up a dozen new academic industries. Meanwhile, we should have identified some keys, but we haven't."

Michael laughed. He had an easy, infectious laugh in almost any situation. Although some thought he did not always take things quite seriously enough, the crew owed him a lot. He had shown a gift, during the long flight, for taking the sting out of almost every problem with some joke. "So we've underestimated the difficulties. We've plenty of time, and so, surely, have they."

"Rick," said Selina Guthlac, "Aren't we making a questionable assumption?"

"We can't expect the translating to be easy, but if their language has consistent rules—and surely it must— we will translate it in the end." The Neuronetic lattices on and in the ship were Lambda Platform. Their cell-connections were beyond counting.

Selina worried Rick. The crew and their successful interaction were his responsibility, and Selina seemed at times to be what another age might have called a misfit. And he had met her brother. Scrawny owlishness in him was in her a hint of watchfulness which reminded one that owls were hunters. Arthur Guthlac's undirected nervous energy was in her concentrated accomplishment. Like all in the *Happy Gatherer* she was a winner. Selina had won her way into Space with the sufferance sometimes accorded genius. Arthur had given up any idea of belonging. She could adopt protective coloration and be accepted by most of the crew, nearly all the time. But interdependence in such a situation was virtually total, and, as on Earth, too many eccentricities stacked up.

Now she spoke carefully, tasting the words and

disliking them as she used them: "What if they do not want to communicate with us? What if they deliberately disguise their speech? Deliberately make it impossible for anyone else to translate it?"

No-one asked the obvious question: "Why?" But here and there expressions began to change.

"Selina!" Peter Brown laughed, "What have you been reading?"

She flinched for a second. Beneath its innocent surface, the question might have dangerous implications. Then she came back at them.

"Another thing: you said the alien ship is big. Look at the scale. It's not big, it's gigantic! And the shape— that might not be for atmosphere entry, it might be to reduce surface area. Why do you think they would want to do that?"

No one answered for a long moment. Then Peter asked:

"What about the *Angel's Pencil*? Have there been any messages?"

"None we've heard." The colony ship to Epsilon Eridani would have passed through this quadrant, but in the interstellar distances no-one had seriously expected to intercept messages from it. Its big com-laser would be tight-beamed back to Earth or the Belt.

"I suggest we all assemble at the end of each watch for updates. The crew of the *Happy Gatherer* dispersed reluctantly, with many lingering glances at the screens. Peter called Rick and Paul aside.

Selina had comfortable quarters, decorated with a number of personal touches. In Space "personal space" was a necessity not a luxury. There was a transparent case of stimulated glass and wood on the shelf, a small grey-painted object within. The model recalled a shared life of the mind light-years away. A reminder too of the dangers the old sea-voyagers and traders of Earth had faced in primitive craft. A good-luck charm, perhaps? Something else? She looked at it as she had many times in the past, but HMS *Nelson* told her nothing more.

The door signaled a visitor. Rick entered.

"Why did you say that?" He asked her without preliminaries, "About alien messages being made untranslatable deliberately."

"I hardly know." She already regretted her previous words, and their inevitable implications. The intimacy of a long voyage could lull one into self-betrayal.

"Selina, I don't agree with what Peter's been saying . . ."

"Why, what has he been saying? Or can I guess?"

"I don't want to be hypercritical, and I'm sure that's not his intention either. Or anyone's. Paul has always defended you, you know. And sometimes Peter says things a little before he's thought them through, perhaps.

"I'm not suggesting you need conditioning or anything like that, but have you thought of having your psych profile redone, just as a precaution. It would be entirely voluntary."

"No."

"Suppose there was some chemical imbalance."

"The doc would notify me and correct it when I have my next check-up. In fact, and as you know, I would never have got past the selection board carrying anything like that. But Rick, both the selection board then and the doc now are of the opinion that I am sane." His self-assurance was a goad to her. She realized she had never liked or respected this smug, complacent, always unsurprising, somehow *herbivorous* man. *Like Paul, only worse, she thought. Well, it's not surprising. There was always a chance we might meet Outsiders. The same board chose both of them as the best representatives of the human race . . . what an error it made when it also chose me!*

"Are you sure you're *happy*?" It was a weighty question as he asked it. This was a culture that took happiness and its pursuit more seriously than any in history.

"What's it to you?"

He was hurt by her words. "We are a team. You know that."

"Thank you, Rick. You've possibly seen my profile as you are in charge of crew records. Since one of my jobs is Space navigation, I have studied something of Space-flight. Since I am also, as you are doubtless also aware, particularly as we have discussed it a number of times, a natural scientist, I do know something about human body and brain chemistry." She paused, measured him with her eyes and added, "And they may have gravity control."

Part of Selina's problem in socializing may have been connected to the fact that she lived in a culture most of whose members had little concept of sarcasm or irony. These people did not insult each other, and it took Rick Chew a little while to work out what she meant.

"I'm only thinking of you," he told her at last. "Anyone who can't get on with people shouldn't be here."

"Shall I get off and walk home, then?"

He flinched.

Something hurt her. She sensed that the atmosphere of conflict was not only alien to him, it was painful. She sought for words to calm the situation.

"I think you're tense, Selina," Rick said, "Perhaps a little current stimulation would help you relax."

He backed away, raising his hands against the murderous rage blazing in her face. He distinctly saw the beginning of a striking motion before she checked it. She spoke as he had never heard anyone speak before.

"My father was a current addict. He cured himself. I was with him. I saw him cure himself. Have you any idea what that means? Do you know how many current addicts have ever cured themselves? Do you know the price they have to pay?"

"I'm sorry. I didn't know." Rick was doubly distressed at giving and receiving pain now.

"Don't you ever, ever, say that again, do you hear!"

Selina had dropped into a half crouch. She glared into Rick's face, now working with signs of consternation, for a long moment without speaking. It was a glare which a generation experienced in such things might have called murderous. Mumbling apologies, he shook his head in bewilderment and left.

How would he behave, how would any of them behave, her thought began to form, *how would any of them look, if . . . if at that moment . . .*

A headache. Stress perhaps. The autodoc had outlets in each crew member's rooms and Selina quickly inserted her fingers for chemical analysis.

Gutting Claw

I fell onto my forelimbs as I crossed the bridge. Zraar-Admiral would have to calculate how much more I could take. It was not my place to comment on this, but to report.

"Dominant One, the enemy know nothing of *Tracker*. They know a little of the Ancients, but of no other thinking life in Space. They have no clear aims except to gather data about anomalous radio and gravity events and other useless knowledge. But they are *kz'eerkti*."

"What radio and gravity events?"

"Probably us."

Monkey inquisitiveness. There were Simianoids on several planets in the Patriarchy, and it was an ecological niche which often led to rudimentary tool-using. Intelligent beings were generally somewhat alike and also generally edible. Slaver-students thought the Ancients had spread common primitive life-forms through much of the Galaxy. But this on the screens represented more than rudimentary tool-using.

"I believe the same type of apes killed *Tracker*. The drives are similar. Omnivores with five fingers like the print . . . The species has established itself in considerable numbers in one star-system apart from its original one, and in smaller colonies further away, using reaction drives. They have hibernation . . ." We Telepaths were expected to understand alien sciences, religious, societies, languages and technologies as well as alien thoughts.

But several inhabited worlds! A Vengeance-Hunt had become a promise of Conquest Glorious! The hunters' minds were volcanic.

"They send messages to us. They call their ship the . . ." I had trouble translating. *Successful Plant-Eater* was how it came out.

But *Tracker* hung in every mind. *Tracker* and the great swathe of exhausted hydrogen which we had been following.

"What weapons do they have?"

"None, Feared Zraar-Admiral. These creatures have never fought. I find nothing of weapons, hardly a concept of war, save in one *female* mind. Even there it is vague." I paused, then spoke again, all around knowing as I spoke that I repeated the words of dead *Tracker's* Telepath: "They have only kitchen-knives."

"Feared Zraar-Admiral," said Alien Technologies, "how could such a race have evolved a theory of ballistics?"

"Ballistics or no, we see them in Space," said Student of Particles. "There is a danger of weapons! I care not what the addict says."

"There is also the Paradox," said Zraar-Admiral, "Do not forget it ever."

Zraar-Admiral had killed enemies in plenty on the ground as the Heroes' battle-legions over-ran worlds, or fought each other, with claw, fang, *Wtsai* and occasionally with beam or fusion-bomb. Not all those battles had been easy, for a true Hero attacked—on the ground or anywhere else—without too much reckoning of the odds. On one planet with wide oceans the locals had had sea-ships hidden under water, armed with missiles with multiple warheads. Heroes died before our Students of Particles developed a heat-induction ray that boiled the seas. *Tracker* had had such a ray. And there were vague stories that came slowly from distant parts of a widespread Empire of other things . . . But Zraar-Admiral had never joined battle against aliens in Space.

Perhaps he never would. The war between the Slavers and their Tnuctipun slaves that wiped out intelligent life in the galaxy billions of years previously might be the only full-scale war of species that would ever be fought in the deeps between the stars, save for the far-distant, almost legendary, Time of Glory when the Jotok had been overthrown. The few races encountered in the Hunt that had interplanetary and poor weapons were hardly substitutes. There was a legend of a Feral Jotok Fleet which had escaped when the Kzin rose, but in centuries no trace of it had been found . . .

The fighting against other Kzin was controlled. Struggles of Kzinti Houses Noble produced exhilaration and bloodshed in plenty and the ambitions of young Heroes for names and territory made for a number of outlaws, rebels and pirates. There was always dueling. Zraar-Admiral had owed his first advancement to his dueling prowess and his trophy-hoard contained an impressive number of ears, but fights between Kzin, in the training arena, the hunting preserve, or even in full-scale military action, were not the Conquest Glorious or The Day. *Gutting Claw's* destiny, he felt, was unfulfilled. Like the whole Navy's. Like his own.

Some priests said Space-faring warrior aliens were a fantasy like intelligent females, a self-evidently heretical denial of the natural order of things. The Jotok alone had been created by the Fanged God to give Heroes access to gravity-motors and High-Tech weapons without shameful dilution of our own warrior culture. But for Zraar-Admiral life with no possibility of The Day, the Triumph Supreme, presented a prospect of doleful dullness. The Battle-Drum on the bridge showed the Navy's view. It had never yet been struck, and for one thing only would Zraar-Admiral strike it.

Alien Technologies Officer suspected dimly the struggle between Priesthood and Military, between religious doctrine and the claims of honor which the Battle-Drum symbolized. I, whom he disdained to notice, knew more than he about the ideas that made him. But instincts less acute than mine would have told him how dangerous a path his thoughts and words might start down. AT shifted to safer ground, keeping matters purely technical.

My report, Zraar-Admiral realized as I did, duplicated *Tracker's* recorder. An alien enemy with no weapons or knowledge of weapons, and *Tracker* sliced by a claw of light. If the enemy deceived Telepaths there was real, and for Zraar-Admiral thrilling, danger. For me the prospect was less thrilling.

Happy Gatherer

"There was a signal coming from Earth," said Paul, "but I've put it on record and left all channels clear for our friends. Whatever it is, it will have to wait on this."

"The headaches . . . do you think . . . ?" Anna left the words unfinished.

"Attempts at direct mind contact? It's the kind of thing one might expect in advanced beings. If so, we're not equipped to cope. I know telepathic ability was a factor in the selection of some of us, but we haven't enough of it."

"So what do we do?"

"I'm unhappy. What if they decide that *we* are too alien for *them* to communicate with and leave? We can't follow. I don't think we can just sit here and wait for them to make the next move. What a disaster if they decided we were a waste of time and vanished!"

"Would they, after all this effort?" Paul asked. "That ship is big. *Really* big. It must have cost them energy to bring it here to meet us." He was instilling confidence. "Look, there are scientists on that ship, people with minds like ours, or better, who look at problems the same way. They'll adjust to us. Perhaps they expected to recognize us. Now they don't. Perhaps," he added after a moment, "they're frightened. I think we'll have to pay them a visit. We'll take a boat across."

"I wonder," said Rick, "if that would be entirely . . . diplomatic? We know we're dealing with alien minds. What if they saw us as some sort of threat to them?" His confrontation with Selina had left him with food for thought.

"Threat? What do you mean?" Anna Nagle asked.

"Did you ever see an animal in a safari park? Go close too suddenly, and it'll often run, though you mean it no harm. For all we know these outsiders might think the same way."

"But," Paul objected, "beings that get into Space must share certain common attributes of social order, co-operation . . . isn't that what the whole history of civilization is about? How could they see us—fellow

Space-farers—as a . . . threat. If it's obvious to us they
are not savage animals, surely it must be equally obvious
to them that we are the same."

"How do we know what they think? I'm sorry now
we've no Belters with us. Even of they do tend to be
paranoiac about Space, I need a different perspective
on this . . ."

"I think we can do without any paranoia here." Peter
said. He may have been looking in the direction of Selina
but it was impossible to be sure. "We are mature adults
and I think we can arrive at sensible decisions."

Peter is an ARM, Selina thought suddenly. *Of course
the technological police would have people aboard. He's
going to have ARM do a thorough job on my files when
we get back to Earth, and this will be my last trip into
space. What am I thinking of? This may well be the
last trip for all of us anyway.*

"As well as the boat, why don't we send across a free
party in suits?" Paul asked. "I will go first." He was
unsure why his position compelled him to say this, but
some deeply-buried thing told him it was appropriate.
"I take the point that they might be frightened of us.
This should demonstrate that we mean no harm.

"Ancient people approached each other holding up
empty hands," he went on. "So civilization started. I'm
sorry we haven't an historian to tell us more . . . Six in
the boat and six in suits. That leaves eight on board to
control all essential systems and the major com-links."

There was a murmur of agreement.

Paul and Rick turned to Selina again. "You won't want
to come, of course."

"I certainly do want to come," said Selina. "You've
convinced me." *Get off the major target!* The voice was
screaming far in the back of her mind.

The crew of the *Happy Gatherer* scattered with final
instructions.

Selina's Space-suit was standard issue, geochronically linked to the ship's planar logic lattices, with large pockets in the arms and legs. There was nutrient under high pressure in waist-cylinders, boot-caches and other compartments, and the suit recycled moisture. The lonely Belter rock-jacks might have had it differently, but in Earth's history of this sort of Space-flight such things had seldom been needed: in an emergency you were usually near help or dead. She could think of nothing more she needed to take. She slipped her good-luck charm, the model ship, into one pocket.

Gutting Claw

Space-suited figures were leaving the enemy ship. Further magnifications brought them into clear view. A port opened and a boat put out. The monkeys made no attempt to conceal their approach. The enemy ship in arrogance or threat was actually shining lights upon them.

The EV aliens moved towards *Gutting Claw* with small reaction jets. One, who I felt Feared Zraar-Admiral mentally marking with his own urine, was ahead of the others. Unless there was something very peculiar about those compact, long-limbed bodies, they carried no weapons.

"Telepath! What is happening!"

"Sire, I detect no warlike intent. But if *Tracker* was somehow deceived, I cannot be sure . . ."

"AT! What sort of tactic is this?"

"I don't understand it, Feared Zraar-Admiral."

"Are they going to attack us with those jets."

"Feared Zraar-Admiral, I do not know, but they are far too small to do any damage to the hull. They are maneuvering jets only. That boat is powered by chemical rockets on the same principle. We detect no radio-actives in it. They still appear to me to be completely unarmed."

Fight them! I caught Weeow-Captain's mind. *What are you waiting for, you old fool? Kill now!* Then a blur. *Noyouaremymentoroldfriend* . . . I broke that very perilous contact.

"They are small creatures."

"And the creatures that killed *Tracker* were also small. Telepath!"

"Sire, still all my skills tell me they have no weapons."

"Do they seek to take us prisoner?"

"They seek to meet us. Sire, that must be the reason."

"I want live specimens," Zraar-Admiral said. "Telepath, is there anything useful in that ship?"

"No, Dominant One. In general the technology is primitive. The creatures have a number of gadgets and devices we do not possess, and their reaction-drive technology is of course developed, but that is all in their minds and can be extracted. The drive is inferior to ours and the materials are insignificant."

He turned to Weapons Officer.

"Destroy the ship as soon as the EV *kz'eerkti* and the boat are far enough away not to be involved. Watch sharply for monkey-tricks!"

The battle proved kittens'-play. Under the converging beams the enemy ship's life-system area melted almost at once. Its fusion plant should have destabilized with a major explosion but the drive was idling and probably some monkey used its dying moments to shut off the fuel-feed in an attempt to save its fellows. Cowards. We knew little of such drives but knew a Hero would have pointed the ship at his enemy and turned off the fusion-shield. I thought of Lord Dragga-Skrull and his last historic order: "The Patriarch knows every Hero will kill eights of times before dying heroically!"

The weedy creatures made no attempt at attack,

resistance, or even evasion. The final explosion was visually fierce but of no consequence. *Gutting Claw* was heavily shielded.

Watching the blue-white glare fading on the screen Zraar-Admiral regretted that the business had been so easy. There had been relatively little honor gained. Whatever had happened to *Tracker*, these omnivore apes, like previously-encountered aliens, had nothing to match Kzin weaponry. But that disappointment also held rich promise—of worlds ripe for the taking by his squadron alone.

"Weeow-Captain!"

"Sire!"

"You have the enemy ship's course recorded?"

"Indeed, Sir!"

"It is, I declare, a Patriarch's Secret. When we have avenged *Tracker* we will follow that course to its home."

"Yes, Sire. They came in a straight line from their first appearance. They seem to have made no attempt to hide their point of origin. If they have changed course since their original take-off Telepath will take the course from their minds." They took it for granted that I could do such things, and that I would, at whatever cost to myself. "In any event there will probably be records in the surviving boat."

"They will have destroyed those by now."

"I wonder. Their behavior is so strange . . . perhaps they are a death-worshipping cult . . ."

"Telepath was not deceived." Zraar-Admiral did not try to hide the contemptuous rage in his voice. He knew all his officers shared it. "They can't fight at all."

Perhaps, despite the similarities in her Telepath's report and my own, *Tracker* had encountered something different to these leaf-eaters. That led to another consideration: as a matter of honor, Zraar-Admiral could not turn aside from the pursuit of an enemy known to be dangerous, and against whom vengeance was owed, to attack the soft targets of this monkeydom. We were on the trail of *Tracker's* killer and that account would have to be settled first. That should not take long, however. Zraar-Admiral turned to Weeow-captain.

"When the prisoners are inboard I shall look at them. Bring my gold armor"—this was hardly a ceremonial occasion but it was what the protocol of Fleet Standing Orders declared for first meetings with conquered prey—"detail two more infantry squads for my escort."

The monkeys had been secured and breathed Kzin air. So we could breathe their air. The monkeydom extended, as I had reported, over several industrialized worlds. Feared Zraar-Admiral could claim the biggest continent of the homeworld for himself. And a Full Name, certainly. A Full Name for Weeow-Captain, too. Partial names for others. Many others, if Zraar-Admiral indulged. Vast fiefdoms. Smells of names, riches, glory, conquest! Perhaps some of the monkeys' less-advanced sub-species would put up a fight on the ground. If so, there could be rich rewards for the most Heroic and ferocious of the infantry troopers. Partial names and estates might not be beyond the claws of outstanding Sergeants.

Nothing, of course, for Telepath. Except burn-out.

Twelve humans and thirty-four Kzin stared at each other in the ruddy light of the great hangar-deck. One squad of eight flanked the prisoners. Zraar-Admiral, with Telepath at his feet, stood at the head of his Guard squads.

Zraar-Admiral saw Simianoids with considerable variations of skin-colors and strangely limited and irregular hair-growth. Their general morphology at least suggested the theory of common life-form seeding by the Ancients. They stood two-thirds of his height and would carry, he judged, a third of his body-weight or less. Some were leaking red liquid, presumably circulatory fluid, where marines had torn their skin in stripping away their space-suits. Frail as well as ugly, he thought. Spindly limbs with puny muscles, branch-grasping monkey-hands, with those five long fingers and tiny, useless horny tips that could not be called claws. Foreheads higher than many *kz'eerkti* species on Kzin, which was only to be expected. No tails, oddly enough. How did they counter-balance when running on branches or leaping between trees?

They would be able to climb trees too slender to bear the weight of Kzinti. Sport there perhaps. On Kzinti worlds the cunning and agility of the beasts made *kz'eerkti*-hunts enjoyable as well as useful training for the young. The odd distribution of body-hair on these specimens suggested an ancestry with aquatic episodes, so perhaps they could also swim. There were two large, grotesquely red-centered, teats on the females. Zraar-Admiral wondered why the males had put the females into Space-suits and led them outside the vehicle. Were the monkeys in continual need of copulation? The gross external sexual organs of the males at least suggested it.

Some of the male monkeys were holding the slightly smaller and generally longer-haired females in a manner that suggested they were either trying to groom them or lay claim to them. Evidently the females had belonged to more than one dominant monkey. Several harems in the one ship? *Kz'eerkti* and other arboreals on Kzin behaved in such ways . . . but the arboreals of Kzin did not have Space-ships. Two were on their knees in an awkward posture. Some were waving their forelimbs and hands as if tantalizing the guards to break ranks and pounce. Liquid was running from the eyes of some, and one, a female with oddly-patterned red hair, gave an unpleasant prolonged high-pitched cry and defecated as Zraar-Admiral watched, in what the Kzin took as a gesture of willful obscenity. A guard snarled and stepped forward. The monkey screamed and rushed at him, fingers extended as though trying to attack the guard's eyes. The guard swiped at the monkey's head with instinctively-extended claws, tearing it partly off. The monkey's body flew across the compartment spraying fluid to hit the wall and fall in a puddle. The other monkeys screamed and jumped about, though no more tried to attack. Some covered their faces and wailed. The guards snarled in the Menacing Tense and most of the wailing stopped. The body of the rude monkey soon ceased to move and seemed plainly dead.

They are even more fragile than they look, Zraar-Admiral noted. A proper *kz'eerkt* would have put up a better fight than that. He would not, he though, punish the guard, who was now looking at him somewhat apprehensively, too heavily. He had used no more than reasonable force. Still, it was all rather disgusting.

He could see Telepath was in no condition to do more at the moment. When he recovered he should be able to discover a lot more with them face-to-face. Their resemblance to Kzinti life-forms suggested they were meat, but proper dissection would put the matter beyond doubt.

Zraar-Admiral returned to the bridge. He ordered the monkeys to be confined separately from one another. After Telepath had gone through their minds thoroughly he would turn a few loose in his miniature hunting preserve to see what sort of running they made. He turned to Weeow-Captain to outline his thoughts.

"When we have avenged *Tracker* it will take us at least eight and three years' real time to get back to

Hssin, more time for a fleet to be assembled. Then we have the journey to the monkey-systems."

"Yes, Dominant One."

"But you are thinking that is a long time? Even in sleep?"

"Urrr." Weeow-Captain gestured assent. They had been together a long time and thought they knew each other well. Zraar-Admiral believed Weeow-Captain was not so brilliant as to be a threat to him, which was one reason he was there. He also believed him to be a completely efficient and reliable officer, which was the other reason. Ambitious of course, like any healthy Kzin. They had fought side by side on the ground and won scars together. Weeow-Captain met his gaze.

"If it is necessary we must take the time, Sire, but . . ." That "but" said it all.

"Obviously that is what we should do, if the aliens were fighters, despite any loss of time involved," Zraar-Admiral told him, "but since it is plain they are not, I say we should leap on with this squadron alone. I will send dispatch vessels to Kzin and Hssin with the operational diaries."

It was phrased in the Equal-acknowledging tense, a request for comment as much as an order. The squadron riding in *Gutting Claw* was already small for its task, but there was no help for it. Radio or lasers were both too unreliable over such distances and too insecure in what might, after all, be a sort of combat situation, disappointing as the *kz'eerkti* were in that respect. Security was more important to prevent a rush for spoils should other Kzin become aware of them. If what he had seen was a fair sample, even a reduced squadron would be more than enough for the monkey-worlds. Let other prowlers like Chuut-Riit find their own. Weeow-Captain's eyes flared with eagerness.

"A Hero's leap! Yes!"

There was nothing unfeigned in that delight. *He is a good companion* thought Zraar-Admiral. They had dreamed together of such actions.

Alone in his quarters Zraar-Admiral meditated upon Conquest and its implications. Honored Maaug-Riit might not like such independent action, but surely the monkeydom would produce gifts to appease the Fleet Admiral and other high nobility. Besides, Zraar-Admiral guessed, the Patriarch would not be too displeased to see a relatively minor noble like Zraar-Admiral improve his position relative to a Fleet Admiral of the Patriarch's own house who had grown very mighty indeed.

I shall have to start culling my sons more rigorously, Zraar-Admiral thought. *Urrr. For more than an Admiral's inheritance.*

Suddenly Zraar-Admiral knew that the monkeys might be leading him on the most dangerous hunt of his life. *What if this, instead of being a simple leap to glory, turns me into a politician?* His tail curled. Now he would have to do something about Telepath.

Zraar-Admiral had power of life and death over every creature aboard—any Kzin commander did—but the Patriarch's family would have other ears and noses. To wantonly silence any Telepath would be highly suspicious. He was confident that even if he was a spy for Honored Maaug-Riit, Telepath could not read his own mind, with its inculcate Authority, but those of his officers were naturally weaker.

He thought of killing Telepath and disguising the act, but banished the idea immediately. To murder Telepath would be shameful, a violation of the honor which to a Kzin commander was virtually a physical reality. He would have Weeow-Captain put him in charge of guarding the apes. It was a logical job for the little Kzin when his special talents were not required on the bridge. Already, with the battleship not having such luxuries as eunuchs, Telepath had shown himself a reliable tender of the small harem, which Zraar-Admiral had had little time for recently. No fighting Kzin would want the degrading task of herding plant-eaters and he could continue extracting information from their minds.

Both Telepath's investigations so far and the first quick dissections of a couple of specimens showed the monkeys were omnivores. That was not unexpected. Pure herbivores had never been found in Space. There seemed no strictly logical reason why the evading of hunters should not have led to intelligence as great as, or greater than, that of the hunters themselves —one, after all, was running for its meal, the other for its life— but it would be blasphemous to suppose herbivores could dominate their environment or defeat and subjugate carnivores! At some time in the past the monkeys had fought and killed.

The two large teats on the females (if that was what they were) were significant. The number indicated small litters, and the bizarre size of the teats suggested prolonged lactation. That in turn suggested the apes' get must survive a lengthy and helpless kittenhood. How numerous must they have become before they controlled the resources to build a Space-ship?

Telepath had said that on their home-world they numbered in billions. So they evidently had no enemies that were a major threat there. Though lacking significant teeth and claws they had some characteristics of a dominant animal—*heiin*, they had Star-ships. They would have had to fight sometime in the past to accomplish that, presumably against real carnivores. The larger size of the males, though nothing like the degree of sexual dimorphism in Kzinti, indicated competition for mating privileges in their history.

Their small teeth were a typical omnivore mixture.

Telepath said their meat had come from automated kitchens, partly burnt in a disgusting manner. Perhaps it was grown from cancers in vats like infantry rations.

Presumably the monkeys' ancestors had been scavengers, and had become used to burning carrion to kill toxic microbes rather than eating their own fresh kills. They must have fought for carrion against large predators, wielded clubs and thrown stones to make up for their deficient teeth and claws.

And ended up with a drive that collected hydrogen atoms from interstellar Space to carry them between stars.

Or had these got their ship from somewhere else? Surely no-one would recruit monkeys for mercenary warriors as the Jotok had once been foolish enough to recruit on Old Kzin.

There was a story of a *kz'eerkt*-band on Kzin that had once seized a Space-craft and performed outrageous tricks and monkey-shines to the discomfiture of certain overly-confident Heroes.

But that was a fable, a joke, an exercise in poets' ingenuity! A piece of entertainment set down by the Conservors to smuggle germs of wisdom into the hot livers of adolescents. It did not seem possible in the real universe. Space-craft were complicated. An idea flicked away from him. Like a kitten chasing the tip of its own tail he sensed something maddeningly just out of reach. Something about monkeys and Telepaths and Kzinretts. Once or twice behavior by Telepath, and also by some of his harem, especially Rilla, the lithest, and Niza who had the biggest vocabulary, had struck a note of inconsistency and puzzled him as the monkeys did. Was the common factor a conditioned species showing less than perfect conditioning. No knowledge of weapons . . . *Was* monkey pacifism conditioned? Had their tails, surely indispensable to free-roaming arboreals, been amputated in connection with their conditioned status?

Were the monkeys slaves of a race that no Kzin except perhaps the late crew of *Tracker* had met so far? The glandular rush he felt at that idea had no fear about it, only exhilaration. Postulate a race that had conditioned the monkeys, and riddles disappeared! It remained only to find the Conditioners, and leap upon them with the Fleet. The ship they were pursuing was the obvious place to start.

He thought of Rilla and Niza again. He had not, he realized, seen either of them recently. Telepath had told him they were pregnant and had dug themselves birthing burrows. Two more sons to compete for the Sire's inheritance. Well, that might be to the good. Two more daughters, useful gifts to superiors or subordinates. A nuisance that his two most attractive females were engaged in birthing at the same time.

But why did he think of Kzinretts now? There was no odor of estrus in the system, he had deliberately had that programmed out, wanting no distractions for anyone at present. He had not been thinking of mating, but . . . Rilla and Niza . . . Was Kzinrett stupidity a product of conditioning too? That was not exactly what either the Priests or the Conservors said. It was a punishment by the Fanged God, with a bit of help from the Priestly Order long ago. Zraar-Admiral's ears folded. The Navy respected the Conservors of the Ancestral Past, some of the history of the Priest-kind it respected less.

Telepath said the monkeys know nothing of other contemporary Space-travelling species. Had the Conditioners, whoever they were, gained control of the monkeys without the monkeys' knowledge?

Where the conditioners *that* good? Or was he discarding Churga's *Wtsai* and breeding entities he did not need? Perhaps the monkeys were simply behaving as Kzin's own arboreals would had they got into Space. Zraar-Admiral was used to exercising self-control. Now he slashed at the bulkhead in puzzlement.

I slept not only because of Sthondat-drug. Sleep was my escape from existence. On the world where I was born I had known my life would be lowly, nameless, despised and short, my minds open to the violating contempt of all warriors. Space was worse. I could never block out entirely the Kzinti minds confined with me. Sleep, some Telepaths believed, helped hold the Death at bay, allowed our minds time to heal. Sleep, I sometimes felt, especially the sleeps when I dreamed of Karan, had taken on some quality of a Hunt, though it was a Hunt for a prey whose nature was dark to me.

Usually I had more or less the run of the ship. The officers did not deign to notice me, the others avoided me. I was unchallenged. My talent which cursed me also protected me. No subordinate would risk destroying such an asset.

Already Zraar-Admiral had delegated me to tend his harem—I was beneath insulting by being given this task normally reserved for eunuchs. Telepaths were hardly thought of as males.

I saw that the Kzinretts were exercised and given space for birthing burrows as necessary. The female tongue is easy and I did not need to read their dim minds to learn their simple wants and problems. Since the harem was small and Zraar-Admiral often distracted there were few kittens, and the males, when they were old enough, I took to Zraar-Admiral's Family Trainer at the crèche. But soon the harem gave me new secrets to chew upon. Now I had added to this my tasks as ape-keeper.

The trail of burnt hydrogen we were following was

growing fresher. It was similar to that of the monkey-ship we had defeated. It did not deviate and we simply headed straight down it.

It became easier with time to enter the aliens' minds, and I tried to learn more than AT could as he picked through the litter of their boat and suits. At first I felt degraded at having to rummage through monkey-minds but Feared Zraar-Admiral complimented me for finding out about toilet-paper, ice-cream and the potential weapons-properties of electromagnetic ramscoop fields. AT liked tooth-brushes and made one, but I should have got the credit for that too.

Ten surviving monkeys to begin with, all yammering at my mind with not only their alienness, but also with pure fear and despair if I raised my mental guard. And fear is a huge part of the Telepath's Curse. All creatures' minds tend to take on what they are bombarded with, to resonate with it. How can we be Heroes, who feel the pain of all, yes, even the secret pains of terror and loss that no real warrior will admit to? Even when I shielded myself those alien minds seemed to crawl around in my consciousness. I had felt shamed, concealed fear in Heroes' minds often, and hated it, but *this* fear was unashamed. Had they no pride?

And they all had names! Full names! Sometimes more than two! They had been born with them! Paul van Barrow (that was a troublesome one) had been the leader (Zraar-Admiral wanted him for himself). Rick Chew, Henry Nakamura, Michael Patrick, Peter Gordon Brown . . . even the females had full names: Anna Nagle, Lee Jean Armstrong (that one tried to ambush and attack me when I brought it food, not knowing I could read its mind as it crouched behind the door with a length of pipe it had found), Selina Guthlac . . . But none were fighters, none had *earned* names. I finally decided they could not be counted as real names at all, rather they were the sort of means of identification we gave to Kzinretts and kittens.

Some of the monkeys had a god, a Bearded God that was a Patriarch of Patriarchs like the Fanged God, but different. Where this image was present, the monkeys concerned were usually beseeching this god to forgive them for having forgotten him and crying to him for help. I tried to follow this further but became lost in monkey-logic and the welter of alien images. Reading their minds when they had been calm and complacent in their ship had been easy by comparison. It did not lead back to useful technology or to monkey secret weapons.

On Kzin the more intelligent types of *kz'eerkti*— those with enough mind to read—often had a kind of playfulness like that of kittens about them with tricks and games. These did not. They were miserable creatures.

They were in general poor performers on the miniature hunting range, too, without cunning, stamina, speed or fighting prowess. Or mostly so. I noticed that once or twice, when I got my tongue round their language and explained to them, their fear somehow diminished. The Peter Gordon Brown male and Anna Nagle female rigged up a makeshift dead-fall trap and did some damage to one of Zraar-Admiral's hunting-party. That amused the others (and me, though I dared not show it) but it also gave me food for thought. Of course, the miniaturized hunting preserve, though it ran cleverly in and out of several decks of the battleship, was hardly a real test of skills.

Those who did not or could not learn to use the excrement turbines with which all cabins were fitted were the first to go, though I did not tell the officers this, of course. Some that I simply took straight up to the officer's banquets screamed and struggled. Some, and this gave me more to think upon, insisted on walking on their own feet and tried, I think, to be dignified. The Peter Gordon Brown died uttering cool-headed curses that might have come from a warrior. His last monkey-words as the hunters closed in on him were: "I despise you." Although I did not know exactly why, it showed some kind of defiance as he ran at them for the last time.

Although I did not use their words with them more than necessary, this behavior made me uncomfortable. Anyway, I was told by the officers that they were good to eat.

Of course for a Telepath speech translation is quite easy. As soon as I heard the monkey-language I recognized that it matched the speech from the *Tracker* recorder.

Zraar-Admiral was pleased when I gave him a report on what this said. Indeed some time later he sent for me for a discussion with him such as I had never had before.

"You are more intelligent than most addicts," he told me. He had received me in his own quarters, in an Admiral's luxury. Then, and rare indeed was it for such as he to ask the opinion of such as I: "What do you think this tells?"

"First, Feared Zraar-Admiral, the creatures which destroyed *Tracker* have the same language as these monkeys of ours," I told him. "They are connected, though ours know nothing of that battle."

"Yes. Go on."

"Dominant One, the words 'They may not be so obliging as to leave themselves in the way of our drive next time' seem of the greatest significance. We know now how *Tracker* was destroyed. It was nothing to do with superior or secret weaponry. It fell in with a monkey-ship like the—pardon me, Dominant One—like the so-called *Successful Plant-Eater*, powered by a reaction-drive, evidently called the *Writing Stick*, or, more fully, *The Winged Undying Shining Monkey's Writing Stick*." The name was not much odder than many other concepts I had taken from the monkeys' minds.

"The monkeys in that craft," I continued, "used the reaction-drive as a weapon. *Tracker's* Telepath picked up no thoughts of weapons because the apes did not know what weapons were. The laser was a function of the drive, or aligned parallel to the drive. Our own prisoners used lasers for signaling back along the way they had come."

"Clever of them to think of that. It sounds as if they are adaptable. Or lucky."

There was a saying, "Monkey-daffy, Monkey-lucky." It was applied to many stories of the scampering *kz'eerkti*. A Hero should not rely on luck unless he or the Fanged God owed one another a jest. Zraar-Admiral looked thoughtfully at the monkey-leader, the Paul, which he had had stuffed for his hoard, as though it might tell him something (Freeze-drying was much more convenient with a universe-sized freeze-drier around us, but Zraar-Admiral was a traditionalist and also had me to do the cleaning and other dirty work involved). The Paul looked back at him quizzically as he sprayed a little urine absent-mindedly on it and several other trophies, though he scarcely needed to mark them again as his own. Even had I not been Telepath his mood would have been obvious to me.

"Dominant One, these Space-*kz'eerkti* may be tricky, certainly. Many of their artifacts are clever, and though I am too lowly to understand such matters in full, AT tells me their boat's computers are more versatile than our own. Their connectivity is such that they have pattern-recognition and other machine-reasoning capabilities which our own computers, however fast, have not achieved—indeed we have never attempted to achieve it. Those properties could confer great advantages, military and medical . . ."—We took military medicine seriously—"Perhaps it is because they are used to looking down from tree-tops and therefore perceive relationships differently to Heroes who once hunted on plains. We have kept one of their programmers, also one of their navigators. It is a female, but in each case I feel there may be useful knowledge still to be extracted."

"*Merrower.* Say nothing yet of this to any other." Feared Zraar-Admiral did not need to use the Menacing tense to me. "In any event," he went on, "their flavor may be a reason to husband them. I am inclined to keep a pair to breed from. Or would tissue be enough? (The Dominant One would not, of course, be an expert in such an unHeroic matter as cellular biology). "Anyway, there ought to be plenty more of them soon. You may pace, Telepath," he added graciously, "if it will aid your thoughts."

"And third, Dominant One," I continued, "We learn the monkeys who destroyed *Tracker* are now warning 'Earth' of our presence. That is their home planet." I felt his conflicting emotions at the thought of the Earth-monkeys' impotent terror when that warning was received.

Then suddenly he spun, whirling upon me so that I jumped back, fearing that he was about to attack me. "TELEPATH!"

I rolled belly upward in total submission. "Dominant One, have I offended?"

"Telepath, repeat to me those first words. Translate EXACTLY."

"Dominant One, the words were: 'They may not be

so obliging as to leave themselves in the way of our drive next time'."

"Do you see the implications of that?" His eyes and mind were flaring at me."

"Only what I have said, Dominant One."

"Stupid. Urrr." But he gave me an absent-minded grooming lick, and now I could feel the pleasure from his mind. He felt he was the first to see something wonderful. Slaver dropped onto my face from the tips of his splendid fangs.

"They speak of 'Next Time'!" he churred. "Feeble as they are, those monkeys think of giving us a fight!

"Remember, too, those other monkey-words: 'Keeping the transmission going is more important than our lives.' What does that tell us about them? . . . No, perhaps that is not a question for Telepath to answer."

Feared Zraar-Admiral stretched his claws. "We have followed spoor into long grass. Telepath, you are loyal . . ."

"Dominant One!" *Fear! Did he suspect my commission from Honored Maaug-Riit? Did he suspect the Telepaths' War? Did he suspect that Rilla and Niza . . .*

"Remember it. You have brains. Of all the Telepaths I have encountered, you are the closest to a warrior."

And where are those other Telepaths now? I thought. Zraar-Admiral had much of benign mood about him at that moment, but with danger always, always. Did he seek to cozen me into games with the family of the Patriarch?

"A reaction-drive . . . Urrr," he churred more thoughtfully. "It is a clumsy makeshift but I do not like aliens having any weapons we lack. Heroes have died in the hunt when a fleeing prey kicked them with hard sharp hooves. Tell Alien Technologies Officer and Weapons Officer to look into the matter. If it is of truly dangerous potential, then they must find out everything about it. Perhaps we can duplicate the principle and better it with our own drive . . . Tell Weeow-Captain in generalities only if he asks." *A new weapon-principle, if it works, may be valuable,* he was thinking, *and I do not know yet where Weeow-Captain may fit into all this new order that may come about it. I hope he will remain my loyal Flag-Captain and friend, but for the moment . . .*

Alone, I took further thought, probed other minds. Waking and sleeping times passed. There were minds whose rhythms I followed. Zraar-Admiral's speculations . . . At last there came a certain time for sleep when, as the ship grew quieter and most minds around me grew still, I knew I had to move, to try to leap the chasm I had contemplated in fear so long.

I went to the cabin where one of the last monkeys was confined.

"You female." Pronunciation was impaired by the construction of its speaking apparatus as well as by its fangs.

"Yes," said Selina, staring up from the corner where she crouched. "I am female."

It was the one which had most often watched her, had pointed out the sanitary arrangements and thrown her food. It was smaller than the other felinoid monsters, not much more than seven feet high, and thinner. The lines of jaw and muzzle were thinner too, adding, with the large eyes and ears, a hint of lynx to the tiger face.

The words were grating and slurred, but she made them out. It was saying: "You are astrogator in the *Happy Gatherer*. Sapient are females of your species."

The first thought that penetrated her fog of terror was: *Give it a human larynx and mouth and it would be speaking good English.*

The second thought was: *It is sick.* She somehow knew

the other creatures she had seen were normal. It all sorts of ways, its violet-edged eyes, its posture, its odor, this creature was not normal.

She found her brain was racing. She could analyze her own observations of the nightmare thing. She felt clear-headed, too. It was as if what had never made any sense to her before did so now. *I felt the universe was out to get us and I was right.* If she could do nothing else, she could grit her teeth and clench her fists.

She had slept when she could, sometimes with dreams of Earth. Sometimes of childhood, sunlight and the sea she had loved, sometimes darker dreams of the deforming torture she and her brother had endured as her father fought current-addiction, the last sight of Easter Island as the shuttle soared towards the *Happy Gatherer* to depart after years of preparation. In some dreams loomed the statues of Easter Island which, she had been told, some people had once believed were made by wise and benevolent beings from the stars.

Sometimes it was the moment their world ended: when, the alien ship looming huge before them, autoshields slammed down over the faceplates of their helmets and they saw the *Happy Gatherer* disappear in a pale-blue glare. Nightmares of the demons, and Rosalind torn apart under their helpless stares. The distant human voices and cries she had heard since. Fewer of them as time went on. Loneliness as bad as terror. In any event it was in the cage of demons that she always awoke.

Several times she had suffered the blinding headaches which she was sure now were induced by the creatures. And now one spoke to her. In English.

She found she was largely beyond surprise. Aspects of the nightmares were compartmentalized from the waking reality. She stood, and forced herself to face the thing.

"Who are you?"

"Telepath. I have no name."

"Telepath? You mean . . . mind-reader?"

"Yes. Be calm. I know, despite posture, you do not challenge me."

"Is that how you know our language?"

"Yes. But time is urgent."

"What do you want?"

"Speech with you."

"I don't mean that. What does your . . . race . . . want? Why have you done this to us?"

"Conquest." For Telepath, it was a statement of the obvious.

"I understand." No surprise now. She stared up into the tired, sunken eyes.

"I not reading your mind now," it said, "But for a time I remember thoughts also language. I do not want to read your mind now. We Telepaths not live long and overuse of talent not help."

We Telepaths . . . I have no name. Yes, this thing is different to the others. An outcast? Why?

Because it is a Telepath!

I know that! How do I know it?

"So what do you want now? I mean you as an individual. Why do you come to me?"

The felinoid almost swayed. Its ears contracted. Its tail rose and fell. It twitched and tried to groom.

"Help." The voice was low. "Help me."

She fought down an urge to laugh wildly. "Help you? What do you mean?"

"Escape. I prisoner as you. Do you not wish to escape? To live?"

"Live?"

"Yes. Alternative is death for both. Even if you male your kind have not fighters' privileges of surrender or honorable death. In soon real-time you eaten. Your species is palatable and non-toxic. Feared Zraar-Admiral toyed with keeping pair to breed but decided many monkeys available soon. Keep tissue-samples. And soon I am burned out. Each new waking I dread first symptoms. Of our two fates, yours I would prefer. I do not know how much time we have—either of us. Zraar-Admiral and other officers have found monkeymeat tasty . . . I have not been allowed any of course."

None of that sank in at once. Then it did.

Selina had decided some time before that she had no chance of getting out alive, though she had blurred the details of her likely end. She had visited zoos on Earth, and, with visual enhancers, had seen captive tigers tearing at meat, held safely on spacious islands surrounded by water and electronic barriers. She had floated in a silent airship over the African Continental Park and seen lions kill. Now she remembered red blood, and muscle and yellow fat pulled away from red and white bones, rib-cages opening like fans, great yellow teeth and bloody muscles buried in the body-cavity of prey.

She had seen holos and dioramas of ancient sabre-tooths at her brother's museum, where children and adults screamed with delighted horror: the leaping bulk of the Smilodon, the replica leopard dragging the limp body of a hairy hominid, streaming blood, along a tree-branch, the cat's huge upper incisors fitting neatly into the hominid's conveniently-spaced eye-sockets, cranial vault fitting with equal neatness between the cat's jaws and held firmly by the lower incisors driven through the skull's occiput.

There had been a skeletal reconstruction of that, with Pleistocene remains from the Swartkrans Cave in southern Africa, showing how neat were the punctures of the leopard's lower fangs in the back of the hominid's

skull, two holes to match those natural cavities the eye-
sockets made for the upper fangs . . . the gnawed skull
dropped or rolled into the cave for fossil-hunters, so
many hominid bones dropped into it that they formed
a geological deposit called *breccia* . . . her mind was
jerking about what faced her . . . Rosalind torn and
flapping on the deck, Paul gone? Rick? All the rest?
The rest? All the *Happy Gatherer's* tight-knit crew?
Her mind spun into a desperate loop, turning away from
that unbearable question.

And she had her deeply-encoded biological inheritance.
She did not need to know consciously of the war of great
cats and hominids on the African savannah that had
impelled her ancestors towards intelligence. The creature
staring down at her was the embodiment of terror. Even
without the drug, Telepath felt something of the effort
with which she controlled herself.

For the first time, a Kzin looked upon a human with
admiration.

She breathed heavily, and wiped the sweat from her
eyes and from her body. Her next question was as brisk
and businesslike as she could make it.

"Where do we go?"

"Steal boat. There is one chance now that may never
come again for us. It is Lord Chmeee's leap, I know,
but we face certain destruction here."

She found an odd lucidity. The prospect of being eaten
concentrated the mind.

"Your people are hunters. They would pursue us,
would they not?"

"That is part of plan. We must make them care for a
mad and therefore useless Telepath and a monkey to
pursue, but pursue wrong way. Monkeys on Kzin planets
have tricks. You are a monkey. You must trick them."

"What do you think our chances are?"

"Perhaps one in eight to fourth or fifth power. But

random mathematics not my field . . . Does contortion of your muzzle signify anger? Or fear?"

"No. Amusement, of a sort."

"I remember. Urrr. But not Heroic for leaping one to calculate odds."

She was silent. She noticed again the endless ripping-cloth sound that vibrated ceaselessly throughout the ship.

"How can I believe you." She was full of fear as she asked this question—somehow she knew (a flash of thought: *how do I know*) that to question the honor of this creature might be a deadly insult. But Telepath answered calmly.

"I could give you my name as my word if my kind ever had names. But name or no name, it is dishonorable to lie except as . . . as . . . you have no word for it. I have so little honor I do not wish to lose any. And you are not going to get a better deal."

"Where do we actually escape *to*? Have you thought of that?"

"I told you, this is our only chance. We escape to your monkeyship, of course."

"I don't understand."

"Your *Winged Undying Shining* . . . The *Angel's Pencil* . . . We are following it."

Winged Undying Shining Monkey's Writing Stick! Yes! Suddenly an image flashed from her mind to mine. I saw our target at last.

A "colony ship", carrying a crew and many embryos to a planet circling a star named something like "Fifth of the River."

A thin cylinder, circled by a halo.

The halo was the lifesystem in which the monkeys traveled, spinning to mimic gravity with centrifugal force. The cylinder housed the drive . . . and the laser.

A reaction-drive, as I had known. Small attitude-jets and gyros. But so cumbersome, hard to turn! Defense of such a thing would be hopeless!

But then, to fight *Gutting Claw* in conventional battle was not my plan.

To reassure the Selina-monkey further, I gave it back (gave *her* back. I reminded myself it was female) the Space-suit which had been taken during examination. It was badly torn, but the creature seemed eager for it, and hastily put it on its body. In its damaged state it seemed quite useless, but of course all females love decorating themselves. She seemed more composed then.

"Why are you taking me?" she asked.

"I will need you to talk to the *Writing Stick* monkeys of course. Tell them that Telepath is a useful companion and will help them remain alive. That is the prime reason, but there are others also. I have read Astrogator's mind recently. I know as much of guiding a vessel in space as Astrogator, but I will forget. The knowledge Telepaths take from other minds cannot stay with us without a . . . bridge. And I only need to forget a little of astrogation procedures—questions for the computer—to be lost beyond all recovery. I will need you then."

"Or do you just want me to eat for yourself. Spare provisions perhaps?"

"I could not eat you personally, unless I was in hunger-frenzy. Perhaps not even then. I have read your mind too deeply. It would be like eating myself. My condition has many disadvantages, one is inhibition in that area. We have too much . . . empathy. Unfortunately, this does not diminish with time. There is an effect. Besides, there are plenty of rations. There are provisions in all boats, and I have identified extra stores and prepared them for loading.

"Also, it is generally desirable to have *a zzrow graff* . . . useful companion.

"Yours was a sea-faring race before it took to the stars, I know. When Alien Technologies Officer and I examined this"—I gave it the thing we had taken from the suit—"we were baffled by its function. It was shaped something like a weapon. Yet once, when I was reading your mind as softly as I might, I discovered it was a small replica of an ancient ship. I do not know why you have it, but I thought perhaps . . ."

"A gift from my brother."

New vistas of alien thought were opened to me. I felt new images from this monkey's mind—of blue monkey home-world oceans, wider than those of Kzin, oceans which the monkeys had crossed for trade or even in order to stimulate some alien sense of pleasure, oceans they had voluntarily swum in and which they had written poetry about. Creatures lived in those oceans and I even caught a taste of them that stiffened my whiskers.

How *alien* these aliens were! And yet . . . the gift from the brother—would a Hero give a Kzinrett sister a gift? Yes, perhaps, when they were young. Bright shiny ornaments young Kzinretts liked. Heroes could feel affection for sisters they had spent kittenhood with, and Heroes could and should treasure mementos of great deeds and give gifts to those they cared for. Heroes who grew up in the households of Noble Sires, as I did not. But no Kzinrett crewed a Space-ship: the vocabulary of the Female tongue was perhaps eight to the power of three words.

The brother had been a museum guard. That was more strangeness. On Kzin Museum Guard was a task for certain old and honored warriors, perhaps heroically disabled in battle, supervised by the Conservors' mystic order.

These creatures had not a warrior among them, nor it seemed to me, a real notion of honor, yet they had museums. It made no sense. What would they display in such places? I extracted images of museums weirdly perverted—displaying not relics of battle but of games, of dances, of the origins of monkeydom and the animal forms that had preceded their own dominance.

Or was there something else? A hint of something secret deeply buried? The model had been preserved as a curio not for associations of honor or glory but for the sake of its age alone. Its name meant nothing to the Selina. A mere sound.

Like their other names that were not names. They gave them to objects, to ships, as we gave names to the vessels of our own Space-fleets.

Names in such a context mattered to Heroes. If not a fine and splendid description of function and purpose, full of poetry, like *Rampant Slayer* or *Conqueror's Fang*, the names of Kzinti ships commemorated the names of great Heroes of the past like Chmeee or the Lord Dragga-Skrull who lost a forelimb, nostrils and eye before leading his force to death and imperishable glory gutting a superior fleet of the Jotok when Heroes rose against them and leapt into Space at the dawn of the Eternal Hunt.

All this passed through my mind in a moment or so. These creatures were not utterly unlike us in some ways, though in others strange beyond comprehension. Selina had swum in those cold salt waves for pleasure! I thought of how much I hated the feel of water on my fur and tail.

I thought at first that Selina would be impressed by the fact that, as soon as I had catalogued the various monkeys' mental capabilities, I had had others rather than her served up to Feared Zraar-Admiral and the officers. But I now suspected this would not increase her trust of me. There was nothing except truth, however, in what I said next:

"But there is another reason I want you, for me

compelling. In your mind is a story of curing addiction. I am an addict. I am going to need that story to have any chance of curing myself even with Admiral's medicine. I will need to cure myself or perish, and in this I will need the example of a monkey. Yes, I foresee I will need to return to that example in what lies ahead. Can a Kzin—even a Kzin such as I—not equal one of your kind in endurance and Will?"

I sat on the floor of the cabin beside her, deliberately relinquishing my advantage in height. Then I continued:

"Those are the principal reasons but there is also another faint, dim spoor. But perhaps a further reason, a . . . *sentimental* . . . one" (that was the word I took with some difficulty from the monkey's mind. I was not sure it was the real equivalent of any Kzinti concept but it would suffice). "Part of the reason I was selected for my talent to be developed is that I have a relatively high but undirected intelligence.

"There is no other role for one like me. I am not a warrior and even before I was made what I am I lacked long concentration, intellectual rigor or even creative flair which would have made me useful in other areas. Yet in your mind I have seen pictures of a world which tolerates the likes of Telepath . . . the likes of you."

"Of me?"

"Yes, the minds of we two are alike at one level, you know." It seemed to me I was stating the obvious, even if it was nothing for me to be proud of. And I felt her accept this fact more easily than I might have expected. "I feel . . . gratitude . . . that such a society has existed even if its future is to be short.

"There is another thing, too, beyond that," I went on, "The thing that gives rise to all my plans, small though their hope is.

"This is a difficult thought, an even fainter spoor, a wandering track in a mind-tunnel not ventured before.

Alien Technologies Officer reached the first prints, and Feared Zraar-Admiral has gone a little further, but only Telepath has really followed the trail. If your race now has no knowledge of weapons or warfare—less than any sapient race we have conquered—yet at some time in the past you learnt to throw missiles so powerfully that today you travel between stars, can it be that, instead of never having had such knowledge, your race has actually *suppressed* it to a unique degree?

"If I had not had long times alone and without duties in which to think I would not have seen this. But you have names of a sort. You have ranks. On your Space-ship you divided time into 'watches' much as we do. What did you once watch for? Where did those things come from? And I know from your mind that there are areas of your past that few of your kind are allowed to study. Why? I know from your mind of the ARM: you even have a . . . police of knowledge. "

"I'm no historian," she said. "I don't know."

"You speak truth here," I replied, "You do not know. But you do not tell Telepath in words all that you think. There is something you suspect, though even to you the spoor is dim. I have read in your mind that there is another monkey, some litter-mate of yours—yes, it is the brother who gave you the small mimicry of the sea-ship—who also hides in its own lair thoughts that it . . . But if what I suggest is true, that knowledge was suppressed for some reason."

"I suppose so. Does it matter."

"It may matter a very great deal. For I can think of only one possible reason that a race—a race whose ships are powered by the fusion of hydrogen atoms—should *suppress* knowledge of weapons and war, and I am the only one of my species it has occurred to."

"I see," she said. And then: "I think I understand. But I do not know if my thoughts are true."

"You do not know of *RRzzinr* . . . of *Tracker*."

"What is that?"

"None in your ship knew of it. I searched for that first of all. But I think of the Eternal Hunt and I wonder if we may at last have stuck our noses into one cave too many. It is only a slight possibility, mind you." I turned from this spoor then, but spoke more of my thoughts, which had grown in the last days. I told of *Tracker*, and of *Gutting Claw's* present vengeance quest.

"When we have killed the *Writing Stick* our fleet will search for your home-world. With your primitive drives it cannot be far away—indeed I can calculate its approximate distance easily. I know how long you live, how long you have been in Space and your course. Alien Technologies Officer has extracted all data from your boat's computer and laid it before the Dominant One. You need not reproach yourself for that. We plotted your monkey-ship's course from the moment we detected you.

"The drives of your vessels and the trails they leave are easily detected. We know most of what you know. We know the composition of your atmosphere, that your home-world is the third planet from its sun, a yellow dwarf, and that it has a single very large moon. We know the other characteristics of your system including the gas-giants. We know of your long-colonized asteroid belt and the distance to your nearest extra-Solar colony world. We will find them without great trouble."

"Then how does it benefit us to get to the *Angel's Pencil*?"

"If the monkeys on board are alerted and if pursuit is slowed, they may escape for a long time. Space is big. Or they could fight. They have done so once. If we can warn them, we can give them time to prepare some defense. Or such was my original idea."

"Won't there be guards on the boats?"

It was a strange question. Why guard boats? Who would leave a Space-ship in the depths of Space? Did Selina think Kzintosh would fear monkey-prisoners from the live-meat lockers?

"What if the others see us?" She persisted.

"They will assume I am taking you to Zraar-Admiral or Weeow-Captain," I reassured her. "I have freedom of movement in the ship since I am beneath having general duties. We must not waste more time. Who knows when the Dominant One may not in truth send for one or the other of us?"

Selina pressed her hands to her head. Hope of escape, I knew, had flared in her mind for a moment. But now she thought I had no plan at all, only neurosis. Still, she did not think it would be a good idea to antagonize me by disagreeing.

"We can gain access to a boat." I said, "Of the small craft Feared Zraar-Admiral's barge is much the biggest, best-fitted, fastest and most powerful. I have prepared various . . . stores and cargo to load.

"If we ran out of other options we could self-destruct, which I think you would prefer to being eaten, and which I would prefer to the discipline I would receive in the event of re-capture, or to burn-out. We will have some counter-measures against missiles. But outrunning a beam generated close is another matter."

"Yes, that would be a problem."

"That is another way I shall need your help, monkey. Think of a way for us to outrun a beam, and it is just possible we may live."

"I see. A simple task." I caught irony in her mind.

"The barge has devices for creating ghosts. I mean ghosts in the electronic warfare sense as well as the obvious one. Electronic replicas of ourselves."

"I need time to think."

Selina sat, head cradled in forepaws. Used to the alien

mind now, I found I could mind-read with a most cautious, almost unnoticeable, entry. She was in despair. *Impossibilities*. And beyond impossible tasks another imperative: her home-world must be warned. I had not told her the monkeys in *Tracker* had already taken this task upon themselves.

No. Not quite despair.

"The other humans. Can you put us together?"

"Why? Do you need to mate? We have more important things to do at present. I know what *kz'eerkti* are like but try to control yourself."

"Together we may be able to think of something . . . I need to pick their brains."

"Anyway, there is only one other monkey left."

I thought I had told her this already but she had evidently not taken it in. Now it shook her like a reed in a storm-wind. She staggered, fell on her knees. There was a storm on her far greater than when I had first spoken to her. I shielded myself against it. Then I thought she was becoming calmer. I did not want to go into her roiling mind until it calmed, but I was puzzled by what she had said.

"Further, You cannot eat brains, if that is what you mean." I told her. "They are delicacy for officers."

"I need to consult."

"The one called Rick is nearby. I suppose I could put you together."

"Is he well."

"He says nothing."

"I must talk with him."

"I do not think talking would be useful. He is a coward. His mind and liver are only fear now. Not like you. But you are more a monkey-expert than I and I will bring him if you think it would help."

"No, take me to him. That is the way it is done with us. I am the female and I must go to him."

Being dragged here by that thing might well be the last straw for him, her real thought flashed out to me. If that was what she thought, why did she not say so? Her thoughts and her words were not in synchronization. She spoke things that were not—*lied*—as no Warrior or Hero would.

But as a Telepath might.

It was useful to be reminded that these monkeys were but honorless omnivores. But why should I need *reminding* of that?

Then a speaker boomed.

"Telepath to the Bridge!"

"Wait," I told it. "If your Bearded God owes you anything, ask him to pay that debt to you now."

"We have the other monkey-ship! It is surely the so-called *Writing Stick*!" Telepath blundered onto the Bridge, looking as always sick and disheveled. The officers drew instinctively away from him, but Weeow-Captain beckoned him instantly to one of the Command couches.

"Get them, Telepath!" Weeow-Captain ordered. "Confirm!"

Telepath sank into the position of the Mind-hunt.

"This is truly the *Writing Stick* and truly the ship that destroyed *Tracker*," he reported after a moment. "They have detected us. They speculate that we are *Tracker's* companion . . . They call us something like . . . *Big Specialized Four-Legged Solitary Carnivorous Hunting Animal* . . ." Zraar-Admiral and Weeow-Captain had expected an obscenely abusive monkey-name. The Kzin felt surprised and mildly gratified that, clumsy as it was, the name these fighting monkeys had given to *Disemboweling Claw* was nothing offensive. Some monkey might receive an honorable death as an acknowledgment of the politeness.

A pause then: "They have Heroes' dead bodies on board, and machinery from *Tracker*. The gravity motor . . ."

Then a strangled cry. A brother Telepath might have detected that Telepath was torn between the compulsion of the drug and a desire not to reveal what he had discovered. "They have *Tracker's* missiles! They have mounted them and rigged *Tracker's* launching console!"

"Urrr. Can they run?"

"They seem to be near maximum speed now. We steadily overtake them."

"Shall we detonate their missiles?" Weeow-Captain asked Zraar-Admiral.

"Not yet. We should be able to intercept such a battery if necessary. But if possible they are to be boarded. There is vengeance to be exacted. And Heroes' bodies should be recovered for honorable disposal. Unless we must we should not send the bodies of Heroes and Monkeys to the Fanged God together in such circumstances. Let the monkeys responsible be properly laid out upon our Heroes' funeral pyres. The meat of the rest will be ours."

Zraar-Admiral stood still in thought for a moment. Telepath seemed unconscious now.

"Weeow Captain, we will not chase them from behind. Divert your course. A large arc." He swiped his claws across the screen, indicating the angle. "I wish to approach this prey from the flank."

He went on: "It will be slower, but it will give the prey more time for anticipation." Zraar-Admiral could feel his officer's keen joy that he was prepared to prolong the pleasure of all concerned. *And keep us out of the way of that drive* . . . Zraar-Admiral thought to himself.

There was more that might be learnt about the enemy, but Zraar-Admiral, seeing Telepath lying prone on the deck, was aware that he would have to be conserved.

He was the last of the three the squadron had begun with. He gestured to an orderly who dragged Telepath away by one foot and dumped him on a shelf in a nearby corridor, slack-limbed, twitching, breathing in shallow gasps.

The orderly had no thought for Telepath. Having to touch the addict's ill-smelling fur was distasteful enough. He hastened back to Zraar-Admiral's side and did not see how quickly the little Kzin seemed to recover, then sprang to his feet, and ran.

Zraar-Admiral had been on the bridge a long time as their quarry was slowly overhauled. He gave orders that he was to be called in the event of any developments and went to rest. Weeow-Captain and the rest could do with a demonstration of the value of the ability to relax before action. Perhaps there would be a monkeymeat feast later, before the final pounce, and, with new monkey-prisoners, a larger celebratory one after the victory.

No-one from the bridge saw Telepath pass by again shortly after, hauling a loaded gravity-sledge. He headed first for the boat-deck, then back to the now nearly depopulated live-meat lockers.

Rick Chew was almost catatonic. Telepath pulled the door closed behind them, curled himself down and knotted his ears for a moment. Then he straightened again.

"It is as I said," he told Selina after a moment. "Its mind is blank. I read nothing. It is male, but it is not a monkey like you."

"Can you bring him round?" asked Selina. Telepath had to probe her own mind to understand what she meant.

"Comfort it? Like kitten? Comforting monkeys is nothing I know. Who has comforted me?"

"Try. Project your mind. Try the ideas of 'Friend' and 'Safety.' "

"I do not put into minds. I take from them. I cannot tell a piece of quivering monkeymeat that it is a useful companion or that it is safe when it is neither. If that is what you want you must do it."

It took Selina a long time to bring Rick Chew to full consciousness, holding and stroking him. It was therapy by instinct. Perhaps the sight of her and Telepath together played some part in helping him accept what was before him.

He could do little more than nod at first as Selina tried to give him a euphemistic and reassuring account of their situation, and when she tried to explain that Telepath was an ally. But Telepath told her that he understood.

Finally, at Selina's instruction, Telepath withdrew and left them, muttering to the effect that time was limited. Rick turned to Selina and, to her surprise, made an attempt at a tearful smile. There was little of the Rick she had known in that gaunt haggard face.

"Aren't you going to say: 'I told you so'?" He asked.

Selina felt tears starting in her own eyes at the attempted joke. But she knew it might be fatal to give way to emotion now. She did not realize that something was making her more receptive to emotion. *He is tougher than I imagined*, she thought. *Perhaps tougher than he imagined, too. Is there hope in that? If not for us personally, perhaps for our kind? Arthur, can you hear me? Can anybody hear me?* She held Rick close, touching his sunken cheek tentatively.

"At least," she said, "we have added a great deal to our knowledge of the universe. We wanted to find out what Space contained. Now we know."

"Yes. And it would be nice to have the results of our research published. Though I must confess the prospects that originally motivated us seem somewhat secondary to me now."

"What a learned paper we could write: 'Notes towards tentative conclusions regarding preliminary results of an investigation into certain inter-stellar gravity and radio anomalies.' "

Rick grabbed her hard. "We've got to warn Earth!"

"I know." Selina suspected the *Angel's Pencil* was already sending off warnings, but this would give him a further motive for action.

"That *thing*!" he shook uncontrollably as his mind filled with an image of Telepath.

"You'll get used to him," Selina told him with a kind of grotesque matter-of-factness. "He's not so bad for a . . . for whatever they are . . ." She repeated slowly that Telepath wanted them to escape with him. She had wondered if this was some cruel equivalent of a house-cat playing with mice, but something told her it was not. Again she wondered at how much she seemed to know about Telepath.

"Yes, he would need us with him to get the *Pencil* to take him aboard. But how?" The voice had relapsed into tonelessness but the words at least suggested Rick was handling data again.

He would not have been selected for this crew if he had not been one of the best, Selina reminded herself. *It is easy to forget that we were an elite*. She told him again what Telepath had said and all she had worked out about Telepath's position. After a time Rick spoke in a different voice.

"It is a question of getting a sufficient start. We must place some distance between ourselves and the ship before our absence is noticed. Given enough distance from the source of a beam, it might be possible to avoid it. They must have counter-measures to beams, too. Devices to throw out dust-clouds, perhaps."

"Yes, he mentioned something about that."

"But if we do somehow get to the *Angel's Pencil*, what then?"

"We are better off there than here. Telepath tells me they used the com-laser as a weapon of their own, and that they have evidently taken missiles from another cat-ship they destroyed. And there is the ramscoop-field."

"The ramscoop-field is generated ahead. The laser points behind. Neither can be moved much . . . Not fast enough . . ."

"We'll have to hope they've got other weapons operational by now. They've had time to think . . ."

They were still struggling with plans when Telepath returned. "Now you have awakened the cowardly monkey, what have you achieved?" he demanded.

They discussed anti-beam defenses and how they could gain time to escape. There were intact hexagons of logic-lattice on the arms and torso of Selina's suit, and on Rick's, which Telepath also retrieved, but at present there was nothing they could ask them.

"No choice but action now!" said Telepath. "We close with the *Writing Stick*! Battle soon! Place for us in that battle! Urrr!"

He struck an heroic attitude. "Let us urinate from the heights on fear! What do all our legends and epics tells us? Lord Chmeee, Krrarrit, Lord Dragga-Skrull, Lost Skragga-Chmee, Ffeelillth-Wirrh! Zirrow-Graff, Grragz's Third Gunner! Kzintosh Heroes without number, all defied prodigious enemies and great odds! So our race may face the Fanged God without fear! Does not even your Bearded God approve of courage?"

"Let us see what capital we have," said Rick at last. "Selina is a navigator-pilot. I know both computers and reasoning machines.

"If I could have one of this ship's main computer

outlets to work on, it is just possible something could be done. Is there an input to a central data-base?"

"Of course. They are all over the ship."

"And in the boats? They are connected?"

"Of course. The boats and also the cruisers and other ships riding in the hull."

"And reasoning machines? Planar lattices?"

Telepath read his mind.

"No," he said. "Heroes use machines when large numbers must be dealt with at great speed, or to enhance hunting senses. We do not use machines to tell us how to make decisions. We are not monkeys."

"That is what I hoped. So you have computers only, with a central computer net?"

"Yes."

"Could that be jinxed somehow? To create an impression that things are not what they seem? We need a . . . diversion. Something to give us time."

"What diversion?"

"A simulated emergency. Computer failure might be easiest. But it would have to be a lifesystem-threatening situation that would occupy all attention."

"The lifesystem has ample back-ups. So does the computer system. This ship was built for battle, though it has never fought aliens in deep space. There are redundancies in all essential systems."

"Never fought aliens?"

"No. Only your *Plant Eater*. We have beaten down planetary defenses and we have landed infantry on some primitive worlds. Some aboard have fought other Kzin. But that does not matter now."

"Oh, yes it does! You mean this is actually a crew without much experience of war! What hazards does your kind fear?"

"None! Heroes fear nothing save dishonor!" The reply was automatic and instantaneous, but Selina felt somehow sure that it was not completely true.

"Then what hazards does your command bear most in mind now?"

"*Tracker* is in many minds. Unknown weapons. Zraar-Admiral and Weeow-Captain are puzzled still how weaponless monkeys could react in time to destroy a Kzin scout-cruiser. They thought your ship would fight, though it did not. Zraar-Admiral has wondered if you monkeys are controlled by hidden masters. There are some who fear ambushes. Even Zraar-Admiral has wondered in secret lately if the recording we found in *Tracker* was not part of a trap to make us think that that battle was a freak only—that the real enemy is formidable and different."

"Then an attack on this ship," said Rick. "That would be a diversion."

"An attack with what?" asked Telepath. "Who would attack?"

"We would. We need to paint a picture of an attack."

"I do not understand, monkey. Is your mind still sick?" Telepath lashed his tail in frustration and disgust. "Heal him!" He ordered Selina. "You may mate with him if that will calm him, but be swift!"

"I don't think his mind is sick," said Selina. "Let him explain."

"We cannot attack a . . ." Telepath spoke for all the control he could muster. There were no words for "capital ship" or "Dreadnought" left in the humans' vocabularies. "Even if we obtained weapons. Suicide gesture only. Urrr. Is that what you intend? . . . Suicide gesture might," he added thoughtfully, "be best option."

"We could attack it through its computers." said Rick.

Telepath stared at him. "Go on," he said at last, "but I do not understand. We could, perhaps, shut down main computers for short time. But back-up computers phase in automatically. I told you there are many redundancies. We would have time to do nothing."

"I would need your help," said Rick, "Can you extract knowledge from the minds of your computer programmers so that they are unaware of it."

"I believe so. I am good Telepath. You hear how well I speak your language. I am good at taking knowledge from Kzintosh or monkey."

"What weapons does this ship carry inside itself?"

"The infantry weapons—guns, beams, chemical weapons, missile launchers . . . The ship's heavy weapons are under Weapons Officer's control."

"The infantry weapons . . . they would have to be comparatively low-yield?"

"There are some chemical bombs, yes. Weapons the infantry carry . . ."

Rick was speaking quickly now: "Any diversion should combine events: bombs exploded inside the hull to simulate missile impacts, and from the boat a program loaded into the main computers. With your knowledge of your computers that should be possible. The bomb-damage would also help disguise the fact the boat was missing."

"Where would we get bombs?"

"Would not the boats carry weapons? The very boat you plan to escape in?"

"How do you know this?"

"I don't know. There is a kind of inevitability about it, once you begin to think in these terms. It would naturally have weapons."

"Your own boat did not."

"No, of course not."

"Yes," Telepath nodded. "It may be as I suspected. But they would not believe if I told them. May be wrong cave at last. Stupid. Stupid."

"Meanwhile," said Rick, "We must do some creative programming. Not disable the main computers of this ship, but Tanj them: place an image of an attacker in them. It must appear on the screens suddenly as we escape. Can you know the ship's computers well enough to do that?"

"I told you I am good Telepath. I can know them for a time. I can read the programmers' and system controllers' minds, take years of knowledge and training and make them my own. Also Navigator, who has access to Fleet computer banks. Everything.

"What none aboard deign to realize is that only I, the addict, may know *everything* about this ship if I choose. I have the ability to read Kzintosh minds by stealth, if need be, stealthy as any lurker in tall grass. For I also have a war, though they do not know it . . . If a computer can be programmed, I can extract knowledge to program it. If boat is to be flown, if weapon is to be operated, I can extract knowledge to do it!

"And yet they would not let me breed. I have read in your minds of monkeys on your homeworld who have a distant glimmering of the World of the Eleventh Sense, the smallest hint of Telepath's power. And you give these monkeys recognition and place and *encourage* them to breed!"

"I am also a programmer," said Rick. His voice had become calm and precise now, no longer with the need to control fear but with the need to discipline and marshal rapid thoughts. *Perhaps even to calm Telepath,* wondered Selina. *How quickly things are changing!* "You can read my mind as well. Given this cognitive array, can you place the image of an attacking ship in the system?"

"It is possible. Displays are diagrammatic. But I do not know how long such a false image would go undetected. Not long, I think."

"Each moment that it was maintained would improve our chances."

"Better if our attacker had alien design-style," said Telepath. "It should not be ship of the Heroic Race, for signatures of all nearby are recorded. Nor could it be another defenseless monkey-ship."

"But what of the thing that waits behind the defenseless monkeyship! The fighting ship that sent it as a lure!" exclaimed Selina. "Let them see that and fear!"

Telepath whirled upon her, claws out.

"What is this? Have you deceived me! Where is this warship?"

"There is none," said Selina. "Read my mind if you would see whether or not I speak truth."

She paused, looking fixedly at the alien carnivore towering over her. "There is none save this," she said. She held up the ancient model of HMS *Nelson*. "Is this strange enough?"

The others stared at her.

"There's the attacker. Can you put a display of it into the computer?"

Members of the Kzin species did not as a rule tend to develop their senses of humor much beyond witticism or ingenious insult. Telepaths, however, needed a sense of humor as they needed all the mental defense mechanisms they could muster, though in general they kept it among their own kind. Now Telepath folded and unfolded his ears rapidly, the Kzin equivalent of a roar of laughter.

Selina laughed too, and then Rick. It seemed the only thing to do, but she was careful to bite the laughter off before it went out of control. In some remote corner of her mind she registered that she had recognized Telepath's laughter for what it was without being told. She had caught his amusement . . . had she somehow, read *his* mind?

"I scout. And I go to programmers," said Telepath. He injected himself with a minimum does of the

Sthondat-drug and his ears contracted into tight knots. He curled upon the deck, wrapping his tail around his nose like a house-cat settling into a basket. His eyes glazed and he drooled from slackened black lips. He twitched sometimes but finally appeared to sleep.

After what seemed a long time of tension-screaming silence Rick moved to waken Telepath. Selina grabbed his hand. She knew without being told that it would not be wise to try to shake him awake. She realized, without doubt now, and with a strange cold thrill like some new fear, that she knew more of Telepath than she had ever been told.

Telepath stirred. His voice was blurred and his eyes unfocussed. Then he brought himself under control. His voice, too, seemed to be becoming easier for Selina to understand.

"Move swiftly," said Telepath, "All nearby sleep."

He rose, and the three stepped into the dim ruddy light of the corridor. The humans felt hideously exposed. They guessed the dimness of the light would be no obstacle to the cats' eyes. Telepath led them to a service duct and they clambered in, like clumsy mice into a hole.

It was not like the tunnels of the Eleventh Sense. This was a passage like a Kzinrett's birthing burrow that I threaded, the monkeys too noisy behind me.

In darkness I felt the monkey minds very close, the Selina's for some reason much closer than the male Rick's. I was fearful, but I pressed on. Death awaited me, but it would be death on my own terms. I might die as Hero, not in foul degradation of burn-out.

Sleeping minds all around. Heroes on duty watch, bored, two fighting in the combat arena with sheathed claws, as Feared Zraar-Admiral had ordered. Junior officers and crew staring at screens that showed energy-pulses of unwavering regularity, or the blackness of space. A brief touch against Feared Zraar-Admiral's mind, and a quick shying away.

The monkey minds: the Rick apparently resigned to whatever might become, but with something else stirring that even the Rick was not aware of, the Selina mind that seemed almost too easy to enter now.

Dangerous always for a Telepath in dark tunnels without sleep or distraction. For all my hurrying (I slowed my pace as I heard the monkeys panting and breathless behind me) it was easy to think too much.

Honored Maaug-Riit had long made plain what was expected of me: to report to him should Feared Zraar-Admiral show signs of overmuch ambition. He had given me his word that, though it might be eights of years in the coming, I might have a posthumous partial name if I performed this well. The Patriarch had many ears into which I might speak.

Yet Feared Zraar-Admiral was my leader. He had complimented me. I would betray him now, but it was a betrayal only to save myself. That was permitted: so many stories said.

The boat-deck was vast, like a plain between mountain walls. There rode whole ships, scouts that needed large specialized crews. I and the humans were almost lost as we moved through a ducting-service corridor to the array of smaller Space-craft.

Gutting Claw carried several ready-reserve battalions of Heroes in sleep who, in the event of an inhabited world being discovered, could supplement and spearhead her crew as infantry. There were ranks of specialized armed and armored landing-craft as well as the normal ship's boats and small fighters. There were bins of spare parts and workshop and machine spaces, at present all secured. I still felt no waking Kzinti minds near.

Zraar-Admiral's barge was parked near the massive doors, ready for instant service. There too was the *Happy*

Gatherer's boat, canted over on one side where the gravity-jacks had dropped it.

"See there," I told the monkeys. "Now I think the Fanged God is minded that our jest with him shall have success. He has given the means to cause enough damage to mask our escape."

In the same floor-space a gravity-motor and its housing had been set up, part of Weapons Officer's project to offset the possible future use of drives as weapons by monkeyships. It was still experimental and very small-scale, but involved generating a tight vortex to in theory either deflect particles or, like a reaction-drive, act as a gun. In this sleep-period it was unattended.

"Help me!" I ordered.

Weak I was but far stronger than the strongest human. Between us we dragged the gravity-motor round so that its field would cover the nearest main entrance. But I did not activate the field yet. That would need to be done, I calculated, from the barge just after the diversion appeared on the computer display and I opened the blast-doors to Space. I showed the monkeys the controls for its traverse and focus. This prototype was based on one of the smallest standard motors, taken from an infantry lifting-sled—the housing of even a boat's motor would be far too massive for power-driver assists of the size fitted here. I had hoped to use it to propel missiles but I now saw with anger that Weapons Officer obeyed procedures and all ammunition was locked away.

There was no problem getting aboard the barge. I had taken the door-codes from Coxswain's mind for my secret loading of the Kzinretts and there was normally no need for great security for an Admiral's personal equipment: unauthorized Kzin would not board without good reason. The barge was ready for instant use. Apart from other functions, it could serve as the Admiral's emergency headquarters in battle. Its central command position was a miniature replica of a battleship's bridge and there were Hero-sized couches round a central computer terminal for a nucleus staff.

I curled down in the Command chair and took another minimal dose of Sthondat-drug. I was prowling through most delicate cover. No vegetable would I disturb so that its crown might sway against the wind and warn that I moved through that undergrowth.

The sleep period was ending. More senior officers were awakening and eating. They would be reporting for their duties soon. My mind touched, dancing on lightest velvet-clawed feet, against one officer and then another. Systems Controller, Navigator, Chief Programmer, First Technical Chief, Lesser Technical Chief, snatching any tiny prey I had not taken previously into my claws with the quickest, subtlest of slashes. Yes, Telepath's claws could be sharp for this work, honed long in invisible caves no Kzintosh warrior knew! More I took from the Rick-monkey's mind, leaping then from a high point to look down upon it all.

Strained and fearful were the humans when I returned from the white tunnels. Well might they fear. Heroes in Space do not like being shut away from any vista, even if it is but a vista of the blackness between worlds, and the barge had bigger viewing ports than the human boat. They were normally clear save in battle. Any Kzin coming onto the boat-deck might have seen them. They pressed themselves down as far as they might and lay in silence.

A combatant Hero might have been surprised to see me then, and the speed with which my claws worked the computer's keys. A visual array of sensors took in the model ship, its diagrammatic image appearing on Local Display a moment later. I rotated it through three dimensions and confirmed the display was consistent. Then I handed it to the Rick.

"It is done," I said, "Part of our deception is prepared."

I consulted the computer again, touched System Controller's mind once more, and the Rick's, linked the image to the battle-alert sensors, then set the program to run. A tunneling thing it was. Time, a little time, it would need yet to burrow its way into the entrails of the Battle-Display tank.

"Do you know how to open these doors?" The Rick asked. Normally I might have swiped the monkey with my claws for the stupid and insulting question, but I thought it necessary that the timid thing be reassured.

"There are officers who do," I said, "and this boat has emergency over-ride for any command to be obeyed when issuing from it. Long ago when he was distracted did I take the code-word from Feared Zraar-Admiral's mind.

"Timing is difficult now. We should load extra stores and what weapons we may."

"More stores? But it is only a short journey, surely?"

This time I nearly did swipe it. "And if we reach the monkey-ship, do you expect me to eat monkeyfood?"

Quickly I climbed down from the barge and began collecting the storage-bins I had prepared previously. The monkeys followed and tried to help, but they were slow and clumsy and could hardly lift the containers. I was fearful that they would drop them. Suddenly the door crashed open.

"What are you doing here? Answer, Addict!" I had forgotten Weapons Officer. Stupid. Stupid. He had returned, of course, to work on the gravity-motor weapon.

What did Weapons Officer see? Telepath and the two loose monkeys, surrounded by bins of stores, standing between the weapon's test-bed and the Admiral's barge. For a moment he was stunned with surprise. He had not come prepared, as he would have come to the training arena. But I knew his battle-reflexes. The next moment he would leap.

Yet I had one *Wtsai* hidden in my cave: the idea of Telepath planning to steal the barge and escape was too insane to occur to him. Weapons Officer was a typical Kzintosh, the same as those youngsters who would have killed me in the crèche when they had taken me from Karan, had not my talent been recognized by the Trainers-of-Telepaths.

The speed of thought! But I did not need to read his mind to see its image of me: I had seen it in the minds of all the officers, yes, and in the minds of the lowliest infanteers and wipers, too, countless times already. To him I was the addict, eunuch-substitute, herder-of-apes, beneath contempt . . .

How could he know how Telepaths thought? But I had a moment, as Weapons Officer stood puzzled, staring at me and at the monkeys, and the image of an alien warcraft burrowed its way into the computer's vitals.

A red jet flared in his mind. No clear understanding yet, but: *The addict! The monkeys! Treachery!* Weapons officer's hand moved to the grip of his *Wtsai*.

I had a *Wtsai* in my belt, too, but to touch it would be fatal. I could not fight Weapons Officer. No addict he, but tall, strong, fast, superbly fit, with countless hours of combat training. There was not a Kzintosh on the ship that I, Telepath, could best in combat. None, indeed, so poor and lacking in dignity as to challenge me in the practice arena. "Fight a Telepath" was a Kzintosh insult.

They did not know the Telepath's Weapon. The light dose of Sthondat-drug I had taken was still in my system: enough to heighten my power, not enough to disorient me. I reached for the pain-centers of his mind, and struck.

Given skill, practice, familiarity with the one whose mind is entered, an experienced Telepath can avoid causing pain at entry. I had read Kzin minds all unknown to them. First Telepath had praised my art. Now I bent all my power not to avoid pain but to cause it: the Telepath's own Hot Needle and Vengeful Slasher.

The agony in his brain Weapons Officer had never expected or experienced. He reeled back screaming, clutching his head, eyes rolling and ears knotted. The effort weakened me, but I was prepared and summoned my will. I stood rampant as Weapons Officer doubled in agony. He dropped his *Wtsai*, its blade clattering on the deck. I leapt upon him and cut his throat.

"That's torn it," said Rick behind me, as I regained my breath and was bending to take Weapons Officer's ears for my first belt-trophy.

I saw what he meant beyond the statement of the obvious. We were committed now. Rick looked pleased. I had no time to read his mind, but the expression on his face, with his little omnivore teeth showing, signified either amusement or defiance.

I could feel Kzintosh minds moving not far away now. "Hurry!" I told the monkeys as I tucked the ears safely away, "Silence has second priority now!"

Selina cried out. Two troopers burst through the door by which Weapons Officer had entered. I could not have held two at once, and for the moment my power was drained. Both carried side-arms.

Selina moved fast for a monkey. She turned the gravity-planer weapon at them and activated it, catching them unprepared, knocking them back and away up the corridor. I took it and spun the controls at random. The monkey-boat, only temporarily secured, broke loose and went smashing away, rupturing cables and ducting. Infantry boats were torn loose and hurtled across the deck. Small-arms ammunition exploded.

Then the huge appalling battle alarms roared.

❖   ❖   ❖

The alarms and the howls of damage-alert klaxons mingled with the screams of Kzin. Zraar-Admiral leapt for the bridge, a standing leap upward from one deck to the next ignoring the vertical ladder, his staff and bodyguards close behind him. He was roaring commands for return fire into his helmet speaker as he came.

Some viewing screens blanked out, but enough remained in the dim-red glare of the emergency lights for Zraar-Admiral, as he reached the bridge, to see wreckage exploding into Space on sensor-screens.

And flaring on one bank of screens and then another was a Thing: an alien craft shaped nothing like either the monkey-ship they had destroyed or the still distant *Writing Stick*. Its bizarre asymmetrical configuration was dominated by what appeared to be colossal triple-banked turreted weapons-systems. Rail guns? The *real* lasers that had slashed *Tracker*? Trap!

The battleship shuddered again as broadsides of missiles blasted away from it. Surging odors of blood and battle, natural and manufactured, filled the air. There was a new scream from an internal klaxon. Zraar-Admiral leapt up onto the battle-drum, striking it so that its Sthondat-hide chambers boomed and reverberated. The Day! The Day at last!

"We have been boarded! There is fighting on the boat-deck!" Weeow-Captain shrieked.

On the boat-deck! But there was the enemy, in Space!

"Monkeys? Identify the enemy instantly!"

"I don't know, Dominant One. The sensors are being jammed."

"Where is Telepath? Why is he not on the bridge?"

"Dominant One, perhaps the live-meat monkeys have become feral and attacked him like rogue Jotok. He was their keeper."

Trap! Trap! Zraar-Admiral would betray no panic to his officers, but again *Tracker* blazed in his mind. Did the live-meat monkeys on the boat-deck know the rarity and value of Telepath, that they had singled him out? Or had they attacked him because he was the smallest and weakest Kzin aboard? But monkeys attacking Kzin! And at this moment! Trap! Trap! Had the live-meat monkeys been deliberately planted in *Gutting Claw* for the purposes of the real attackers?

With battle-shielding activated real Space could not be seen, but visual-display screens were aflame with missile explosions and the multi-colored bars of beam-weapons. And in the middle of it all the enemy warship, with its weird configuration and monstrous weapons. It appeared untouched by the star-hot claws of destruction slashing at it. Kzin gravity technology and the investigation of ancient Slaver stasis-boxes had led to various theories of force-fields. Did the enemy have them? Beams burned at it like solid light. Banks of ready-lights flashed and flashed again as salvoes of missiles were discharged, launchers re-loaded too fast for even Kzin eyes to follow and new salvoes discharged again in barrage, exploding in a nova-like vortex of fratricide.

Suddenly the enemy ship's image disappeared. Its shields collapsed at last? A cloaking device?

There was another series of flashes, then the enemy's outline alone reappeared The outline reduced to a skeleton, then a scroll of numbers. Behind them on the screen there were images of stars again, as the Kzinti missile explosions roiled away into empty Space.

"A false spoor!" cried Systems Controller. "There was no enemy ship! It was an image in the computer! A worm in its guts!" Human and Kzin physiology and technology had led, in an example of convergent evolution that would have interested a philologist, to the same imagery for the same situation.

"Our own computer was infected. Liver-worm within

it! A *rRrarrknarraraaw* seed! There was no enemy ship, but an image generated here! Dominant One, the back-up computers have now found this anomaly and killed it."

No enemy ship. Not The Day, but . . . a monkey-trick! He had struck the drum for Nothing! Snarling, slaver spraying from his jaws and fangs, Zraar-Admiral gathered himself to leap at the lying screen. Again he controlled himself: what good would it do to expend his rage upon machinery?

Not The Day. But there remained a real enemy indeed! Who had done this thing? Were the remaining monkeys loose?

Weeow-Captain punched up a diagram of *Gutting Claw's* entrails. There was no lie here: the boat-deck was in chaos: flames, a gravity-reaction.

"Forward!" roared Zraar-Admiral, "I lead my Heroes!"

Anything else would be unthinkable. The warriors of his personal guard leapt to him.

"Lead us, Feared Zraar-Admiral!" they cried.

"They are coming!" cried Telepath. "The diversion did not hold them!" The Dominant One's mind was on him like a tidal-wave of lava.

The image of HMS *Nelson* was gone from the monitor. "No time! No time!"

"Go!" Rick shouted. Selina stared at him, uncomprehending for a moment as he turned to the gravity-motor again.

"I will delay them! Selina, run! Fly!"

She hesitated. "I *order* you!" He whirled upon Telepath. "Go!" he roared.

He leapt away from the boat, and ran to the gravity-motor, spinning the focus-controls. The gravity-field tightened to a thin tube. A storm-wind roared through compartment and corridor. The Kzin attack force burst in.

Zraar-Admiral leading the way, the armored Kzin advanced against the howling whirlwind, clutching at claw-holds.

Rick aimed the gravity-motor and threw the model ship into the vortex of its field, tightening its beam and increasing its force towards maximum with two blows on the control-surfaces.

Zraar-Admiral, braced against the pressure with every atom of his gigantic strength, saw for an instant the image of the enemy warship hurtling at him with colossal kinetic energies. Impact. There was a multi-colored flash as Zraar-Admiral disintegrated. The Kzin by him were smashed against the bulkheads by the force of the explosion, one beam-rifle firing at full charge. Fragments of metal and Kzin were hurled at bullet-speeds.

Another cache of charges for small-arms ammunition exploded in sympathetic detonation. Rick was knocked back by the blast. He rolled across the deck, then rose hunched over broken ribs and stepped forward. The surviving Kzin were getting to their feet. He advanced to meet them bare-handed.

The field of the gravity-planer slashed across the boat-deck in a snake-shaped pattern of random destruction, dragging flame-filled atmosphere in a roaring typhoon behind it. Then a shot from a trooper's beam-rifle smashed the gravity-weapon. The embryonic fire-storm vanished in an instant. Automatic jets of inert gas smothered the remaining fires. There was a sudden echoing silence. The armored troopers, products of superb training and discipline, did not scream and leap. They fanned out almost slowly, surrounding Rick on the deck and Telepath and Selina in the barge.

Telepath punched in the order to release the locks on the main doors, a complex, multi-staged process.

Selina stared helpless from the port as the Kzin closed

in. Rick still stood facing them. Others were leveling their weapons at the barge, coolly, without haste now. Then Rick raised one arm, pointed to his sleeve and to the *Happy Gatherer's* boat. Selina nodded. She raised a hand to him and they looked at each other for a moment. She activated a sensor-point and shouted an order into a fragment of lattice on her sleeve. Aboard *Happy Gatherer's* boat an attitude jet fired, turning the boat so that it was parallel to the barge. Kzin leapt back from the clouds of flaring gas. She shouted an emergency override code and a second order. The boat's main engine fired, vaporizing everything organic and unprotected on the deck. Flame washed towards the barge. Missile warheads exploded in the same instant. The boat itself flew through the hangar to explode against the main doors, blowing them into Space.

Flame and air blasted into vacuum. Other doors flashed shut, activated by emergency triggers.

Aboard the barge neither Selina nor any other human could have moved fast enough. Telepath fired the retaining bolts and kicked in the motor. Propelled by both its own oversized gravity-planer and the explosion of air from the boat-deck, the barge shot into Space, the edge of a fireball just behind it.

Telepath leapt to the weapons console. Even had he wished, there was no time for arming nuclear warheads but he was firing all that could be brought to bear of the barge's other weapons into the cavity of the docking bay.

Even if Selina knew the controls, her hands could not have matched the eye-blurring speed of Telepath's claws. To venture near him would only have invited injury. She climbed to the upper viewing bubble and looked back. Behind them, the battleship's boat-deck was a glowing crater, venting rose-colored fog and incandescent debris. *Gutting Claw* had been hurt.

But the battleship was growing rapidly smaller as the barge accelerated away. Biggest of the smaller vessels carried aboard, it had oversized gravity-engines, not only to give it the best speed in the fleet, but also so that it could act as a tug. Now *Gutting Claw* was a red star among the stars. Telepath, firing the weapons, flying the ship and needing all his alertness, had no time to read the minds of *Gutting Claw's* officers, but no beams or missiles flashed out to destroy the craft: perhaps in the damage and confusion, the flight of the barge had not yet been noticed.

Telepath activated defenses: a cloud of metallic dust, a small robot craft generating a false signature, computer-stabilized mirrors which might in theory reflect a laser back to its source.

Selina became aware again of the sound of the gravity motor all about them. It was a moment of relative tranquillity, even if only the tranquillity of exhaustion. *Gutting Claw* was no longer in visual range: the inferno in the boat-deck could not be seen, possibly because the battleship had turned its wounded side away from any possible enemy.

"You are brave for a monkey," Telepath said to her at last.

"And you are brave for a Telepath."

"Do not grieve for the Rick-monkey too much." Telepath said. "It too was brave at last and the bearded monkey-god will take its soul. We could have done nothing to help it . . .

"I know the liquid discharged from your eyes is a sign of grief," he added after a moment, "but you are affected by something else I do not understand. We are companions, monkey who is not quite a monkey, Kzin who is not quite a Kzin. Should I not try to comfort you?"

Admiral's Barge

I was outcast now from all of the Kzin species that I knew. But I had slashed the deepest wound that any Telepath had struck in all the centuries of our hidden and so far largely futile war.

Still no beams leapt out from *Gutting Claw*. According to the screens before my eyes, no missile-signatures were detected by the instruments.

I cast back now to read the minds aboard the ship. Weeow-Captain spitting and shrieking orders to damage-control parties, junior officers and sergeants leading Heroes against fires where robotics had failed. Rage and shame of Damage-Control Officer in his cabin flinging himself at a cabin-door warped shut by explosions. Zraar-Admiral's remaining Kzinretts yammering in his harem as explosions rocked them and sirens screamed and toxic fumes poured through ventilation ducts. *Gutting Claw* had not been closed up at battle-stations when the alarms went. *Yes, though we could conquer by sheer power and ferocity, we were unused to alien ways of war*. But what had they been taught at damage-control courses? *Of disasters, a fire out of control in a loaded capital ship's hangar-deck calls for the greatest Heroism!*

I caught, briefly before I broke contact, death-agonies of a troop of Heroes propelled suddenly into vacuum. There was worse agony to leap at me from other minds: as well as the gravity-motor gun, Weapons Officer had been developing a hydrofluoric acid spray as a way of hosing monkeys out of trees on "Earth." The tanks ruptured and a mist of acid flowed up ducts and corridors, penetrating tissue instantly to devour bones from within. Too late other armored doors and emergency air-locks were crashing shut. *Gutting Claw* was truly in a space-battle at last, against chemical demons from its own guts. The boat-deck and all access ways to it were sealed off now.

Feared Zraar-Admiral was plainly dead. Though I had seen him die I had hardly believed it, but he could not have survived. It is said among Telepaths that the very greatest of them can contact the minds of the dead, but I dared not try that. I had not wished to betray him or be a spy upon him, and he had paid me compliments, but he had destroyed First Telepath, my teacher and only friend, my leader and commander in our war, and he would have destroyed me. As for the rest, when had one of them given me a good word or a gesture of respect? They had treated me, one and all, as a despised tool to be used and broken. As a Sthondat-lymph addict. I had hated them all. And now I had slashed back.

There was no trace in any mind aboard *Gutting Claw* that they knew what had happened on the boat-deck. On the bridge the impacts of the missiles I had fired from the boat had registered unambiguously for what they were. Now Systems Controller and Alien Technologies Officer, with Zraar-Admiral's orders forgotten and Weeow-Captain pre-occupied with damage-control, were fighting a death-duel to resolve the question of whether the enemy ship image had been real or not.

And still, as Heroes sealed red-hot doors shut with naked, charring hands, and, naked or in armor, advanced into holocausts with chemical fire-killers, as they leapt shrieking their battle-cries down corridors in lurid flame-lit darkness, and fought the demon-claws of hurricane winds that would drag them from the ship, as fire-storms hurled white-hot knife-edged debris, as clouds of choking fumes poured into the air-space of the bridge itself, as Weeow-Captain spat and roared his orders in the Battle Imperative (and wondered with a mixture of blazing ambition and a shameful touch of private grief and fear if he had succeeded to Supreme Command) Zraar-Admiral's barge was fleeing at the full thrust of its motor. There was no eye upon it.

I realized slowly what I had done. I was racing into the darkness of empty Space, to a dim and uncertain goal—a weak ship of alien omnivores—and with a mighty enemy behind.

More than an enemy. Zraar-Admiral had made the location of the monkey home-worlds a Patriarch's Secret, not merely hiding it in the computers but removing it from them. Now that secret, aboard *Gutting Claw*, had died with him and the Rick-monkey. I had hoped that with both vengeance and the defenseless monkey-worlds with all the rewards of a High Conquest beckoning, the warriors of *Gutting Claw* would give little heed to as useless an object as a mad Telepath. I had miscalculated: not only had my escape done immensely more damage than I had anticipated, but the Selina-monkey and I were now not worthless but were the only keepers of a secret beyond price. Further—the constant use of the Sthondat-drug in the last few days had clouded my mind so that I had been foolishly slow to see the implications of this—we were heading for the *Writing Stick* which was in any case *Gutting Claw's* first-priority target.

Torture if we were re-captured would be one of the few things worse than burn-out. Heroes may despise torture for its own sake as an indulgence of the weak, but have no hesitation in using it either as condign punishment or to extract secrets. I knew the instruments, and had sometimes had to read the minds of torture-victims. I felt my own fear like a solid thing. There was fear from the monkey's mind, too, fear of fangs and claws, fear that was in some ways like my own.

Too like my own! And now I was aware of thought leaking not *from* Selina's mind but *to* it: a leak that was broadening to a torrent. I felt-saw walls collapsing, a thing lunging out, growing between me and this female ape.

The fabric of the pale tunnels was suddenly tearing. My fear and Selina's fear merging. I felt other things merging, too: I knew what it was to have a flat whiskerless face with tiny teeth, udders, a soft, boneless, vulnerable stomach, well-padded rounded tailless buttocks. And a name. Zraar-Admiral had wondered why their tails had been amputated. I now knew they had not had tails for millions of years. They did not live in trees. More than the idea of salt oceans now—the stinging cold of salt waves. Swimming in a tumbling green ocean under a blue sky lit by a yellow sun, wind drying salt-crystals on exposed skin, darting silver fish in the water, quick as *viiritikii*, yellow ground and green vegetation behind. Weird memories of human mating. Memories of human kittenhood . . . childhood.

More. Emotions which I had analyzed and reported previously had changed as if from two-dimensional to four-dimensional things. A nameless blend of loss and excitement at the sight of a blue and white planet dwindling into Space. I saw myself, saw Telepath, grown taller and more terrible than any warrior, and fear like a *Wtsai* of black ice in the liver—in the *heart*, and then Telepath again but changing.

The viewer and the instruments moved far away. And as I returned to them, I was not the same. *Nwarrkaa Kishri Zaaarll* . . . the Double Bridge of Demons.

It is a term of Telepaths' Art, to describe an event that is not rare. It is particularly common when dealing with a subject that itself has some telepathic ability, latent or actualized: when the Single Bridge of Demons is erected, the Telepath loses his own identity and *becomes* the subject whose mind he has entered. With the Double Bridge the process is mutual but may be only partial for each party. Perhaps with the communality of our hopes and fears as a catalyst, that is what had happened here.

I had felt too much empathy with Selina before to regard her as prey, but Selina was truly in my mind now. Because I was Telepath I had never thought entirely like a Kzin. Now I no longer thought entirely like Telepath. There was a monkey—a *human*—in me too. I was reading the alien thoughts and feelings from *experience*.

The Bridge, once erected, is not completely broken while both of the two parties live.

I could now enter Selina's mind without the Sthondat-drug.

And she could now enter my mind.

While both of the two parties live. I could end that in an instant, with one sweep of my claws. Yet I did not. Could not. There was now too much of Telepath in Selina too.

"You know what has happened," I said. It was not a question and needed no answer.

We were silent for a time, but each mind was assimilating what had flowed to it from the other. The motor snarled and rippled and purred behind us. A long time passed as the two bruised minds recovered. I think we both slept at some time. As in a dream, I rose at last and wandered to the barge's trophy-drier and preserved Weapon's Officer's ears for my belt. Selina watched me.

"Do you still feel a duty to warn Earth?" I asked her at last.

She knew from my mind now the fragment of human speech that Zraar-Admiral had ordered me to memorize in a time that suddenly seemed long ago.

"It seems the *Angel's Pencil* has done that already," Selina said. "I wish I did not think it so likely that it will be disbelieved. But if they disbelieved the *Angel's Pencil*, they will come to know that *Happy Gatherer* has disappeared in the same part of Space. We never answered their last signal. Let them make of that what they will."

Selina thought of Earth and of her brother, guarding and herding gangs of children through the strange human museum, her brother with a secret collection hoarded as a Kzinrett might hoard playthings. A collection with a purpose I now began to understand truly for the first time. Crumbling pages of forbidden books and "military" paraphernalia.

A secret history—or set of false legends—of Earth that the government had *banned*. "Banned" was a strange concept (Or was it so strange? How much of Kzin's own history was in the control of the Priests and Conservors?). But was this brother a secret rebel against the dominant humans? Both he and Selina thought of something called the Military Fantasy: a forbidden cult that suggested the humans had once been something very different to what their histories told. I followed this a little way, some of it over ground I had previously guessed out for myself. Many of Selina's own thoughts were not clear on the matter, but when her thought combined with mine a picture emerged.

Then, perhaps because I had touched the image of her brother in her mind, I felt her thoughts flare with something almost Kzin-like: *Your destiny is upon you! Rouse them! Rouse the silly sheep before the tigers spring!*

Sheep? Brainless quadruped grass-eaters, I saw. Herds of them had once been husbanded by monkeys for food or to make clothing from their fur. They were almost displaced on Earth now. A few were reared as delicacies and others were kept on hunting preserves called *zoos*, but these latter were not hunted. Humans came simply to watch them. Strange. Strange.

And tigers? What were they? *Merrower!* There was an image there! Kzin, and something else. Fangs, and leaping and eyes like fire. The images became conflicting. But the overwhelming impression was unambiguous: I knew what she thought of tigers.

Or did I? For in the images of blood and death and fangs and slashing claws, all the splendid rampant slaying, there was a strange claw-point of something else that Selina herself was hardly aware of, to do with my attempts to console her for the death of Rick, something that contained the words: "poor creature!"

What did this mean? Did it matter? Why?

And other thoughts: *I know their reaction will be disbelief, denial . . . And then panic?* Gangs of humans swarming through hive-like cities . . . *and screaming in terror and then . . . and then, perhaps . . .*

Overwhelming all again came the image of the sheltered sheepfold and the tiger leaping from the stars. But even if the sheep were roused, what could they do? Then I thought of *Tracker*, and the wound blazing in the side of *Gutting Claw*.

And another Kzin-like thought leapt in Selina's mind, perhaps triggered by own. A leap against Fate, a thought that in the Heroes' Tongue might have been expressed in the God-Defying Tense itself: *The launching lasers!* In the human system were giant laser-cannon used for boosting the launch of reaction-drive Space-craft, some on the planet nearest the sun of the human home-system, a few on the human home-world and its moon, some in the human-settled belt of asteroids and the moons of the outer gas-giants. And then another thought, Kzin-like but of a different kind: *they are obsolete. They are being phased out and not replaced! Time! Time! Will there be time?*

And then: *Nothing I can do*.

For an instant she tried to keep these thoughts from me, knowing it was futile. In any case, what did it matter now, driving into black Space, death behind us and death, surely, before us?

That took my thoughts back to *Gutting Claw*, and Weeow-Captain on the bridge, in command, determined now to make an end of the *Angel's Pencil* straight away, once and for all, without toying with it.

The *Angel's Pencil*!

If Selina and I conferred, it was at a level too high and at a speed too fast to record. From her mind came the radio frequencies used by the human ship.

And then I cast my mind back to the *Claw*, and knew what Weeow-Captain planned.

Angel's Pencil

"Explosions. And Big Cat is moving at a tangent." Crouched over the makeshift weapons console, Jim Davis shook his head as if trying to clear it. The autodoc was good, but it was not intended to keep a man keyed to this pitch for so long.

"What does it mean?"

Steve Weaver made a gesture of incomprehension. "I can only guess . . . somebody else is fighting them."

"It can't be one of our ships. Nothing human. Not against that maneuverability."

"Were you expecting a human ship? Why do you think there were anti-missiles on that ship we struck? They were expecting attack from . . . something else. Something worse than they are, perhaps. Something higher on the food-chain."

"Steve! Steve! Jim!" Sue Bhang leapt to the console. "There's a message coming through!"

Fingers flickered at keyboards. The comscreen lit. A picture rolled, slowed, stabilized. A human woman, haggard, eyes huge in black, sunken pits, clad only in the torn scraps and under-strappings of a Space-suit. And behind her one of the felinoids, huge and alive.

"Who are you?"

The woman and the felinoid were in a small compartment, obviously in a cat Space-ship. The fittings and design they could see were cat not human. Panels behind her head showed stars. The reply came quickly. Either she was very close or she had anticipated the question.

"I am Selina Guthlac of the *Happy Gatherer*. There is no time to talk. Fire your Kzin missiles now! Jettison them! They are slaved to the Kzin battleship's computer. It can detonate them whenever the enemy wishes! Inside your own hull! Do it! Do it!"

Steve and Jim stared at each other in horror. They had been braced for a battle against odds since the huge pursuer had been detected, but not for this. The comscreen shouted at them again:

"Do it! Do it now!"

Her voice propelled Steve's hand to the firing button. Jim snatched it away.

"Don't! You see she's a prisoner! The cat is forcing her to say that. You can see she's been tortured."

The face on the screen was still speaking.

"This is an ally. We escaped in a boat from the Kzinti ship. Listen to me!

The felinoid's lips moved. It spoke in a hard, grating English:

"Zelina zpeakz trruth. My wurrd az my honorr."

Then again the woman spoke.

"This is a Kzin Telepath. We read your thoughts. You think we want to disarm you. But we can prove we are your allies. We have struck a blow against the enemy. See! This is our escape!"

The screen rolled again. There was film of a ship, apparently an oversized version of the one *Angel's Pencil* had encountered, burning with internal fires and spewing wreckage into Space.

"It means nothing," said Jim. "It could be a virtual reality simulation."

"Jim!" Sue held her voice as low and steady as she might, "There is some activity beginning in those missiles."

On the control-panel that had been fastened to the *Pencil's* main console lights were glowing. Green lights, the alien color for danger. That panel had been taken from the alien ship, as had the missiles it controlled.

"The missiles are arming themselves!"

Jim Davis stabbed the firing button. The *Pencil* lurched violently as, eight upon eight, the missiles fired. Propelled by Kzin gravity-planers that left no drive-flame, they were invisible from the viewing ports.

"Now we're disarmed." There was no question of using the ramscoop as a weapon unless an enemy with suitable physiology flew into it. Its conical field covered a vast area of Space, but it projected ahead of the ship. The laser, intended to beam messages back to the Solar System, could only be adjusted within a narrow cone behind them. The small attitude jets and gyros could be disregarded as measured against the total, inertialess, mobility of a ship powered by Kzin gravity-planer.

There was a heavy, fearful silence in the control-room. Then black visors crashed down over the ports. Across the gulf of Space, blue-white spheres were swelling like new suns.

"Where are you?" Steve asked the screen. "We'll take you aboard."

"No time for that. The *Claw* is coming. And it thinks you are clawless now.

"We are. When we armed ourselves with those missiles, we gave ourselves hope and courage."

"No. You are not clawless and it is time to fight. Your laser is still a weapon . . . wait!"

The watchers in the *Angel's Pencil* saw her turn to the felinoid. Something without words was taking place between them. The bulk of the Kzinti battleship was returning a bigger echo on the radar screens now, almost directly behind them. There too was a smaller echo, a little closer and to the Galactic north-west. Then the screen spoke again.

"Are they in range of your laser yet? We do not believe they know this frequency or that they could translate these transmissions."

"Extreme range for damaging their hull-material, I think. We tested it on wreckage from the other ship."

"No good. The Kzinti fight each other a good deal. They attack head-on and they expect to take enemy . . . slashes . . . head-on. The bow of *Gutting Claw* is designed against beams as well as bombs. It is mirror-finished and in battle other mirrors and dust projectors are deployed. It is made of super-hardened materials and has super-conductors to lose heat. This is a capital unit, not a scout-ship."

"The *Pencil's* laser is Tanj big. Bigger than they might expect."

"Hit the bow and you might burn through eventually, if they kept still for you. But it would take more time than you have. And there would be beams and missiles coming the other way. The sides and the damaged area are less well-protected but you cannot maneuver to attack them. Be thankful she can launch no fighters from the boat-deck yet. Your best chance is to hit the Command Bridge or the center of the damage in the side if they are presented. But they are small targets and they do not present when *Claw* is head-on.

"What can we do?"

"Keep your laser on the target but do not fire yet. You must let her get closer. And we must make her turn."

Admiral's Barge

There was *Gutting Claw*. With radar, infra-red and sense enhancers and my own senses guiding me I could find the hull now. The human ship was no problem to find on the end of its vast column of exhausted hydrogen.

The vented material that *Claw* had trailed like a blood-stain had tapered away. The hull was cooler with fires under control, and the hangar area had been sealed off. The motors were undamaged, and the weapons capacity was still colossal.

Time moved slowly. But the Selina's chatter with the *Writing Stick* humans became instantaneous as the distance between us decreased.

The barge's computer and weapons-systems could not be over-ridden from *Gutting Claw*. It had been the Admiral's own. I armed a fusion-missile and fired it at the *Claw*. Beams and anti-missiles converged on it and destroyed it. Another. It got no closer. I sent a stream of ball-bearings at the *Claw*. Its meteor defenses could cope with that but it took up more computer capacity. They must have identified the signature of the barge's motor now. They had some idea of who was attacking them. Rage on the bridge was moving out of control.

The blind noseless fools! Never to think what an enemy a Telepath might make! They had no conception that I was reading the minds of Weeow-Captain and the whole bridge and attack-team! It was easy after the minds of aliens. They might have felt pain in their brains—I had no time for the subtle dance—but the *Claw's* lifesystem was still full of noxious fumes which would explain that.

Weeow-Captain's rage engulfed him now. I punched up the visual comlink to *Claw's* bridge. He saw me. He would not understand Telepath insults, so I did my best with ordinary Kzintosh ones. But coming from a Telepath at all, they must have been shattering.

"Eat vegetable matter from the dung of the Sthondat that *chrowled* your mother! You seek only to *chrowl* the female monkey!" I snarled at him. "Where is Weapons Officer, you wonder? His cinders float in Space, but see, his ears hang from Telepath's belt! And from my belt hangs the path to the monkey home-worlds! Try to take them if you dare! Come and fight me! Fight Telepath, if you dare, Coward-Captain!"

The screen went blank as Weeow-Captain leapt at it. He had less control than Zraar-Admiral. My last picture was of his fangs. And *Gutting Claw* was turning towards us. I was already breaking contact. No Telepath could long stand that intensity of rage and hatred tearing directly at his own mind. I sent the rest of my missiles on their way. If some by chance got through the battleship's defenses, so much the better. But no missiles or beams were fired back at us yet. Weeow-Captain still wanted us alive.

Gutting Claw and the human ship were much less than a light-second apart now. One flash of thought to Selina, one command from me, one word from her. *Gutting Claw* had turned its bow away from the human ship now, and had at that moment no attention to spare for it. The loss of Zraar-Admiral and many other officers was like a brain-wound for it.

There were the *Claw's* missiles! I fired our anti-missiles. They would probably stop the first wave, but the first wave only. The humans would have to be quick.

In the darkness of Space ahead and a little below us a green nova-like light flared, impossibly bright. Then there was another light-spot in space, another incandescent green star.

Gutting Claw was hit side on. I felt it in my mind as the laser hit the bridge, then it began a slow slicing move into the hull. But it still took armored bulkheads and the massive bulk of the main gravity-engines and their containment-fields long seconds to melt. I had told them *Tracker* had been far more lightly built. It was moving out of the laser's field: the green star that was *Gutting Claw* faded. Then the ravaged containment-fields failed and it exploded.

There was agony in my head. It was the Death. I had burned my brain too much. But when I died Selina would lose all my knowledge of piloting the barge. Honor demanded I get her to her fellow-monkeys . . . fellow-humans.

Green light flashing! A missile fired from the *Claw* in its last seconds still alive and heading towards us.

I had to leap again, to trigger our remaining anti-missiles. A huge, blinding explosion, too close. The stars spun, the meteor-defenses activated. There was an indescribable sound as something hit the bulk of the gravity-motor behind us. I thought that bulk had saved us but then came the dreadful howl of air escaping from an hull-puncture. I struggled with a meteor-patch. On the dials lights and wave-bands were showing engine malfunction. Power would be gone in a few heat-beats. Think quickly! From Selina's mind I snatched what no Kzin astrogator trained on gravity-motors would have had ready enough: a knowledge of inertial forces sufficient to turn the barge with the last of its power and align its course towards the human ship.

I had done what I could. My claws slipped on the

control panel. I saw them tearing strips from it as my muscles began to convulse. Then pain . . . pain . . .

"I think your cat is dying," said Steve Weaver. As he saw her face he added: "I can't be sure. I'm only a human doctor."

The human and Kzin seals could not interface, of course, but four of the *Angel's Pencil's* crew had crossed in suits.

There had been embraces, greetings, some explanations between the humans. Telepath lay on the floor of the barge, not curled like a sleeping cat, but with his limbs sprawled out, violet eyes a quarter open, unseeing, breathing irregularly.

Selina stared at the *Pencil's* crew around her. Her movements were like the twitches of a cornered and desperate feline. *A hunted animal*, thought Steve.

"Yes," said Selina, "Dying with withdrawal from addiction, perhaps from burn-out. But that is not all.

"Kzin normally have no guilt about killing each other, if requirements of honor have been met. Young males kill each other often. Death-duels are a recognized way of advancement. Telepath has been trying to convince himself that he owed nothing by way of comradeship or had any other obligation to the crew of *Gutting Claw*, who had treated him like dirt. He loved and feared the Admiral, but it was not by his hand that the Admiral died, even if he had set up the situation. But he is not quite convincing himself. The tragedy of all Telepaths: too complex and vulnerable to be a Kzin, psychically damaged and then forced into a life that worsens all that damage. He's always been neurotic and now he's going mad. He'll die unless I can save him."

Let it die, then, thought Jim. *Another cat less in the Universe.*

"He's been trying to shield me from what he is going

through. That is weakening him also. He feels an obligation to me. Once they accept them the Kzin take their obligations seriously."

"Well, what can you do?" asked Steve. "I can't treat it. Nor can our autodoc."

"There's a doc here. Put him in that. He's beyond resisting if you lift him. If I stay in touch with him, whether I'm here on in the *Pencil* I feel . . . I don't know . . . After all, we owe him something. But . . ."— There were tears again suddenly on the sunken skin below her eyes—"I'd rather like to get aboard a monk . . . a human ship again."

I was Telepath. I was in the medical unit of Zraar-Admiral's barge. It was a scene of wide cold plains. The grass tall so a hunter must stand of hind legs to see above it, even a hunter used to growing on all fours. Scrabbling slopes of red sandstone, of scree, of red ironstone. There were distant mountains and somehow there were also forests, with leaping arboreal animals. Cliffs. Ironstone walls. I knew I was looking at a planet I had never seen: Old Kzin, as it had once been.

But now tunnel after tunnel was opening to me, opening and expanding to flash away. I saw scene after scene in a lattice-work.

Barer landscapes, stony heath. The strange landscape of dreams, clearer than I had seen it before. It was a great plain I wandered now. Alone? Or was someone with me? Zraar-Admiral? Karan? Selina? Gullied stone now, rock ridges, red under a red sky. Deeper gullies, rising about me, turning to caves, to tunnels . . .

Karan? Karan? Was she here? I felt her presence surely.

Recognition like a membrane tearing! I saw the blackness of the birthing burrow. And then a sudden light and what seemed a memory of the Harem. Karan was with me, grooming me as I played and kicked with my tiny, clumsy feet. I felt her tongue rasping at my fur. Then the grooming stopped and I lay back, full of contentment. The last contentment I would know.

I was small, small, my fur still spotted. We were alone, with the female kit, my sister, asleep. Karan's belly and teats swollen with her next pregnancy. Then I knew my last day with her had come, and I tried to cling to her.

And then the scene changed to madness! The dream of an addict in withdrawal! For it was a dream of Karan speaking to me, and speaking to me not in the Female Tongue, but in the kitten's version of the Heroes' Tongue itself! The tongue no Kzinrett spoke!

But did I imagine now, or *remember*? Karan's eyes shone above me huge and luminous as moons.

"Remember! Remember! Brave little spotted Kzin. I will plant a memory of words with little hope, but I must bury that memory in your mind deep, deep.

"Telepath they may make you, if you live. Little do they guess. Certain kittens they will test for Telepath talents. Rare kittens. What if they tested the mothers of those kittens? And the mothers of those few mothers?

"The few, the few . . . But the enduring. Not quite every line of female brains did the priesthood kill. Not yet. But soon. The speechless, mindless Kzinrett is the Kzinrett that lives and breeds. Each generation we, the secret, secret Others, grow rarer. Remember, though you do not understand my words.

"Someday you may find a sapient female. If fortune lets that happen, let that trigger your memory of these words. For a Telepath and a sapient female could do great things together . . ."

Karan's tongue rough on my fur again. A purring in her throat so loud I could barely hear the words she chanted.

"A great secret. The greatest of all. And each of we few must plant it deep at the bottom of a few poor minds, hoping against all knowledge that one day it will shoot.

"The priesthood bred Kzinretts to be brood-animals before ever the first Jotok ship landed upon Kzin and our kind leapt into the stars, as they bred Kzintosh to be Heroes that laid worlds waste. Conquest, Empire, world upon world. And the Kzin becoming a race to smash itself at last, as it smashes all else. So small is our hope that we can save it, and the Telepaths and their war so poor and flawed a weapon. No more can I say but: Remember, when the time is right, that the way of the Eternal Hunt is not the only way. So small a word to whisper! So poor a hope! And yet, as we may, we keep alive a tiny flame, we tend a tiny seed."

Seed? Tend a seed of vegetable? Who spoke of tending seeds. Our herbivorous slaves and prey-animals tended seeds. And yet—why did this image not sicken me as it should? The dream-voice of Karan again, chanting as she purred to me in her rippling throat.

"I cannot prophesy. Hunt in the glades of sleep. Remember . . ."

Karan's eyes filling my eyes with their light. And I falling into sleep, my face against her fur for the last time. for indeed they came to take me to the crèche and the training-ground that day.

It was imagination, not *memory*! For no Kzinrett used that tongue. A mad dream. And yet I wondered, as the scene changed.

Telepath alone.

The blue-gold sky of the human world. Green vegetation and that blue above.

Telepath within a human dwelling, and knowing it for what it was. There was a smell of charred meat and a smell of the partially-burnt eggs of some flying creature. A day fixed in Selina's memory, the day she too had left for a training crèche, something called an Advanced Astrophysics Institute.

A human speaking: "I know we'll be proud of you. We've stiff with pride for you already. I know you wanted to do biology first, but keep that as a second string for your fiddle. You're like your brother—each has brains enough for two."

An old female human. Mother of Selina, I knew. And now came a single certainty in one part of my mind, one doubt dissolved: as I knew that I moved not in real-time or real-Space, so at one level at least I knew the things I was experiencing to be only monster-images of wandering imagination, not memory from Selina's mind or my own. For the presence of an impossible animal made this that I saw, even on a human world, impossible: it appeared as if, curled and asleep upon the old human's legs, stroked by the old human, there had been a goblin-creature like a tiny Kzin.

What tortuous symbol was this from Telepath's sick brain? But it proved that the scene had no reality. Bridge to Selina or no, this scene could not be from her memory. And as this vision was unreal, the delusion of a poor addict's mind lost in the tunnels, so the earlier scene must be dream and delusion too. There were no tiny goblin-creatures in the shape of Kzin, so Karan had never spoken to her kitten save in the few soft words of the Female Tongue. And Karan knew no other than those few soft words.

Then Telepath alone once more, Telepath stumbling over a rocky landscape, the pale tunnels ghostly and transparent, and then the pale tunnels fading, a dark stalker, whose shape could not be told, appearing and disappearing. I felt my mind dissolving, and knew I had at last seen the approach of the Shadow, the End and Last Despair that First Telepath had warned me would come like this.

I cried out for help. To First Telepath, to Karan, to Zraar-Admiral, to Selina.

An empty space, and then arches like a high-roofed cave. Naked sky. A gigantic face. I fell into the position of supplication. It was the God. Fanged, rampant, come for Telepath's soul, and Telepath was not the warrior to fittingly defy Him. Or was it the Fanged God. The face seemed to shimmer, and was bearded like the face of the human god? Fanged God or Bearded God, or somehow . . . both?

I mewed like a kitten. Stars whirled about me, and *Gutting Claw* exploded.

Angel's Pencil

"And those females? It's obvious what he loaded them for."

"Wouldn't you, in his position?"

"Give you a continent to breed cats on? Selina, are you insane? A colony of Kzin to attack our colony the moment they've got the numbers?"

"Hear me out." Selina half rose, as the senior crew of the *Angel's Pencil* fell silent about her. "Telepath is highly abnormal. You can see that. If he lives—and he may not—he has a chance of being the first of his kind even allowed to breed. What he breeds may be something quite new.

"The Kzinretts are unintelligent. They can do nothing to educate their children in any real sense. I can. I know Telepath's mind, and I know that no other human can come close to the knowledge of the Kzinti that I have. Dammit, I doubt many *Kzin* know as much about the Kzinti as I do! Few but the Telepaths have a multileveled picture of their own make-up, and the Telepaths have it only flickeringly and without proper context.

"I think I can guide such a colony. You can keep watch on it—put a satellite above it with camera, sensors, weapons. If I fail and it becomes a threat, you'll know in good time. You can help me guard it, guide it, trade with it, maybe. Visit it before aggression and xenophobia can take hold in the culture. Of course I can't give guarantees. If necessary you can discipline it and if necessary you can wipe it out. Obviously with the Kzin in space the human colony must be on a war-footing always. But here we have a chance to create a Kzin society as it ought to be."

"A chance to play god, you mean? I don't like that idea."

"What else are you going to do? Kill them here and now? Helpless prisoners? One of whom you owe? A desperately sick Telepath and two females in hibernation? Isn't that playing god, too? I am offering the human race an asset. No-one else has it to offer."

"If Earth is conquered by the . . . Kzin, what good will having a few tame cats do?"

"Almost certainly no good at all. But then nothing will matter anyway, unless anything from the more distant colonies can flee further into Space. And I do not think the Kzin will find Earth as easy a conquest as Zraar-Admiral imagined. Unarmed and surprised as we were, we have met them twice and beaten them twice already . . ." Her voice trailed off. She suddenly understood what Telepath had meant when he spoke of the wrong cave at last.

"I think it is likely the war will be long. I suppose there will be prisoners taken, but I doubt Earth can deal with Kzin prisoners. That's another reason Telepath and the females are precious."

"Your motives sound very patriotic, Selina. But is that

all your agenda? It comes down to breeding Kzin."

"To breeding Kzin you can talk to," she corrected him.

"Is that really an asset?"

"It could be a bigger asset than you can imagine. Not only for this colony . . . There can be interchange between the two kinds right from the start. Humans will have the advantage of numbers, and Telepath's children will not be the Kzin of the Patriarchy.

"When I learnt Telepaths were not allowed to breed, I wondered: when the gift is both so rare and so valuable a military asset, why is every effort not made to increase the strain, as it is among humans when even the smallest trace of such ability is found? I think I know why: Telepaths are introspective, empathetic—qualities that could be a deadly threat to the Patriarchy, if they became common among Kzin. Even if the proportion of Telepaths to the general population was only a little higher than it is now, they could be an intolerable influence for destabilization. So they cannot be allowed to breed.

"And I think they would breed true. That is the First Secret of the Telepaths. My Telepath thinks the breeding prohibition is because they are too 'shameful'. But I think the . . . Patriarchy . . . also prohibits them from breeding because at some level it knows what a danger they could be were they not rigidly controlled. As well as needing them and despising them, I think it also fears them.

"Kzinretts . . . female Kzin . . . usually have one male and one female kitten in a litter. You know female Kzin are morons. But the female kittens of Telepath may be a wild card, and we are going to need all the wild cards we can pull out of our sleeves. A collection of non-Conformist Kzin could be a great threat to the Patriarchy. Some Telepaths already see themselves as at war with Kzin culture, but from what I have gathered their war is pitifully confused and disorganized, almost completely futile.

"I get a feeling there has been some kind of intervention, something inculcated in some Telepaths, perhaps an integral part of the whole syndrome that allows them to survive as Telepaths, that makes them at odds with Kzin . . . rigidity, but the chance and the motivation for them to actually *do* anything comes rarely.

"They're not morally better than ordinary Kzin, whether by our standards or theirs—often they are worse. They are not necessarily more intelligent. They are not happier or more stable—quite the reverse. But they are different. The actual quality of their resistance or non-conformity has a great deal of self-delusion in it. We might change that.

"I gather from Telepath that the worlds of their empire have a great deal of local independence—I suppose that is inevitable with the limitations of light-speed— but they all conform to a pretty basic set of common values and culture. Here we have the chance to plant something different enough to make a real change. At the same time, humans can learn an enormous amount from these Kzin—things we'll have to learn, and learn quickly, too.

"And I can't come back to you. Not without Telepath. There is too much cat—neurotic cat—in my brain now, and too much of me in him. You need not look disgusted. Believe me, you have no idea what an asset the human race has in that relationship."

"Assuming that is true," said Steve, "how could we make the human race aware of it . . if we've made them aware of the Kzin at all. Even if we still dare advertise our presence by signaling?"

"We can only think in the longest term," said Selina. Her words hung in the air a moment as the assembled humans thought upon what the longest term might be.

Steve Weaver stared at the map-display with an ashen face. The controller of the *Angel's Pencil's* laser was suddenly a sick man. He swallowed, choked, then raised eyes of despair to Selina, Jim and Sue. "It doesn't matter," he said, "Don't you see? Nothing matters. We are dead meat."

"We've won a battle!" Jim said, "That matters! We've won two battles!" He jumped to his feet and struck the table. "If we meet another Kzin ship we'll fight that too. We're armed with knowledge now."

"Meet another? Oh, we'll do that all right. Don't you understand? It's obvious enough, isn't it? These maps only confirm what we should have known—what we did know." There was something twisted in Steve's voice, "Only we haven't let ourselves think about it because it's so Tanj obvious!

"Encountering one Kzin ship might have been chance. But we've encountered two, and Selina tells us they are part of a Navy and an Empire, and coming from—there!" He pointed forward, through a port and past the great Collector Head and fusion torus at the "point" of the *Angel's Pencil*.

"We are heading straight into Kzin space! We are heading towards what the ramrobots tell us is a roughly Earthlike world in order to establish a colony. There will be no colony. An Earthlike world is a world Kzin can live on. A main-sequence K2 star—of course they would seek it out! It even has handy gas-giants with their own large moon-systems for bases and mines.

"We know they have been in Space far longer than humans. We don't need Selina's knowledge to tell us that apart from their aggressive instincts carnivores that size need elbow-room, territory. They will have settled all possible worlds within reach."

"Yes," said Selina. "And their hibernation technology

for Space-travel is at least as good as ours. Probably better."

"We are heading into a part of Space where Kzin ships will be more and more frequent. And even if we miss them—Space is still big enough for that, I suppose—one thing is sure: when we reach Epsilon Eridani they will be there waiting for us . . . We should have realized it long ago. After the first one . . ." He buried his face in his hands.

There was silence as his words sank in. Military Command Psychology was a long-forgotten science among humans. There was shame now that they had not let themselves see anything so obvious. Horror as they allowed themselves to realize the implications.

"We couldn't have known. Not until now . . ."

"I think I did know," said Sue. There were tears on her cheeks. "I didn't let myself think about it. The doc was treating me for depression and it was increasing my medication. Maybe that happened to us all. I bet if we checked the doc's supplies we would find that tranquilizers and anti-depressants are way down. It's been keeping part of our minds in a Zombie-state. Not to disable us against the immediate threat, but suppressing the symptoms in our sub-consciousness of the implications. But I had an inkling. I should have spoken before."

"The doc wasn't programmed for war," said Steve. "How could it have been? It was doing the job it was programmed to do on Earth: to identify neurosis and relieve the symptoms while the neurosis cured itself. If it identified a psychosis like paranoia it would treat it. And it had no was of telling if that neurosis or paranoia was justified. You might say its job was to unfit us for war, and we achieved what we did in spite of it. We're not used to this. I knew we weren't used to physical pain. We turned away from it. I should have realized we weren't used to any kind of pain. The doc was only doing its job by deadening it. But, Selina, you didn't see it either."

"You're forgetting. Your doc gave me a going-over as soon as I got aboard. Filled me with stuff. I didn't ask what. Like you, I'm still the creature of our culture."

"Another thing. Relativity. With time-dilation effects we will be there even sooner from our point of view."

Words like a low upon a wound.

"Another thing. Those two Kzin ships got *behind* us. It's against the odds that that would happen again. We can't expect our weapon to be any use at the next encounter."

"It we had a Kzin gravity-engine we could turn and fight them. Or use the ramscoop-field, if it affects them like other chordates."

"If . . ."

"If we had a gravity-engine we could turn and run. Head for the colonies on the other side of Space. Or head back to Earth . . . Warn them in person if they have ignored the messages . . . Pity about the physics."

There was no need to spell out what the physics were. They all knew that with the *Angel's Pencil's* forward velocity the turn-around time ruled it out.

"Why talk of impossibilities? We haven't a gravity-engine."

Despair filled the room like fog. It was not hard to imagine, once the obvious had been spelt out, what their reception at Epsilon Eridani would be. *Think! Think!* Selina told herself. *Think like a Kzin! Think like Telepath.*

"We do have a gravity-engine," she said. "The barge is a tug. It could turn us. With the delta-v we have plus the gravity-engine we could turn quite tightly and still keep enough velocity for the ramscoop to function. The Kzin use the gravity-fields to shield themselves from acceleration effects. We could do the same. The gravity-motor is damaged but we can repair it. Even with losing some delta-v that would give us the capacity to maintain constant one-G acceleration. In a year we would be back to .8 Light . . . or run our own drive and the Kzin engine together. If we can control the gravity-field we can accelerate as fast as may be without medical problems."

They looked at her as though they might not be dead meat. Then Steve said:

"We can't use a gravity-engine. We sent Earth all the specifications we could of the first ship's engine. It is still stowed here in pieces."

"Then we have two. Even better!"

"No. Hear me out, Selina. The engine we have was also initially damaged by our laser, although we salvaged all we could of it. We can describe most of the parts. We can film them and transmit the pictures. If Earth and the Belt believe us they can duplicate them. That's all we can do. A steam engineer of five hundred years ago could have described the shape of the parts of a Bussard Ramjet, but do you think he could have understood it from that? I'm not saying repairing and operating them is beyond our intelligence but the technology is too different, given the time we've got.

"We have two damaged engines that we don't know how to repair. We don't even know how to make the tools to work on them. Even if we had an engine in one piece we can't understand it. We can't operate it. It's like trying to build the Dean Drive. Tanj! Maybe it *is* the Dean Drive, or its descendant.

"Ours has melted parts, yours has holes in it. They have massive energy-containment fields and if we were to activate them without those fields fully functioning . . . well, that would be that.

"Oh, I grant you that perhaps we could learn, given years and research facilities and skilled teams. But we are a small specialized crew, and our colonists are frozen embryos. How many years do we have? We are getting deeper into Kzin space every moment."

"Then it lies with Telepath and me," Selina said. "He had Weapons-Officer's knowledge. If he still has that, we have a chance."

"If he still has it?"

"Telepathically-acquired knowledge decays much quicker than ordinary memories. Telepaths would go mad much more quickly otherwise. But he was in Weapons-Officer's mind not long ago.

"I have some of it, thanks to the Bridge . . . Weapons Officer was working on gravity-motors. Between us we may be able to retrieve something."

She was speaking in a peculiar mumbling monotone now, with the grating Kzin accent surfacing in it.

"But this makes it a bigger, harder thing than I thought. Rearranging his chemistry to cure his addiction—or to stop the withdrawal syndromes killing him—is complex enough, but it's something the Kzin autodoc and I may be able to do, if I can give him psychic support through it. He/we knew that—Kzin reparatory medicine is good. But to do it without scrambling his addict-acquired memories as well . . . If I can reach him, talk him through it, you might say . . . but it's much more than that . . . I haven't the human words . . . But to cure him of his addiction without breaking the bridge . . . I feel it can be done—Telepaths have secrets and I know some of them now. But it's not going to be easy."

"If he's still alive."

"He's still alive. If he were dead I can assure you I would know."

Jim suppressed a shudder. This woman's bonding to the cat made him physically disturbed.

Selina's face was changing now. Color was draining from it. Her features were twisting into something like the Leonine Mask of leprosy. "But he's sick. He's very sick. He's in great pain . . . He's not strong enough. Urrr."

"What should we do?"

"I must go back to the barge," said Selina. "I should be as close to him as possible."

Admiral's Barge

Stars whirled above me. I entered a new space: a bowl like the arena at the training-crèche. And the cliffs. I stood about it, and I knew they were minds to which I must cling.

The cliff of Zraar-Admiral's mind. I clutched it, knowing he was dead, and felt my claws pass through empty air, as when they had tried, long ago at the crèche, to make a fighter of me. But they had taken me from the other kits and let me live, like the science-geniuses and other despised ones, for they saw that I was a Telepath ("You may be the greatest of us." First Telepath had said, one sleep-time aboard *Gutting Claw*).

Something held me then. Was it something from Zraar-Admiral's mind? Had I indeed touched the Dead?

"You are the closest to a warrior . . . hold yourself like a warrior then . . . fight like a warrior. Earn the compliment I paid you."

Was it he? What was that other mind that held me like the mind of First Telepath? Or Karan?

"The way we were made was not the only way."

I could not tell. Were they all come from Telepath's poor sick mind?

And then, in the cliffs and tunnels, the running white lattices, and bare plain and the grass that was both the orange of Kzin and the green of Earth, I saw Selina coming towards Telepath, towards me, bending above me, and felt her holding me. And somewhere a yellow sun was rising.

GALLEY SLAVE

•

Jean Lamb

Dr. Marybeth Bonet swore softly to herself as she tried to get two different sets of computer codes disentangled from each other. If Lt. Thomas Dalkey hadn't been so handsome, she would have killed him. He was navigator of the *Cormorant*, a heavily armed packet ship patrolling the edges of the solar system against the enemy. He'd earned a number of medals for courage and heroism defending human space against the sudden invaders. Unfortunately, he had also had the brilliant idea of tying the autochef into the main computer so it could be programmed from the bridge in emergencies. Why didn't people read the manual?

She was used to this kind of thing. This wasn't the first time she'd had to fix these little problems, especially since she'd designed a lot of the food programs in the first place. Admittedly, Dalkey hadn't complained about the eternal diet of waffles the autochef now seemed to favor. He'd asked for help only when the roast beef and gravy sequence had showed up in the star charts. As a civilian expert, she was more used to hearing grumbling about the food.

Marybeth had three main options. One was to exercise her global search and destroy option and restore both computers to their original configuration through manual recovery procedures. Unfortunately, that wasn't possible in the middle of this mission, or she would never have been sent out here from Terra in the first place. The giant felines that called themselves the kzinti were an ever-present threat. As she thought about them, she bit her lip with anger. The human race had finally learned how to live with itself—and *they* came. They had disrupted everything in less than a generation. She glanced down at the knife she wore in its sheath on her thigh. Even that was a sign how far the kzinti had driven the humans out of their new Garden of Eden. Anything she could do to make the aliens pay was worth it. Granted, humans now had decent gravity systems on ship since adapting stolen kzinti ones—but it was a poor trade.

Her second option was to make Tom's plan work without disrupting either system. There wasn't enough time, though. She copied off his preliminary attempts, in case she could do something with them once she was back. The idea itself wasn't so bad, but the execution needed work. Marybeth proceeded as swiftly as she could on her third option, which was to delete any extraneous material from both systems. She had already designed an override sequence to allow the autochef to accept new menu items now, while Dalkey had nearly cleaned out the nav computer. Unfortunately, the override sequence was rather unwieldy. If there was enough memory left, she could boil it down into a macro, or even install it to the normal add menu, then dump it once it was no longer needed.

Marybeth closed down her work, sighed, then stripped in the small changing room next to the even tinier shower. If she was going to get sweaty, she'd rather do it with Tom Dalkey, and not slaving over a hot autochef! All the crew members had shown interest in her when she'd transferred to the *Cormorant*. Being recognizably female helped, though she sometimes wondered if that was an absolute requirement on a ship starved for new faces. Still, as a pale office blob she rarely got such attention except on temporary duty jaunts, and she enjoyed it.

The only one she felt anything for, surprisingly enough, was Tom Dalkey, the handsome, dark-skinned navigator who'd caused the problem in the first place. It'd started as pure pheromones, but she wondered if it could be something more eventually. She'd liked the way he smiled at her when he ducked his head to get into the galley, and had learned to like everything else about him, too. She grinned to herself as she hung up the knife in its sheath by her clothes. She'd had to "accidentally" forget it three times before Tom got brave enough to proposition her.

Her smile faded. Another social change chalked up to the kzinti. Leaving the Golden Age had put a lot of women right back where they'd started. Warrior instinct expressed itself at home as well as out in space. A compromise made in the region once known as the Pacific Northwest was to allow only women to have knives sharp enough to cut durasteel, easily spotted by the blue-green tinge of the metal on their edges, as if the rattlesnake sheath wasn't enough. Fortunately the gossip shows adored focusing on the custom, while Detective Darla Dagger was the most popular character on *Cascade Cop*. It certainly saved time explaining things.

Marybeth snickered when she remembered the combination hygiene and knife-fighting class she and her friends had taken as young adolescents, known as "The Miracle of Life and How to Avoid It." The Alderson boy had been lucky to lose only two fingers when he'd picked on the class wimpette after her first lesson. All the girls had thrown Jenny Hooks a party, once she and the boy had gone through the inquiry process. Jenny could have lost her right to carry the knife for up to three years if she'd done it maliciously. Marybeth remembered hearing about a woman who'd lost it for life after killing someone in a robbery.

She gently patted the knife's hilt and draped her clothes over it. The one time she'd had to use it to defend herself, she'd thrown up afterwards. It still beat knowing she was at the mercy of anyone stronger than she was. Besides, the court had cleared her completely.

And it made wanting someone all that much more fun when she *knew* it was her idea!

She smiled to herself as she squeezed into the shower tube and turned on the water. If she positioned herself just right, the jets hit exactly where she meant them to. A pity these things weren't big enough for two! Marybeth fantasized what she and Tom were going to do when the computers were all tucked in their beds. The hot, soapy water rushed over her body . . .

She heard an enormous bang. The shower's emergency seal whirred shut. Marybeth hit her head hard on a sprayer as a jolt sent her into the wall. Some of the water turned pink as it ran into the recycler. The small compartment tilted all the way to the side, then righted itself. Just as well it was so small. The walls helped support her. She felt sick and dizzy as the gravity wobbled and she lost consciousness.

After a time, the door opened. A furred, clawed nightmare glared at her. She shrieked and hysterically cowered in the little room she had. An enormous, tufted paw reached in. She attacked it with her teeth and fingernails as she felt herself being pulled out. She got in one good bite, mostly a mouthful of fur, then was flung toward the bulkhead. She barely covered her head with her arms before she hit.

. Marybeth collapsed as soon as she slid to the floor. Something warm and wet trickled down her shoulders. Perhaps if she played dead . . . She lay with her face against the bulkhead. She heard screams and blaster fire. She just lay there for a while. The noise moved away. She moved her head carefully and cautiously looked around. Nobody was there. She stood up slowly. The walls kept blurring in front of her. She felt better when she closed her eyes and felt her way along. The galley was close. She knew her way around it well.

Marybeth opened her eyes when she turned the corner. An enormous furry horror with a ratlike tail squatted on the floor and gnawed on something. Something red and white. A few cloth scraps were by its feet. They were blue. The kzin picked up a watch, sniffed it, and tossed it on the floor. It was gold, like the one Tom Dalkey was so proud of. He'd gotten it from his father when he'd graduated.

Part of her understood what had happened. She ducked into an empty storage locker and moaned softly to herself. Then she curled up into a ball and fled into unconsciousness.

Ship-Captain of the *Claw* conferred with his officers, as impatient as ever. Syet, the ship's telepath, still had a headache from helping the others track down stray humans on the captured ship. Mental contact with ordinary humans was bad enough, but the human-*rett* in heat had been disgusting. He'd heard rumors that the alien females were always that way, but hadn't believed them till now. No wonder their enemies were outbreeding the Hero's Race.

Of course, the others of his own kind despised him no matter how he suffered in order to help them. Part of it was jealousy. Fewer demands and more allowances were made in training.

It was only right, though, that even without prowess in combat he was allowed to think of himself with a Name rather than just a title. That was necessary when several minds met. He was rather proud of his. *Syet* was the position of a cocked ear of a hunter listening for his prey, and there was no one better at that than him. Oh, he took full advantage of his position—he'd be a fool not to. In return, though, he pushed his abilities to the breaking point when needed. Few of his fellow telepaths bore the touch of alien minds as well as he did. Those he knew spent most of their waking time in the bottle or taking dreamdust.

Syet began listening to the conference with all his ears again. The captain was ranting as usual about their glorious conquest. As if twenty humans could stand up to a squad of the Hero's Race! Still, the *Cormorant* was a valuable prize. Much knowledge would be gathered about human capabilities once the ship was returned to be examined. The captain might get half a Name once he returned. That was sufficient reason to be proud.

The captain then ordered Argton-Weaponsmaster to command the prize crew to return the captured vessel to the main fleet. Ship-captain also ordered Syet to go along, ostensibly to take what remaining mental impressions he could from the ship. The real reason was much simpler. The weaponsmaster was ambitious and from a noble line, and might take the ship on a foolish suicide mission. Syet knew he was supposed to prevent it somehow. He could have told the captain it was hopeless. Argton despised all telepaths, and any suggestion from one was as good as a command to do the opposite. Unfortunately, that didn't remove the responsibility. The weaponsmaster was unpleasant, even compared to most of his highly-placed kinsmen. He didn't blame the captain for wanting to get rid of him for a short time. In a serious emergency, the telepath could make contact with one of his mind-fellows on a picket ship just outside the human solar system. It'd cost him a day's blinding headache—or his life, if Argton caught on. Yet his duty to the Hero's Race was more important.

Ship-Captain added, "Keep an eye on the *rett* Argton-Weaponsmaster found. She might be useful."

Syet thought it was a mistake leaving her alive, but said nothing. He was supposed to advise the captain, even when it was unwelcome, but he was no fool, either.

The captain narrowed his eyes as if he knew what Syet thought anyway. "You yourself told me what impressions you got from her," he said. "She's certainly not a threat. Prize vessel duty is usually dull. The crew should be amused by her, and she might be trainable enough for some of the easier maintenance duties. If we get her to the main fleet alive, we could use her to get some of the prisoners to cooperate. If it doesn't work out, her meat should be tender enough, but you'd better have good reasons before you or anyone else disposes of her."

The telepath sighed. "Yes, captain," he said. It'd been a long time since he'd been allowed any live meat. Only those who'd actually fought had feasted this time. Still, it'd be nice to have someone lower in status than him around for a change.

Marybeth gradually awoke. Her head pounded, her bladder was full, and every joint was cramped from being in the storage locker. She peered out the tiny vents. No one was there. She silently crawled out, though it hurt even more to move. She almost fled back in when she heard growls and curses from the galley. Then she slid forward a bit to see what was going on. She couldn't hide forever on a ship this size anyway.

She crept into the galley from the back way she normally used, and ignored the mess on the floor. One of the aliens was hitting the panel, obviously frustrated. Maybe this was a chance to make herself useful. She had no illusions about striking back. Right now she just wanted to survive.

Everything went gray for a moment, then cleared. A *slight concussion?* she wondered. She'd better use what brains she had left now, before she ended up as dinner. Marybeth tiptoed forward, carefully bowed in a submissive position. The kzin growled at her. His nose wrinkled. Marybeth cringed back while pointing at the panel. "This my job!" she said, over and over. Would the alien understand her? The giant feline swept out a paw, though with claws retracted, and pushed her at the panel. She tasted blood as her mouth struck the edge, and squealed. Let them think her as frail as possible! Without another word she picked up the odd-looking disk on the counter and put it in the reader. Amazing that it fit, or that the reader got anything out of it at all. Either both types of computer systems showed convergent development, or everybody was borrowing from everybody as the war went on.

The notation system was completely alien, even after the computer did its best. There was no way she was going to be able to replicate this. She took out the disk, then selected what she thought they wanted. She was rather proud of her Kobe beef analog. She already knew they liked their meat raw.

The galley synthesis machinery powered up. The alien growled again. Marybeth made pleading gestures, and showed her bare throat. The orange, fluffy fur on the alien settled back down. Soon the first meat began coming through the output slot. The automatic cutter refused to work, though. A dent showed where the alien had struck it, too. Marybeth wearily set the indicator to manual, pulled out the blade by its handle, and began slicing the meat into large chunks as it came down the processing counter near the serving area.

She almost threw up at the sight and smell of the red beef streaked with white fat. It reminded of her of Dalkey—or what was left of him on the floor behind her. She barely controlled the impulse to slice up the alien, though she knew the penalty for any threatening move.

The alien sniffed one large chunk, then ate all of it in one bite. He purred, obviously pleased with the result. He lightly patted her. At least he probably meant it to be light, though he left bruises. He went off while Marybeth was still at work, ducking carefully under the overhang over the back entrance. Pity he didn't smack his head on it. A dent in *that* would probably disable most of the electrical conduit for the engine room. She would have designed it so it was out of the way, but it probably made things easier for the maintenance people. At her height, she rarely noticed the thing.

She put chunks of meat on platters and set them on the two small tables outside the preparation area. The serving counter was hinged to be open or latched closed. Then she checked the drinks dispenser. All she got out of one was diesel-grade coffee, which she gratefully gulped down. She could retire if she learned how to synthesize something decent. She looked back into the galley and shook with anger. There had to be a way to do *something*. Marybeth filled up another platter with meat and cautiously left her sanctuary. It was a longshot, but worth checking out.

Unfortunately, the weapons lockers were already guarded. She should have expected it. Better to find out now, though, than depend on anything later.

Marybeth approached the guards with the meat, bowed, set it down a fair distance from them, then fled. Her terror was not an act.

She made a quick run for the sanitary facilities. She shuddered when she looked at the shower cubicle, and washed herself in the sink. Her clothes were in a pile on the floor. She reached for them, then hesitated. As uncomfortable as it was, she'd be safer naked. Despite feminist pride, it was better to stay alive. If that meant letting them think she was little more than a beast, like female kzin, she'd just have to put up with it. It might make the aliens feel superior. Those who did so often made useful mistakes. Being a visible threat meant getting eaten. She was glad she'd had her shots, though. She couldn't begin to imagine the fun she'd have coping with a period in this situation.

She bundled the clothes up to throw them into the disposal to remove temptation. The sheathed knife fell on the floor. Marybeth dropped the clothes and clutched it to her. Then she paused. What good would it do her? She still couldn't bring herself to get rid of it. She had to get it to the galley somehow. She watched the hall for traffic, then spotted a couple of blankets in a doorless storage locker. Marybeth oozed over to it and put the knife in with the blankets. Then she took the whole bundle to the galley. Maybe she could establish the place as her territory. Even a beast deserved some kind of bedding.

She nearly panicked when she saw other aliens near the galley devouring the meat. There was a difference between pretending to be a coward and actually being one, though. Instead of vomiting on the floor, her first choice, she gulped and hastened back behind the counter. She put the blankets on a corner counter and began cleaning things up. Every stain, every bone fragment reminded her of Dalkey and how he'd died.

She knew the rest of the crew was dead, too. Perhaps with the floor clean she might be able to sleep.

As she scrubbed, she ignored the slobbering noises outside. When she found Dalkey's gold watch underneath the bottom edge of a cupboard, she put it up to her face and cried a little. Then she went back to work. With her head out of sight, she opened each cupboard and took inventory. You never knew what could be useful. Her eyes ran over the usual cleaning supplies. If the aliens had a keen sense of smell, they wouldn't like the detergent. She'd better keep that tightly capped. The big jug might make a good club, though. She hefted it experimentally, then put it back. It'd probably work better if she just threw it. Marybeth paid more attention to the broom. A knife attached to it with a length of cord would make a pretty decent spear, but she wouldn't be able to fix it up ahead of time without risking one of the aliens seeing it. She searched the closet for a tube of Sticktite but didn't find one. She could leave a sticky strip of it on the broom that'd stay that way until she placed something on it—the knife's handle, for instance. Sticktite would hold almost anything forever till the proper solvent was applied. There had to be some on this ship, but it certainly wasn't anywhere in the galley. A pity she didn't have access to her own lab kitchen at home. Some of the attachments to her food processor could be seriously dangerous in the right hands.

She found more knives in one of the drawers. Marybeth crawled over to her blankets, slid the sheathed knife across the floor, and put it into the drawer unsheathed like the rest. She'd have to dispose of the sheath. For now, she stuffed it in a junk drawer just below.

The noises outside the galley stopped. Marybeth peeked out. The kzinti were all looking at another one that just came in. She couldn't believe this one was the captain! This alien was skinny, scraggly, and more like a half-drowned rat. One of the others made sniffling sounds, only to have someone next to him stick a claw in his arm. It was almost like they wanted to laugh at him, but were too frightened.

Then she felt a funny tickle in her head. The kzinti had telepaths, too, just like humans. She began humming a popular commercial jingle just under her breath. That might annoy him. Then she picked up Dalkey's watch. That drove anything else out of her head. *Red blood, white bones, the gold watch on the floor* . . . The scruffy kzin shook his head, as if someone had splashed water on him. Yes. She had to watch out for him.

Syet held his head. It pounded in agony, but he had to eat. Then he could return to his room and silence the hideous voices inside his head with the bottles of whiskey he'd found in a small locker. He paused for a moment as the delightful aroma of proper meat filled his nostrils. Maybe the human-*rett* should live after all. He wished she'd shut up, though. Her mental singing was worse than Argton-Weaponsmaster's. Besides, he had absolutely no interest in what passed for thought in the little bitch. As long as she kept the food coming, he didn't care.

The weaponsmaster summoned him as soon as he'd finished eating. Argton made up for his lack of height in utter ruthlessness. "A pity the captain doesn't see the opportunity now placed in our hands," the weaponsmaster began.

Syet knew the rest already, but listened politely. He had respect for his superior's claws, if not his brains.

"Though much of the navigational data for this system is in code," the weaponsmaster continued, "I'm certain our techs will be able to decipher it. We still have enough to avoid most of their defenses. I do not understand why the captain wants us to flee like cowards."

"I believe the captain has his reasons," Syet said. He hated seeing disaster come his way without being able to avoid it. He might as well agree with everything Argton-Weaponsmaster proposed, though, no matter how idiotic. It was safer that way.

"Possibly." The weaponsmaster flexed and unflexed his claws. "One who wished to keep all the honor to himself might also act this way. Too bad. There might be enough of it here for even someone like you to acquire a true Name. All *you* would have to do is keep quiet. Yet that might show enough courage to report your valor when we return in triumph."

The telepath could easily see themselves being blown into floating debris instead. Syet was tempted, though. Telepaths had informal designations on their mental searches, but they were not true Names at all. "One wishes to know the extent of the plans," he said, "to advise and assist as is the duty of all the Hero's Race."

Argton closed his eyes briefly, a clear sign of approval, which Syet received mentally as well. "As far as the techs can tell, we're on a course to rendezvous with another human ship in thirty of their days. If the human-*rett* is still alive, we can use her to lure them in. We should record her voice soon just in case. Once we have *two* ships . . ."

Syet filled in the rest silently. One ship could return, as per the captain's orders, while the other rampaged through the human system—a rampage that might open the way to an outright invasion by the rest of the fleet. As long as Ship Captain got a human ship to examine, the telepath saw nothing wrong with the plan—just as long as he was on the ship that returned. "Glory," he whispered.

❖   ❖   ❖

Marybeth fell into a mind-dulling routine in the next few days. She awoke, sneaked in and out of the refresher, cowered when one of the aliens came near, and hid in the galley. Her arms didn't hurt as much from cutting meat as they did at first. One "morning" she laid out more Kobe beef. That was still the aliens' favorite, though she occasionally varied it with fish. She gave most of the kzinti nicknames, though she'd learned a few of their words. Furball was the tech who'd first tried to use the autochef. She took care to cringe in fear whenever he cuffed her around, though he didn't hit very hard. It was worth it, though. One of the others had tried to claw her up for no reason, and Furball had cuffed *him*. After that she made sure Furball got the first serving each meal time. He'd earned it. She gave names to others, too. Snaggletooth was the telepath, or so Marybeth thought. She kept Dalkey's watch close to her when he was around. He didn't spend much time in the galley, though, and she didn't think he could read her without being nearby. The only one she was really afraid of was a magnificently tiger-striped kzin with a gloriously fluffy coat. Evidently both humans and kzinti made up for lack of height with attitude sometimes. Everyone else was scared of him, too. She nicknamed him Hobbes—nasty, brutish, and short. She disappeared into her nest of blankets whenever he showed up.

One night she began to analyze the kzinti rations while preparing a meal for herself. Since she had become a sudden convert to a vegetarian lifestyle, she thought it was unlikely she'd be interrupted. It was like waking from a terrible dream to start using her mind again. It took several hours to crack their notation system. Fortunately, their style of structural charting was similar to the human standard. Once she'd spotted a familiar-looking lipid she was home free. Once she and the computer knew where the carbons were, the rest was easy interpolation. No wonder the kzinti enjoyed beef and fish—as well as fresh human. Their metabolism was like that of other Earth carnivores. The autochef food was clearly superior to the kzinti rations, as far as she could tell from the small amount she synthesized. The stuff was probably well-balanced and so forth, but it was clearly mulch, ready to eject as far as texture and flavor. The aliens' nutritional experts probably had the same slogan as at home: "Food will win the war—but how can we get the enemy to eat it?"

She concentrated on fat ratios. Lipid metabolism was a great deal simpler than protein, and seemed to work the same way for the aliens as it did for humans, judging by the rations. She wasn't surprised to find most of the fats were polyunsaturated. Kzinti probably got less exercise in space than they did on the ground. That was the standard for human food synthesis, as well. She examined the carbons in the kzinti ration fats again. There was something odd about their number, but she couldn't figure it out. Marybeth hastily ate her soysteak and fake broccoli. Since the kzinti were using up the protein and fat reservoirs, she had free run of the carbohydrates. It might even make her smell less threatening.

Was there anything she could do to the kzinti food? With their metabolism so close to human, anything overt would be stopped by the autochef's poison control program. Furball watched her too closely when she chopped the meat for her to add anything then. He also inspected the salt shakers. Could she reverse-engineer the kzinti rations and find something that'd be bad for them without getting the autochef to lock down?

There were a few things she could do now. Marybeth changed all the fats to saturated ones. That called up a nutrition flag, but went through. Then she increased the sodium to just under the max allowable. Just for fun, she converted one of the drink dispensers to grain alcohol. If that didn't increase their triglycerides, she'd like to know what would! A pity they were also hooked into the poison program, but such was life.

She poured herself a drink to celebrate still being alive so far, though it was only a combination of alcohol and a hideous orange drink substitute. She retired to her blankets with it, head blurry as she tried to piece together the molecular structure for a banana daiquiri in her head. When she was done with it, even the cold metal of Dalkey's watch brought back only good memories. His kindness, his sense of humor . . . the warmth of his touch whenever their fingers met during repair work. *Wonder what the rest of him would have felt like?* she thought fuzzily. The blankets were firm and warm, but not the way he would have been. She slid into sleep still wanting him.

Syet sat straight up in his bunk and nearly retched. He didn't know what to do. This was worse than the time three shipmates had killed each other in a mutual duel.

At first his head had been full of black-and-white thoughts. Maybe the techs were wrong and there *was* an AI aboard. He didn't care as long as nobody made him try to read it. Then he'd gotten really confused when the thoughts blurred into whirling, skeletal shapes, and then into the brain of that damned *rett*. He shuddered at the impact of her lustful impulses. How those flabby, hairless humans found each other attractive was beyond him. Where did those other thoughts come from? The *rett*'s impressions had been so clear. Was she really imagining her partner?

Maybe she wasn't. Maybe there was a reason he'd gotten those computer-like thoughts at first.

One of the human crew was still alive! Mostly likely the *rett* had believed everyone was dead at first. Her grief still burned his soul. What if one of the others had survived in hiding, though? Of course the *rett* would help him—and naturally the little bitch would demand her reward. The human was undoubtedly plotting mischief.

Syet dug deep for courage and woke Argton-Weaponsmaster. The commander was angry at first, then concerned. A human on the loose was dangerous, and might keep them from fulfilling their mission. They both went down to the galley. Syet ducked beneath the low ceiling, while his superior barely had to nod. The *rett* emerged from her blankets with a squeal. Argton tore them away, in case she was hiding someone in them. They found only a glittering bracelet. The commander broke it in his rage. The *rett* began crying and gathered up the shining links. Syet didn't get anything besides terror from her. He couldn't find clear thoughts of anybody with that wall of emotion she was projecting. Both kzinti tore open the storage bins and lockers in the galley. They found nothing worthy of report. The commander clawed the *rett* in annoyance, and she collapsed in a corner. Syet was embarrassed. He knew something was going on, but he'd never find out this way.

Weaponsmaster clawed him, too. "You'd better stop drinking so much! Or find yourself a different brand of dreamdust!" he shouted. "I'll have the ship searched again, just in case. If they don't find anything, I'll make you pay for this!" he shouted as he stormed out of the galley.

Syet considered reminding the weaponsmaster that they were still in range of one of his friends on picket. He decided it'd push his superior too far.

There was more than one way to earn a Name. The

next time he felt those thought patterns, he'd deal with it himself. A human pelt would convince anybody he was right!

Marybeth limped to the autodoc, whined and cringed till the kzin on guard let her use it, then slinked back to her lair. With luck she'd convinced Hobbes she wasn't a menace. Snaggletooth might still be a problem, if she'd interpreted him correctly. Simply staying under cover wasn't going to keep her safe. She could die at any moment from an alien's whim.

She thought longingly about her fighting-knife. The odds were slim that she'd take out even one of the aliens, let alone more of them. She wanted them all dead. Marybeth had no idea what course they were on. For all she knew they were headed out of the solar system entirely. Suddenly she didn't care.

How much time did she have? When the ship had been captured, they were about a month away from rendezvous with the *Peregrine*. She wasn't sure how long it'd been since then. She had to assume they were still on course. If they weren't, it didn't matter as much. She might as well plan for a worst-case scenario.

She needed more information. She couldn't sleep now. A grate that led into the air vent system yielded to a mixing spoon handle used as a pry bar. Marybeth quietly made her way through it. One part led to a grate near the weapons locker. It was still guarded, of course, though probably to keep the aliens from killing each other, judging by what she'd seen earlier. She backed away hastily when one of the sentries wrinkled his nose in disgust. Well, she didn't like their smell, either. She returned to the galley and rested. What was she going to do?

A few days later she cleaned up the spatters from a minor duel—no one died—between two of the kzinti.

She took the soaked rag back to the galley and analyzed the blood. She wasn't sure what was normal, but spotted a high ratio of triglycerides in the blood fats. There was a difference between the aliens and humans, though. There appeared to be more carbons—about one-third more. The computer wasn't sure where they went. Of course it wasn't. It was programmed to follow human metabolism as its default template. She went back into the system menu and reset it. The carbons resolved themselves into glorious triples, as did the fats in the kzinti rations.

Of course. Coenzyme A in humans made use of fats by cutting off two carbons at a time. The kzinti equivalent plainly used three. If she could design a receptor molecule to gather up the triglycerides in the kzinti bloodstreams into clumps that blocked circulation in vital areas, she might be able to get it past the autochef poison control program.

Just as she finished figuring that out, it was time to serve the first meal of the "day." Hobbes came into the galley and swaggered over to the drinks dispenser. Well, it'd certainly taken him long enough to figure it out why all his crew used the one in the corner. Even Snaggletooth had used it to fill his bottle.

Then Hobbes ripped it out of the wall and howled with rage. A stream of pure grain alcohol flowed onto the floor. She thought Furball was going to cry. Marybeth threw up her hands and looked as bewildered as she could manage, then shut off the outlet valve. The aliens stared at her as she mopped up the mess. Wonder what they'd offer for the first squeezing? Hobbes threatened her with his claws again. She kept from screaming at him only by imagining him as a rug. He'd make a pretty one, since his coat was longer and glossier than ever. She took care to limp on the leg he'd clawed before. Maybe he'd lose face by attacking someone so much weaker.

It worked. He turned from her and ripped a pawful of fluff from Furball instead. The poor fellow cringed nearly as hard as she did—though his eyes told another story. She wasn't the only one acting a role for self-preservation. And maybe she wasn't the only one who'd like Hobbes better as a floor throw. But it'd be stupid to count on any of the aliens as allies.

The next days and nights passed quickly. She spent all the time while fixing her own meals on planning molecule design. Whenever Snaggletooth came in, she gave him a full bottle as well as a platter of meat. She'd stored bottles of alcohol from one of the remaining dispensers but left the default innocuous. Furball got the credit, but she didn't care. Other bottles were also handed over, but only to aliens she and Furball approved of. Her head whirled sometimes with lack of sleep, but it didn't matter. If she failed, she'd get all the rest she needed anyway. Fortunately, she could do some of the design work mentally while she worked. Marybeth had always had an internal 3-D screen, which had come in handy at school when the computer was down or unavailable. Snaggletooth looked at her oddly sometimes, but she didn't think he ever caught her telepathically while she used her computer. She was getting rather tired of synthesized broccoli, but that vegetable seemed to be the most effective in keeping the kzinti away.

One "evening" she thought she was bringing up the menu to work on the receptor molecule and got the nav computer instead. *Oh, Tom,* she thought ruefully. *I thought we'd gotten all of that fixed by now.* It helped sometimes to speak to him mentally, even though he was dead.

If the screen was right, though, a ship was approaching and would rendezvous in less than twenty-four hours. She'd wasted enough time tinkering with the stupid thing. It was time to take her chances with it. Having aliens control the *Cormorant* was bad enough. What could they do with two ships?

She finally bailed out and got the right program up. She ordered synthesis and input. *There, Tom. It's the best I can do. Just wish it could be nastier, . . .* she thought to herself.

A tufted paw lifted her out of the chair and into the wall. She slid down it, stunned. "Where is he?" Snaggletooth growled. Marybeth just let her jaw hang open. Then she leaped for the drawer. She had to get the knife.

Snaggletooth struck her again. "Where is he?" he repeated.

Oh, shit. She landed near the cleaning supplies. Without hope she reached in and grabbed the detergent jug, stood, and threw it at him. He clawed it away. Cleaning fluid splashed on him as he inadvertently sliced it open. He gave out a thin howl and shook his claws to get the smell away from him.

Marybeth used that momentary distraction to go for the drawer with the knife. Without thinking, she leaped forward with the hilt in her hand and attacked Snaggletooth's claws before he could use them against her. She was astounded at how easily the knife cut through them. His blood spurted out on her. She whirled quickly and went for the other side as the kzin swung at her. The knife worked just as well the second time. She stabbed for the throat, but Snaggletooth swept at her with his arms and the blade went high. He howled as the point scraped by his eyes.

Suddenly she went flying as a blow from his clawless arm batted her away. Somehow she managed to hang onto the knife. Then Snaggletooth starting coming at her again, and raised one hind leg to kick. Marybeth panicked. She couldn't see! Her eyes and hands hurt as if she'd been cut. It was as if she suffered from his own wounds. Then she saw him approach nearer as her vision slowly returned. If she attacked again, he could easily switch legs and get her with the other one. She turned and fled out the back, and never noticed the overhang two inches above her head. Perhaps if she got to the air vent . . .

Snaggletooth approached the galley. He couldn't believe it. The *rett* was actually talking in her mind, not just indulging in emotions better suited to a cub not yet weaned. This time he'd catch her with the male she'd been hiding all this time. He imagined himself presenting the pelt to Argton-Weaponsmaster, and being praised in front of the rest of the crew for his diligence in protecting the Hero's Race. He was startled to see the *rett* by herself again, but not very much. No doubt any human who'd lasted this long had good reflexes. Where was the monkey-boy this time?

Then he caught the true taste and smell of the *rett*'s mind. He hissed in astonishment. How stupid he'd been! Just because females of the Hero's Race were properly docile, he'd assumed those of the enemy were that way as well. The depth of her duplicity awed him. She'd even used his weakness for liquor against him.

It took only a moment to realize this and act. She planned something evil for the food they ate, he was sure of it. The crew and commander must be warned— but not until he'd destroyed the enemy and removed her menace forever. She might all too easily convince the rest that she was just a silly *rett*, while he was only imagining things. He had been drinking more than usual lately and he knew what the weaponsmaster thought.

He snarled and batted her against the wall. He might as well get some decent amusement out of it. Then she flung a jug at him, clearly desperate. He clawed it away, only to gasp in horror at the acrid stuff that came

out of it. Once he was halfway free of it, the human
faced him with a knife in her hand. He almost laughed.
No puny blade was a match for the ones the Hero's
Race were born with!

He roared in shock and horror as he watched his claws
fall onto the floor. He instinctively struck with the other,
only to lose them as well. The human came close enough
to thrust at his face. He beat at her with his arms, only
to feel the knife brush lightly at his face. Blood poured
down and ruined his vision.

Syet had been in duels before. Not even telepaths
could avoid them all the time. He jumped into Marybeth's
mind as he assumed a fighting stance that allowed him
use of his hind claws. He had learned long ago to watch
himself without losing track of where he was. It was
odd looking out of the alien's eyes and watching his own
blood stream down onto the floor, but no odder than
realizing her long, deadly plans to poison them all. He
left just enough of himself in his body to make it hop
toward the human. He had no idea he appeared so large
and terrifying to the female. Then he squeezed her mind
from the inside. As he hoped, she panicked and fled.
One blow from a hind claw would rip her spine from
her body. He had to act quickly, though, before she
reached the vent system.

He was shocked back into his body as he ran into
the overhang. Syet mewed with pain and astonishment.
What a fool he'd been to forget how much smaller the
alien was. As much as he hated to, he was going to call
for help. The crew's safety was more important than
his own humiliation . . .

Marybeth turned around as her mind was suddenly
free of the overpowering shadow of fear that had
possessed her before. She hadn't been thinking. If she
hid in the vents, Snaggletooth would be free to warn

the rest of the kzinti about her. As a telepath, he might warn them about the food, too.

Snaggletooth just stood there in back of the overhang. Then he began to move away. She couldn't let him get away, even if it cost her life! At first she'd just wanted to live. Then she'd wanted revenge. Now she just wanted to kill. Even if she was caught, she had to silence the telepath before it was too late.

She swiftly ran back into the galley, her feet sticky with Snaggletooth's blood. For a moment, he turned toward her and began to open his mouth. Marybeth thrust the knife into the alien's throat and slid it as far in as possible. The blade scraped a little on the thick vertebrae in back and then kept going. Snaggletooth shuddered, then fell forward. She tried to get out of his way in time, but couldn't, though she did get her knees up. She was nearly suffocated by his weight, the same way she'd been the one other time she'd had to use this blade. . . .

He wasn't moving. The smell of his blood nearly made her throw up, but at least it wasn't hers. In fact, it was still slick enough underneath for her to wiggle to one side. Fortunately her knees kept her from being totally crushed. She turned so she was on her side. Snaggletooth's body fell further, but the hilt of the knife caught on what was left of the telepath's neck and propped him up as she braced it on the floor. It only left her six inches to maneuver in, but it was certainly better than being pinned down forever.

She finally dragged herself out from under Snaggletooth and took a big breath of air. Her ribs hurt some, but that appeared to be all. *This was not a fun date,* she said solemnly to herself.

Then she heard the hum of lights that signaled change of shift. She didn't have much time till the others would start coming down for breakfast. If there were only some way she could retrieve her knife, but she didn't see how. She decided to bluff her way out. First, she cleaned herself up. She had new bruises all over, but they blended in nicely with the ones she'd had before. After a moment's thought, she smeared some blood on the drawer that held all the kitchen knives.

As soon as Furball showed up for his serving, she went hysterical. She wasn't acting. She mimed a big, nasty fight, showed him the dent in the overhang where Snaggletooth had hit his head, and tried to indicate that "the other one went thataway." When Furball tried to question her, she sketched out a height not that much higher than her own. She didn't think that kzinti could go pale, but Furball did his best as he apparently came to the conclusion she hoped he would. After all, Hobbes fit under the overhang. Furball picked up the body, but stared at the knife. Marybeth hastily pantomimed the drawer holding all the knives being pulled out and knocked onto the floor, then quickly huddled into one of her blankets to show that she was hiding during most of it anyway. She didn't have to force herself to start crying.

With any luck, Furball would be too frightened to ask Hobbes anything till it was too late. They cleaned most of the mess up. Marybeth washed and put the deadly knife back in the drawer once Furball got it out of Snaggletooth's body. Two other kzinti came down and carried the telepath's remains off. She began slicing up the morning rations. Furball kept watching her. He probably had his suspicions, but not as much as if he'd caught her taking the body apart herself. Then he took one platter and set it in front of her. She gagged down a few mouthfuls so as not to make him suspicious. Fortunately the beef was salty enough for her to stand it. Um . . . did humans have any processes that involved triple carbon bonds? She didn't think so, but hoped that her vegetarian diet would protect her from most of the receptor's effects. Making sure *they* ate it was more important. She just hoped the DMSO-type delivery molecule would get the enzyme through kzinti mucous membranes as well as her own.

After the meal, she finished cleaning everything up. It would take hours for the molecule to take effect, if it ever did. She trembled as she picked up the platters. At least she could *think* what she wanted to about them now!

As soon as the place was clean, she went into the air ducts with her special knife. Perhaps she'd smell like a meat-eater from this morning. She was certainly sweating hard enough. Then she picked off a clump of fur from a screen in the vents and rubbed it all over herself. That might help. Marybeth listened for complaints. She was ecstatic when she heard gripes about headaches, chest pains, and numbness from the aliens. At least that was how she interpreted their gestures as she caught sight of them through the grates over the vent outlets.

Then someone roared in anger as a kzin fell to the floor. Given the anger in the voice, she thought she'd just learned the kzinti word for *poison*. She heard lots of comments with *rett* this and *rett* that. A good thing she wasn't in the galley! They probably thought a dangerous human was running around. How right they were.

The next few hours were a nightmare of roaming from air duct to air duct as the kzinti scoured the ship for her. She thought the engine sounded odd, but figured that was because she was closer to it than usual. A good thing the kzinti were too big for the vents! Lethal or sleepy gas would disable them, too, unless they blocked off just one section, so she was probably safe from that danger if she kept moving. Once she screamed out a vent, "I killed him! And now you're all going to die, too!" Then she laughed.

The ship rocked as something hit it. Of course! The *Peregrine* must have come, and the kzinti couldn't answer the challenge correctly. Then she heard the sizzle and clang of weapons as men from the other ship boarded. She peered out of a vent. A dead alien lay by a weapons locker without a mark on him. She kicked the grate out, grabbed a disruptor for herself, and slid back in the duct. She headed toward the loudest noise, then peered out again. Hobbes was fighting two marines, and was winning. Marybeth popped open the vent and blasted him right in the back. Two other kzinti were already on the floor, but she shot at them anyway, just for fun. Besides, they might be faking. The marines gaped at her. She waved at them, then crawled back into the duct to look for another fight. The ship's gravity cut loose again. She banged her head right on the old sore spot. She felt herself blacking out, but didn't care. She'd won.

Lt. Aziz helped the unconscious woman into the autodoc. At first he'd thought she was dead. After the mopping up was done, two marines had sworn they'd seen a naked female come out of an air vent and join the battle. Even though the commander had been skeptical, they'd gone looking anyway. Armed. The ducts were designed to fit humans, not the aliens, but one never knew.

Aziz had been very surprised to find her. The only woman assigned to the *Cormorant* had been a civilian specialist sent to fix the autochef. The skeletal figure who'd damned near bit off his ear when he'd tried to put her into the shower hardly resembled her picture at all. He sincerely regretted having to sedate her.

Dr. Bonet looked a little better once she'd been cared for. She'd have to undergo major surgery back on Earth for muscle repair and scar removal, as well as diagnostics for her head injury. How she'd managed to live so long as a prisoner of the kzinti was beyond him. Her internal status had stabilized once she'd received several pints of universal blood substitute.

The next day, she was able to sit up and ask for something to eat and drink. She laughed hysterically when he offered something from the autochef. He decided to humor her and fetch something from the other ship. For all he knew, the kzinti had gotten their rations programmed into it. He'd had a taste of them once, and didn't blame her if she'd gotten tired of them. Especially if a bad batch had been responsible for killing the kzinti they'd found dead without any wounds on them.

She stared at him as she huddled in her blankets. "I've contacted Earth," he said, trying to make her feel better. "I can offer you anything within reason, including the captain's best whiskey. You've gone through a terrible ordeal. Once you're back on Earth you can ask for anything, reasonable or not. They say the rehab program on Hawaii is very nice." He wondered if she'd ever make it out of it, or join the permanent residents. It was too soon to tell.

Dr. Bonet smiled at him, though he thought she put a little too much teeth into it. "All I want," she said, "is a decent cup of coffee, my clothes, a hot bath in a real bathtub . . ."

Lt. Aziz nodded briskly. "No problem. We're heading toward a station with its own spin and a little more room. You can have the first two right off, though I recommend a slug of brandy to go with that coffee. Anything else?"

"Yes," she said with another smile. *Definitely too much teeth this time*, Aziz thought. She leaned forward and whispered, "A fur coat."

JOTOK

•

Paul Chafe

The planet overhead was breathtaking. Planets always were. Especially the ones with atmosphere. This one was a life-bearing oxygen world, swirled in clouds with nearly three-fifths of its surface area covered in ocean and dazzling icecaps. Cities sparkled on the night side as the terminator slid slowly past. It had started as a pinprick on the one nav screen that was currently imposed on sixty percent of Joyaselatak's field of vision. It continued to swell until it was no longer a planet but a place as the laws of motion carried the tiny ship inexorably toward its final destination.

Outwardly Joyaselatak was calm, secure in a resilient anti-acceleration bubble full of oxygenated fluid. Inwardly its torochord buzzed with chatter between its five self sections. The beauty of the view belied the danger. This planet was the citadel of the enemy. In order to evade detection, the ship would enter the atmosphere at meteoric speeds. The larger and more powerful pair of the ship's gravity polarizers would be used—and burnt out—in a massive last-instant surge to check its fall. Secrecy was essential. The enemy's sensors and weapons were crude but effective and getting better all the time, augmented by technology stolen from captured Jotok merchants. Attempts to reconnoiter with ultra-low albedo satellites had failed. The enemy detected the remote spies and destroyed them before they even entered orbit, thus the need for a risky ground-based scout mission. Joyaselatak hoped it would reach the surface intact and undetected. What the enemy lacked in technology they more than made up for in unrestrained aggressive energy. And as they mastered what they stole, their technological deficiencies diminished. It had taken a fifth of a lifetime for the news of the predators to reach the Jotok Trade Council at the speed of light and two-fifths more—unaccelerated times—for the probeship that had brought Joyaselatak to arrive at this distant star. Who knew what tricks the aliens might have developed in the meantime.

"You mock my honor!" Swift-Son of Rritt-Pride snarled the words through a fanged smile and dropped to attack-crouch in the dust of the pride circle. A pair of frolicking kits startled and bolted for their mother. Pkrr-Rritt watched from the den mouth with mild interest as other kzinti backed up to make room for a challenge duel.

Opposite Swift-Son, Rritt-Conserver shifted only slightly, but his new posture balanced him at once for attack or defense. "I taught you honor, kitten," he snarled back, deliberately insulting. "You mock yourself."

Swift-Son circled slowly, watching his opponent, looking for an opening. He was worthy of his name—his claws were faster than lightning, and his teacher was old and slow. Swift-Son could take him, perhaps. Hadn't he already two sets of ears on his belt? His anger told him he could win, but Rritt-Conserver smelled so calm.

"I will go east for my Name. I will steal the Mage-Kzin's totem!"

The old kzin pivoted slightly to keep his eyes locked on Swift-Son. "You will defy the Fanged God and destroy us all. If this one has taught you no better, it deserves to die. Come claim your due." Rritt-Conserver purred the words in the humbled tense but his meaning was clear, and *his* belt held more ears than a tangle-tree held leaves.

But to back down today of all days, and in front of the pride and the Patriarch, that would be too humiliating. Swift-Son held his crouch and let his rage give him strength. "I am an adult and I choose my own Namequest." He breathed rapidly through his mouth, priming his blood for battle.

His teacher abandoned sarcasm for the mocking tense. "You are a fool. You would refuse a name from the Fanged God for a kitten's dream."

"Only a fool would die in the desert for another fool's prattlings." Swift-Son gathered himself for the killing leap. But the old kzin's move had brought a rock from the fire circle into Swift-Son's touchdown area. A poor landing was quick death, and so he did not leap.

Rritt-Conserver noted the young kzin's restraint and relaxed his snarl but not his posture. "Remember the portents," he said, almost gently. Swift-Son stared back at him, eyes locked and muscles tensed for attack.

The tableau held as Pkrr-Rritt and the other kzin watched in silence. This was the critical moment. Swift-Son was acutely aware of their gaze. He could not back down now! But his teacher's words rang in his brain. Never in his life had the Fanged God sent portents, though the pride-ballad spoke of them. Then, on the eve of his Namequest, the Sky Streak had fallen in the east with thunder to shame a cloud burst. And that very morning he'd watched with his own eyes as the

Fanged God's talons raked four cloud-slashes across the sky from west to east. Strong portents, indeed, and the Fanged God was not to be denied.

And Rritt-Conserver was still so *calm*, and perhaps he had a right to be. Too many of the ears on his belt sheaf had once belonged to Swift-Son's playmates. Wild-Son's challenge hadn't lasted as long as his leap; their teacher had disemboweled him before he hit the ground.

Swift-Son had reacted without thinking and now had to pay with honor or blood. *Sheath pride and bare honor.* Rritt-Conserver had taught him that, too. It was the hardest lesson of all. For many, too hard. With an effort that made his limbs tremble, Swift-Son settled onto his belly from his attack crouch and lowered his head to expose his neck.

"Forgive this one's insolence, Honored Teacher," he choked out in humbled tense. "If the Fanged God wills it, I will go west for my Name." He waited for the symbolic neck bite that would confirm his master's dominance.

To his surprise it never came. Instead Rritt-Conserver grabbed Swift-Son's paw and drew him upright. "The Fanged God has marked you for special honor, Swift-Son. You are the *krwisatz*—the-pebble-that-trips-pouncer-or-prey. From today you will have a verse in the pride-ballad."

A shocked murmur went through the gathered watchers and Swift-Son's sense of humiliation evaporated. A verse in the pride-ballad! In each generation, only one, the Patriarch, was assured such tribute, and only after he died. In four generations only eight verses had been added, three of them during the Great Migration, when the pride moved west into the heart of the savannah. He groped for words, but a rake of his teacher's paw through the space that separated them cut him short.

"It is time."

Swift-Son, still trembling from the confrontation, fought himself under control and turned to Pkrr-Rritt. The other kzin had drawn in closer now—his brothers, his seniors—pridemates and friends, all wanted to share this moment with him. He drew strength from their presence and spoke with confidence. "Sire, I hunt a Name of Honor for Rritt-Pride." He intoned the traditional formula.

"Clean kill, Swift-Son." The Patriarch answered with a formality seldom accorded one who had not yet earned a Name.

The young kzin raked his claws across his nose. As the bright drops of blood that affirmed his fealty beaded, he turned and shouldered his hunt pouch. Then, without a backward glance, he disappeared into the long grass of the savannah. When next he entered the pride circle, he would be a stranger to it.

Rritt-Conserver watched him go with a mixture of pride and concern. In all but size Swift-Son was the pride's best—proud and *smart*. Rarely did he need to be taught a lesson twice. But though he was a more than promising youngster, even he did not possess the gift that Rritt-Conserver had been born with, a gift he had not realized was a gift until he learned that his pridemates did not share it. That gift had told him long ago that Swift-Son was *krwisatz* for Rritt-Pride. Now the Fanged God's portents confirmed it. Swift-Son's success smelled of fat game for the whole pride; his failure would bring—who knew? All he was certain of was that whatever the Fanged God had in store for Swift-Son in the deep desert meant change, great change that would be shared by all the pride. Of all his pupils, it was well that it was Swift-Son who had to carry that responsibility—but change never came without a price.

❖   ❖   ❖

It was a hard day's lope to the western edge of Rritt-Pride territory where lay Swift-Son's watch-rock. As a hunting blind the site was ideal: it jutted from a small rise just below the crest and facing the prevailing wind, with a view over the long grass to the game trails by the pool in the rivulet below. Beyond that the golden savannah sprawled to the curtain of the sky, now painted a brilliant red-gold by the burning solar disk that had just touched the western horizon. Behind him the crest dropped away steeply, securing his back. The rock was just the right shape for comfort, and sandy-orange, a fair match for his pelt. When he jumped to its surface he could *feel* himself donning the land like a cloak.

His watch-rock was not just a favored hunting spot, it was his refuge. Swift-Son felt more need to *understand* than did most of his peers; many times he had come here to mull over a problem undistracted, or just escape from the rough and tumble of pride life. Today might be the last time.

Many young kzin went numerous seasons wandering the wide savannah before returning with a Name. Many young kzin didn't return at all. Some found homes with other prides. Some became nomads who'd been able to claim a Name at the pride-circle but not a place within it. Still, far fewer returned to pledge fealty than left to seek a Name, and Swift-Son knew how his Patriarch and the other adults dealt with the hapless vagrants they caught on Rritt-Pride territory. Pride-kin or not, he knew how they'd deal with him.

A Namequest didn't *have* to take that long. Last year Eldest Brother had left on his Namequest, and by the next Hunter's Moon had brought back a tuskvor herd-mother eight times his weight, with tusks as long as his arm and razor-sharp horns. That he had killed it was amazing enough; that he had survived the deed bordered on mystery. On his return he'd dumped the huge skin triumphantly into the pride-circle and claimed the name Iron-Claw, following the legend of Graff-Trrul, who had challenged the Fanged God and nearly won. Iron-Claw now carried an iron *wtsai*, the symbol of adulthood and his fealty to Rritt-Pride. Eldest Brother was strong and cunning and his name proclaimed his ambition. One day he would be Graff-Iron-Claw, and one day after that he would challenge the Patriarch for leadership of the pride. If Pkrr-Rritt was wise, he would yield with only a token fight.

Not yet though. Pkrr-Rritt was strong himself, and what age had taken from him in speed it had given back in experience. If Iron-Claw was wise, he would wait until victory was sure. If not, he would never live to become Graff-Rritt.

Swift-Son wasn't as large or strong as his brother, but he had the eyes of the Hunter's Moon, and moved like a shadow in the night. He did not covet the double-name of a Patriarch, but he had dreamed of a Name-quest that would bring him even greater honor—the Namequest Rritt-Conserver had just denied him. He had planned to journey east beyond the edge of the world to the stronghold of the Mage-Kzin and steal their magic totem. What name could he not claim with such a triumph? He already knew his choice. Even now he secretly thought of himself as Silent Prowler—following Chraz-Mtell-Huntmaster-of-the-Fanged-God, he who with infinite patience stalked the ever-fleeing *ztigor* across the summer skies. His chosen quest had honor enough and more for such a name—the Mage-Kzin were dangerous adversaries.

Old Ktirr-Smithmaster often told the story of the destruction of Stkaa-Pride at tale-telling. His words conjured the flames of the pride-circle fire to life as he told of great monsters that devoured the land, and death magic that burned as it killed. More unbelievable still, he claimed that the Mage-Kzin females could talk and duel like males. His tale might be a fable, but the old crafter's ropy scars lent weight to his words. He was Stkaa-Pride's sole survivor, and many logs would burn while he related the fall of his pride and his own escape.

The story haunted Swift-Son, for the Mage-Kzin spanned the gap between legend and reality. Their powers were beyond imagining, but the dust clouds on the horizon that marked the passage of their demon-beasts were real, and grew closer every year. And every year the pride moved west to avoid them, away from the fertile heart of the savannah and toward the fringe where the desert began. Pkrr-Rritt was a wise Patriarch and he didn't want Rritt-Pride to follow Stkaa-Pride into the worlds of myth. Privately, Swift-Son wondered how much farther they could go; already game was much harder to come by. No longer could the pride's hunters rest and yawn for seven days of each eight-day cycle. In two or four years, there wouldn't be enough to support the pride at all. But if Swift-Son could gain the Mage-Kzin's magic totem, Rtitt-Pride would gain the power the Mage-Kzin possessed, would *become* the Mage-Kzin. No longer would the pride be driven into the desert like prey over a kill-drop—and Ktirr's long dead pridemates would be avenged.

He'd dreamed of that quest for years, right up to this morning. Of *course* he had challenged Rritt-Conserver. His reflexive honor required it even though his laggard thoughts had finally overruled his fanged hind-brain. It was only now, a day's march behind him to cool his blood, that he fully realized what he'd been given in return. *Krwisatz*-portents in the sky. Could it be that he was to become a fated warrior, like those in the ancient sagas?

He watched the sky fade from red-gold to indigo to

black, and the stars begin to wheel across the heavens in their eternal patterns. What might not come of this Namequest? Already he was promised a verse in the pride-ballad, even before he'd earned a Name.

But honor brought responsibility. A *krwisatz* could be bane or boon. Rritt-Pride must benefit from the role fate had given him. Only then would he prove himself worthy of his destiny and his name.

Were it not for that destiny he might have turned away. He was poorly equipped for the hazards of the deep desert—his belt hunt pouch held flint, iron striker, and tinder, his bone skinning knife with its granite whetstone, and his carefully hoarded store of iron tradeballs. On his back he carried a section of tuskvor skin for a shelter, a waterskin, and a larger pouch of dried meat. Better perhaps to turn north, avoid both the desert and the Mage-Kzin. He could live off the land and with great luck avoid the prides that held it. Perhaps eventually he could claim a Name somewhere else. Surely even life as a homeless nomad would be better than death in the desert?

To voice the question even silently in his mind was to answer it. His doubts held no honor. He was Swift-Son, chosen *krwisatz* of Rritt-Pride by the Fanged God, and none were as silent or stealthy as he. He was Silent Prowler, fated warrior stalking with the spirit of Chraz-Mtell-Huntmaster-of-the-Fanged-God and the night belonged to him. He purr-growled deep in his throat and slid off his watch-rock into the shadow, picking his course westward under the silent stars by light of the High Hunter's Moon.

Thirty-two sunrises later found him deep in the desert. As the initial excitement had worn off, his doubts returned. On his fourth day, perhaps inspired by Elder-Brother-Iron-Claw, he had been rash enough to stalk a young *tuskvor*. Just as he crept into pouncing distance, his prey's mother had appeared, scented him and charged. He'd had to scramble ignominiously for his life or be impaled, then crushed, then trampled to mush. He'd spent the night hungry in a lone tangle-tree, and the very next day he'd narrowly avoided ambush as he crossed Dcrz-Pride territory. It had taken half a day crawling paw by paw down a maze of dry gullies to avoid the hunters stalking him. Twice they flushed him and he'd fled like a *ztigor* while *wtzal*-hunting spears hissed past. Only when darkness fell had he finally been able to lose them.

He'd recognized two of his pursuers, Pouncer and Furball of Dcrz-Pride. He'd sparred and joked with them at the yearly Great-Pride-Circle, while Pkrr-Rritt and the other patriarchs pledged fealty to Graff-Kdor, the Great Patriarch of all the wide savannah. The memory of happier times weighed heavily on his mind, for it underscored his outcast status. True he could have made a border gift and crossed Dcrz-Pride as a guest, but he couldn't afford the tradeballs, and he needed all his kills just to keep himself fed. A Namequest was a test, he knew, and if it were easy there would be no honor attached to it.

On the eighth day he'd left the savannah and with it danger of attack, but simply traveling the desert was dangerous. He never ventured more than a day from a waterhole and it often took many exploratory probings to locate the next one to westward. Game was vanishingly scarce, and he was reduced to digging *grashi* from their burrows. They were tasty morsels, but not much nourishment for the time involved; eight were barely a mouthful. Thus he spent his days just getting enough to eat. Moreover, the digging filled his nose and pelt with sand. No matter how much he groomed he was never entirely free of the grit. He'd lost his skinning knife in a sandstorm. Four or eight times a day he *needed* that knife. Four or eight times a day he used his claws instead. They were quickly becoming ragged and torn from the abuse. Claws were for killing, not cutting roots in pursuit of burrowers.

It was not at all his idea of what a warrior did. True, the sagas often told of long and arduous treks, but when curled up by a crackling fire in the warm den, a journey even twice around the seasons was over in a few words so the tale-teller could get on to the exciting parts. Swift-Son was beginning to realize that it was not just courage but tenacity that made a Hero. Even both qualities might not be enough. Perhaps his role as *krwisatz* was simply to walk until he died—perhaps the portents were meant for the pride—to keep a rash youngster from bringing the wrath of the Mage-Kzin down upon them all.

As he left his watch-rock, Swift-Son had been sure he was fated to become a legend. But now, alone in the vast, uncaring desert, it seemed a faint hope at best. Normally he preferred only the Hunter's Moon for company. Now he yearned for a pridemate. Somehow the verse to his honor in the pride-ballad now seemed a poor return for a slow, lonely death.

Thus he pondered gloomily as he trudged through the shifting sand on the night of the thirty-second day. Already the sun was starting to peep over the horizon behind him. Soon he would have to stop and take cover from its burning glare and he had yet to find a waterhole. If he didn't find one soon he had nothing to look forward to but a day of fitful rest beneath his *tuskvor* skin with a few mouthfuls of *grashi* and not enough water. Then the next night he would trudge back to the last waterhole and spend the morning digging the last *grashi* out of their holes there. He estimated that there were enough burrowers left for one more journey westward and then if he didn't find anything, he'd have to go back to yet another waterhole for food. He desperately needed a genuine kill to provision himself properly, but he hadn't seen so much as a *ztigor* since his third day in the desert.

Suddenly he realized that something had been tugging at the edge of his awareness. Instantly Swift-Son crouched behind a nearby bramblebush, ears swiveling up, nostrils flaring, lips twitching over his fangs as he scanned the crest of the dune ahead. Awareness grew in him that the texture of the sand was wrong. The desert floor had become loose and crumbly, as though it had become the spoil mound of some gigantic *grashi* burrow. The smell of hot dust and bramblebush ahead was not quite right.

There was no prey-scent, but there was sound, faint but clear. Something was moving on the other side of the strange dune ahead. His ears strained forward as he strove to identify it. It was unlike anything he'd heard before—a semirhythmic pattern of dry clicking. Swift-Son tried to imagine what could cause such a sound.

He began to stalk slowly, moving parallel to the dune's crest without coming closer. Cover was scarce, but he took maximum advantage of it, slipping quickly and silently from bush to stone to sandhill, exposing himself as little as possible. As he moved he instinctively triangulated the sound source. He carefully positioned himself downwind and up-sun of his target. Only then did he start his approach.

As he drew closer the depth of the disturbed sand grew. *Something* had moved an immense amount of sand to build the dune. There was no more cover, but a couple of bramblebushes that had been uprooted in the digging process and lay partially buried in the sand uphill. With nothing to hide behind, he moved up the dune on his belly, using a slight depression in the slope for what little concealment it provided. He shifted barely a paw-span at a time, listening at every pause, his tail

unconsciously twitching hunt commands to nonexistent
pridemates. His goal was an uprooted bush at the crest
that would give him cover as he surveyed the other
side of the dune. He moved with the sounds, stopping
when they stopped. A prey animal pausing to listen
for danger would hear nothing.

Here was the bush. With infinite patience he lifted
his head until he could see over the dune's crest.

Nothing he had experienced before prepared him
for what he saw. It was *wrong*. The dune was the rim
of an immense bowl-shaped concavity and all of it was
freshly-dug sand. Swift-Son didn't want to contemplate
the size of the creature that had dug it. Arcane artifacts
lined the bowl, set in concentric circles a rock-throw
apart from each other. They looked vaguely like the
tall cache-signs a trail scout would build from sticks to
mark a kill or a route change during a trek, but they
weren't. These had a symmetry of construction that
he'd never seen before, and where cache signs were
blackened with charcoal to make them stand out
these . . . things were a dusty yellow that made them
hard to see against the sand. In the center of the bowl
was—something. It seemed to be a pile of sand until
he tried to look right at it, and then it shimmered into
the background like a mirage. The entire tableau was
unsettling.

Then he caught sight of the demon. A cache-sign-
thing had obscured it momentarily. It was a nightmarish
shape with five multijointed limbs with *eyes* on them
and no head at all. It was standing on three limbs while
the other two worked at the artifact with some strange
tool. The tool was making the rhythmic clicking that
he had tracked. Perhaps it was a magic totem? He would
kill the demon and bring it back to the pride. Rritt-
Conserver would know what to do from there.

One thing was sure: the old kzin had read the portents

correctly. Swift-Son *was krwisatz*. He had been guided to this desolate spot by the Fanged God himself. This would earn him a greater Name than "Silent Prowler" if he lived, and a place at the Fanged God's pride-circle if he died. Banish that thought; he would not fail! What name would he choose? Chraz-Hunter—no—*Chraz-Warrior*! He snarled the name beneath his breath. It tasted good. The exultation in his liver washed away the fear and fatigue.

The demon was coming closer, to perform its ritual on the next artifact. Swift-Son studied it carefully. His first blow had to kill; otherwise it might bring magic into play.

It had no vulnerable neck to snap or head to tear off. It seemed to be all limbs, but he couldn't see himself pulling them off one by one while it attacked him with the remainder. Its featureless central body must be its weakness. Strike there, fast and deep, and all the limbs would be rendered useless at once.

His target was oblivious to his presence. That was as it should be. His stalk had been as silent as a zephyr and he was downwind and directly in front of the rising desert sun. Not even a demon's eyes could see into that dazzling blaze. Swift-Son gathered himself for the leap.

Joyaselatak was pleased with its progress. Touchdown had been successful. The next morning four enemy fighters in formation had dragged contrails across the sky, but by then it had its wide spectrum camouflage canopy erected over the ship. Of course nothing could be done about the impact crater, if searchers could pick it out amidst the rolling dunes. It was an acceptable risk. The nearest outpost of kzin civilization was a mining complex well to the southeast.

That afternoon it began to deploy its sensors. Information began coming in. Once the transmitter was set up, the data was uplinked in microbursts to the probeship lurking in the primary's cometary halo. But even before the first transmission, Joyaselatak had gained an important piece of intelligence. The contrails meant the kzinti still used turbines for in-atmosphere flight. That meant that grav polarizers were still too expensive to be used anywhere but space, and that meant this species might not have to be exterminated to halt its expansion. The Jotoki were a far-sighted race. Annihilating enemies was wasteful. If an enemy could be contained, then in time it could be converted to a valuable trading partner. Joyaselatak's primary mission was to determine if in this case such restraint was possible. If its initial estimate of the enemy's technology proved correct, then indeed mercy might once again prove both safe and profitable.

Not that it could head home yet. Much analysis remained to be done. Closely allied with the main task was the question of the most economical method of control. Of course the predators would be charged containment costs, service fees, and interest when they finally became trade partners, but the process was a long one and conversion didn't always occur. The Trade Council wanted to minimize their investment risk.

Its mind sections debated possibilities as it adjusted an element of its transmitter grid with a ratchet. The impact crater provided a fair basis for a parabolic antenna form and the grid was designed to take advantage of this. It was a clever design, although each antenna element required quite precise alignment. Though not planned for, the shifting sand had posed no problem; it had been simple enough to bury each element's supports, then douse the sand with liquid adhesive. Once set it was a simple, if meticulous, job to ratchet the elements into position. Even so they tended to drift out of alignment as the sand settled, with a resultant drop in signal. Joyaselatak didn't mind resetting them.

It made a pleasant change from evaluating the never-ending flood of information from the sensors.

Swift-Son screamed and leapt, taking the Jotok completely by surprise. Four of its self sections were concentrating on the tricky antenna adjustment. The one left on danger alert was watching a portable display board with the ship's detection systems remoted to it. Blurred somewhat by the impact crater's rim, the ship's sensors had still picked up life-form readings from the approaching kzin, but in the absence of corresponding metal or power indications, the computer hadn't even assigned them a threat priority until Swift-Son exploded over the dune. The scream shocked the watching self section into action even as the others realized the danger and jammed the torochord with warnings. The first section overrode them all, throwing the display board and ratchet at the enemy with two limbs and dodging the leap with the other three. It was too little too late. Swift-Son's pounce had been perfect and there wasn't enough time.

The ship's AI, belatedly recognizing the threat, sifted through a decision tree. Since the threat was immediate, it could act without Joyaselatak's authorization. It selected the weapons turret that covered that arc of the ship. Since the threat was biological, it chose a stunner. Since Joyaselatak was within the beam's spillover cone, it set minimum power for the target's mass and offset the aim-point to spare the Jotok as much of the radiated energy as possible.

The turret accepted the targeting data from the AI, computed Swift-Son's trajectory, swiveled to track him, locked on and fired. His kill-scream cut off with a gurgle as he went limp in midair. Unable to control his touchdown, he landed in a heap atop his target. Kzin and Jotok went down in a tangled pile of limbs.

❖   ❖   ❖

Joyaselatak recovered first. Swift-Son's shock became fear when he found he couldn't move a muscle, then terror as his intended victim rolled him over on the sand. His horror only increased when the demon began to drag him downslope, beneath the shimmering not-mirage.

The Jotok's spindly limbs belied its strength and it quickly hauled its prize under the filmy camouflage and tied the kzin to one of the canopy's supports by looping a mooring cable around its ankles, securing it with a burst from the sonic welder in its tool smock. Then it retrieved its display board from upslope, sat on its undermouth, and went to work. One self section maintained a watch around three hundred and sixty degrees for more intruders, borrowing eyes around the torochord as necessary, and three more began accessing the ship's sensor logs to find out why the AI had missed the danger. The remaining limb stripped its captive of its meager possessions.

Swift-Son felt his panic recede somewhat when he found he could weakly move his bound legs. As the weirdly shaped demon took his hunt pouch and tools, he tried to make sense of his surroundings. Only the sand beneath him was familiar; everything else was strange and intimidating. The sand pile mirage was held up on poles, like a travel-tent. It covered a huge, blunt cone, unnaturally symmetrical and thoroughly scorched. Smooth cords snaked from an opening in its belly to every one of the cache-sign things in the sand bowl and a number of larger, more oddly shaped arcana deployed beneath the canopy overhead. And that was the strangest thing of all. It no longer looked like a wavery sandhill. From underneath it was just a faintly bluish filminess, rippling like a pool in the desert breeze. He knew it was impossible, but he could see right through it into the clear and cloudless sky.

Examining the sensor log Joyaselatak carefully noted the points where the AI had registered the kzin and decided it represented no danger. Threats were too narrowly defined as weapons or weapons carriers, with an implied assumption that these involved power sources, heat production, EM emitters, or other technological fingerprints. Clearly someone at base was far too solicitous of the sensibilities of local animals. A few brief commands expanded the definition to prevent future surprises and for the local fauna. That done, the Jotok transferred all its attention to inspecting its prize.

It had never seen a live kzin before. The thing was a killing machine—all fangs and talons with a crossbraced endoskeleton and lean, powerful musculature. Its eyes and ears were large and set forward for hunting prey, and the chances were good that its nose would penetrate even a Jotok's sophisticated scent suppression and camouflage. Its self sections compared notes on the shock of the kzin's attack scream and the sight of the carnivore bearing down on it from nowhere, like fiercely intelligent death incarnate. The Trade Council was right to fear this race.

After retrieving Swift-Son's kit, Joyaselatak learned that the carnivore wore nothing but leather boots with holes in the toes for its claws and a leather cape. Its only weapons were its claws and teeth. Searching through its equipment revealed a waterpouch, some skinned and dried rodents in a bag, and a large folded skin. A smaller pouch on a belt contained a flat, jagged rock, a larger, smoother rock, a small bar of crude iron, some shredded vegetation wrapped in bark, a length of sinew cord, and a number of small iron balls stored individually in a greased leather pouch—metal, but not enough to trigger the AI.

The clothing and equipment were made with obvious skill from natural materials. That suggested that it really was a primitive subsistence hunter rather than a technological sophisticate following some ancient ritual. The very existence of such a kzin was noteworthy. The reports Joyaselatak had studied indicated a homogeneous civilization profile with quite advanced technology. The evidence indicated that the kzinti had forged a single civilization between five-squared and five-cubed generations ago. Analysis indicated a highly stable social structure, though built in violent conflict. Transmission intercepts revealed a single language. Their government was based on a semihereditary leader who had dominion over the entire species and dynasties lasted many inheritances. Certainly their interstellar ventures indicated a unified civilization rather than parallel and competing efforts.

Of course worlds often evolved unevenly. While the highly social Jotok had unified their planetary tradeweb early in their development, it was not unusual for one part of a species to be colonizing stars while another part had only rudimentary tool use. Certainly the aggressive, asocial, and thinly populated kzinti were prime candidates for a fragmented social pattern with distinct subgroups and wildly varying technology levels. Or perhaps the primitives were suffered to exist as a sort of cultural repository, worth the small cost of the wasteland they occupied. Whatever the explanation, clearly the researchers had been seduced into unwarranted generalizations by the paradoxical stability arising from the aggressive individuality of the carnivore's society. Primitive cultures were notoriously hard to detect, especially when they were small and masked by higher technology in operation.

Or, volunteered a self section, in this case by a sand dune. Joyaselatak's integrated thought-chain was interrupted as its other self sections berated the hapless watcher for its carelessness.

The internal argument ended when a self section noticed the kzin moving. It had recovered motor control surprisingly quickly. It would not do to underestimate this dangerous predator. Time to begin the interrogation.

Swift-Son, still partially paralyzed, was sawing with desperate determination at the mooring cable with his foreclaws—taking advantage of his captor's seeming preoccupation. The cable was far tougher than anything he'd seen before and his already frayed talons were beginning to bleed. He ignored the pain. Sooner or later the cable had to give. Hopefully it would give in time.

"I am being Jotok you are being kzinti."

Swift-Son sat bolt upright, as if stung by a *v'pren*, the mooring cable forgotten. He hadn't expected the creature to speak. It had an odd lilt to its voice, almost as if it were singing. Its accent was strange and its words hard to understand. At first Swift-Son didn't even try to comprehend; he was simply too shocked that it could talk at all.

"I am being Jotok my name is being Joyaselatak. You are being kzinti your name is being?"

This time understanding seeped through. He slowly relaxed his grip on the binding cable and regarded his captor with a strange calm. Despite the unusual phrasing, the question honored him. Perhaps this strange being was a servant of the Fanged God, such as the sagas spoke of.

For a moment he thought of claiming a Name. The question hinted that he might, and had he not earned it when he sprang fearlessly to attack? But he had not completed the kill and was now a captive of his prey. Perhaps the compliment was also a test. *Sheath Pride and bare Honor.* Better to be found worthy than boastful.

"I have no Name. I am Swift-Son, of Rritt-Pride." His answer was humble, but he acknowledged the honor by speaking formally, as a guest on a neighbor's territory.

"Your name being Swift-Son-of-Rritt-Pride." The creature seemed pleased with itself. "Your reason being?"

Swift-Son was puzzled by the question. It didn't seem to have any meaning.

After a long pause waiting for an answer, the Jotok elaborated. "Your reason being for attacking of myself?"

Ah. He *was* being tested, and the Fanged God had selected a battle of wits. He must be true to the honor-of-the-captured-warrior, always the hardest to maintain and made doubly difficult by his Nameless status, while the demon tried to trap him into violating it. He would rather be tested claw to claw and fang to fang, with victory to the strongest and fastest.

He *had* been so tested. His careful stalk, his unhesitating pounce had demonstrated both his hunting skill and courage. Clearly his captor controlled magic enough to kill him with a glance. The creature would gain no honor through such an uneven duel. Swift-Son had simply been frozen in midleap so that the second test could occur.

He composed his next answer carefully and spoke with pride, but not arrogance. "Hrrr. I am Namequesting in the spirit of Chraz-Mtell. I am a fated . . ." He paused, considering whether to claim himself as a warrior. He decided he had not yet earned that honor. ". . . hunter of the Fanged God. I follow the Portents of the Starstreak and the Skylash. They have led me here and I have challenged-claimed your totem."

Jotoki were excellent linguists, their multibrain structure naturally parceling out the tasks of phoneme parsing, word identification, vocabulary translation, syntax deconstruction, and meaning recognition. Nevertheless Joyaselatak wasn't exactly sure what Swift-Son meant. The dialect was oddly different from what it had learned and many of the words were unfamiliar.

As far as it could determine, the primitive kzin was saying that he had been out hunting and something, the Jotok didn't know what, had happened to a sky god. Therefore, the kzin, driven by visions from its god, had attacked Joyaselatak for the sake of some religious object. The self sections bubbled the question around for a moment. What object was it? Perhaps the iron balls held some special symbolism?

And the word the kzin had used actually meant *formal* attack. That was an odd usage, especially for an unprovoked killing leap. Some clarification was called for.

"Why is being use of *'formal* attack'?"

Swift-Son was growing wise to the demon's tricks and at once understood the test. It was suggesting that his challenge was incorrect, offered to an unworthy foe. He was being deliberately insulted, yet to maintain the honor-of-the-captured-warrior, he must answer with dignity, not rage. He spoke carefully, in the Formal Tense.

"You are a demon of the Fanged God's pride-circle are you not? What challenge could I offer that you would be unworthy of?"

Joyaselatak buzzed the kzin's words and several possible translations around its torochord, looking for the most valid interpretation. The kzin thought it was a supernatural creature—an unsurprising mistake—and for that reason the attack was formal, which still meant nothing. Better understanding would have to wait until the basics were covered.

The demon waved one of its arm/legs at the massive artifact beneath the shimmering travel-tent. "I am being a Jotok. This is being my starship." It gestured upwards, indicating the clear blue sky. "In it I am arriving from the stars. To be speaking to you I am traveling a distance of great lengths."

Swift-Son followed the gesture and looked with new awe at the "starship." The creature was only confirming what Swift-Son was all but certain of. It had come from the stars of course, from the pride-circle of the Fanged God, and it *had* come specifically for Swift-Son. But that it had traveled in the huge—artifact—that truly savaged credibility.

Of course he knew what a ship was. The pride-ballad spoke of them. Ships were driven by the wind across a savannah of water called a sea, like sailseeds over a pond. Rritt-Conserver had said the ballad was their ancestors speaking, for those wise enough to listen. Swift-Son had dutifully memorized his daily verses, but only now did he understand why. Life in the larger world contained much that wasn't found in the pride. If his ancestors could float ships to distant lands, he had no doubt this demon could sail the skies to the stars.

When the demon interrupted his thoughts, Swift-Son realized he'd been staring at the starship and ignoring his host/captor. Not the best manners.

"You are being a kzin. Where are you being from?"

Well, that question was easy enough, if redundant. "I am Swift-Son of Rritt-Pride. I am on my Namequest."

Joyaselatak looked at its prisoner through three eyes at once. "What are you being hunting?"

Swift-Son began to relax. Another easy question, and asking about his Namequest was another honor. Clearly he had passed the demon's tests. It was hard to keep the pride out of his voice as he answered, but perhaps the almost unearned honors were another, subtler test.

"I am in search of a magic totem for my pride."

Joyaselatak was pleased. At last a response that didn't raise more questions than it answered. True understanding couldn't be far behind.

"What is for magic being by you sought?"

"Hrrr. The Mage-Kzin force us from the savannah

to the desert like harried herd beasts. But with a magic totem we will regain our names and be warriors again. The Mage-Kzin will tremble at our might!"

A surge of comprehension/excitement ran around Joyaselatak's torochord as its self sections realized the import of the kzin's words. Trying to find meaning through the language barrier had delayed Joyaselatak's realization of the goal of the kzin's quest. Its use of the term "magic" had led the Jotok to believe the kzin was on some sort of religious journey. Of course the carnivore meant "technology." It didn't know the difference. That didn't matter. What the primitive wanted was weapons. It clearly belonged to a marginalized breed that was in the process of being pushed from its last remnant of viable territory—no doubt the mining operations to the southeast were expanding and it wanted "magic weapons" to push back.

That offered possibilities. One of the best ways to contain a hostile species was to disrupt their home planet. The normal technique of inciting dissent by supporting competing factions had already been judged unlikely to work here. The Patriarch's court was already awash in plots, counterplots, honor feuds and no small amount of blood. What little fuel the Jotok could add to that inferno of intrigue would make no difference at all. There was no question of gifting one group with Jotok technology; the kzinti had already proven their ability to turn what they'd captured against its inventors. Furthermore, the Trade Council was wary of interfering with the ruling cliques. Currently most of the highly aggressive conquest effort was being made by young, ambitious but not well-connected kzin. The Jotok leaders didn't want to provoke the higher echelons into throwing their full weight behind the drive to space.

And therein lay the prisoner's promise. Supporting one kzin leader over another was hopeless; the names

might change, but the interstellar expansion program would continue. The prisoner, however, existed entirely outside of the dominant kzin technosociological matrix. A push from external barbarians, suitably armed and trained with weapons and techniques they could not maintain on their own, might be just the thing to destabilize the kzin hierarchy. At the very least a swarm of such barbarians would make the kzin leadership turn much of the resources they now so offhandedly flung into space toward internal pacification. At best the primitives would actually triumph and take control— becoming thereby grateful and cooperative members of the Trade Council. Trade would flow, very profitable trade, and in the meantime containment costs would be kept low, increasing long-term margins on the entire operation. Best of all, the next time a race of upstart space-farers stuck its head up, the kzinti would be waiting for them as mercenary representatives of the Trade Council.

And if all that happened on the basis of Joyaselatak's recommendations, it would be a much needed success for the probeship clanpod. That would be good for the Trade Council, of course, but it would also put an end to the powerful cruiser clanpod's attempt to subsume the probeship role—and the probeship clanpod, too.

Joyaselatak considered its prisoner. "You are being seeking weapons?"

Swift-Son rippled his ears at the simplicity of the question. "I will earn a *wtsai* with my name, of course. Rritt-Pride observes the traditions."

"What is being *wtsai*?"

The test purpose of such easy questions eluded Swift-Son, and he hesitated before answering, suspecting a hidden trap. Finding none, he spoke. "It is the symbol of honor and fealty. It will prove that I have earned my Name."

Joyaselatak's frustrated self sections bickered over the translation. Every topic seemed to lead back to the creature's religion. The language barrier was proving too difficult. A demonstration was in order.

"You are being shown weapons. You are being waiting here," it needlessly admonished the bound kzin before clambering up the side of the ship and through the airlock, leaving Swift-Son to ponder the vagaries of the Fanged God.

The spyship was cramped but not too cramped to carry several weapons. Joyaselatak chose a plasma blast gun. It was a short-range weapon designed for boarding actions, ideal for hull breaching, devastating in close combat. Acting in an atmosphere reduced its effectiveness considerably, range and destructiveness being lost to some rather spectacular visual and aural effects. The plasma violently stripped electrons from the gas molecules, rapidly giving up energy to produce a searing cone of superheated air that crackled with its own lightning bolts and left rolling thunder and the taint of ozone in its wake. Range was reduced to a good bowshot, but within that distance the target would be impressively immolated and combustibles near the line of fire would burst into flame.

It was just the thing to impress a primitive.

Joyaselatak lugged the heavy weapon out of its storage niche and outside. The kzin was still there, waiting impassively. The Jotok raised the plasma gun and pointed it at a sandstone boulder embedded in the side of the crater bowl. It aimed carefully, then in quick succession pressed the stabilizer switch, closed the eyes facing downrange so as not to be blinded by the flash, and pulled the trigger.

Swift-Son had no idea what was about to happen, so when the world exploded he was more shocked than terrified. At first there was only the searing afterimage of the plasma cone and the thunder of the blast wave. As the echoes faded, fear crystallized in his brain, but his belated reflex leap simply pitched him face-first into the sand. Fortunately, the sudden impact of his nose on a half-buried rock served to jolt him out of his blind panic. He took a deep, shuddering breath and managed to focus his eyes. Across the dune bowl, a massive boulder had been reduced to pebbles, some of which were still raining down on them even at this distance. The dry desert air smelled like the aftermath of one of deep summer's storms. His very fur was standing on end, snapping at his skin with residual magic.

He suddenly understood how a grazing *ztigor* felt when it heard the hunter's killscream. He knew this must be the magic that had destroyed Stkaa-Pride, and suddenly he mourned for Ktirr-Smithmaster's pridemates, kzin who'd been dead before he was born. The legends said that one day the world began, and one day it would end. This, he realized, was how the world would die. He could not imagine a more terrible weapon.

"This is being magic such as is being object in your hunt?" The demon's oddly inflected voice broke the breathless silence.

Still shaken, Swift-Son managed to stutter out an agreement. It was one thing to know one was in the presence of the Fanged God's servant. It was another entirely to have its might demonstrated. Was there any power the demon did not possess?

"Yourself are being wanting of this weapon?" his captor asked.

Swift-Son could hardly believe his ears! The demon was offering him a weapon! It was asking him to pledge fealty to the Fanged God! Where Rritt-Pride would have given him an iron *wtsai*, the demon was offering this totem of magical fire. That alone was beyond dreaming, but to sit at the Fanged-God's pride-circle! That was an honor unheard of in all but the ancient sagas.

"It . . . it would be a privilege beyond price!" He somehow managed to find the words.

"You are being agreeing to not being formal-attacking of myself and I am being freeing of yourself and being giving of this weapon to yourself."

Without hesitation Swift-Son leapt to his feet, a little unsteadily due to the restricting cable, and raked his claws across his face in the age-old gesture of fidelity. "I vow fealty to you and to your Patriarch, Demon-Servant of the Fanged-God." Four crimson lines on his nose made the pledge a blood oath.

His response seemed to satisfy the demon. It did something to the flat board-artifact it carried, then removed a talisman from its garment and touched it to the loop of cable. A sharp pain bit into Swift-Son's ankle and was gone before he had a chance to react. The cable fell free. And then he was holding the magic totem, caressing it reverently as he half listened to the creature's instructions on how to release its magic.

The demon tried to show him how to hold the weapon, but it wasn't made for his arms and his grip was awkward. He pointed it at a bramblebush on the dune crest and pressed where the demon had indicated. The world exploded again as the weapon sent a burning bolt skyward. Static crackled through the startled kzin's fur, and he dropped the weapon and dived behind a boulder. He emerged moments later much ashamed of himself. Bolting like a startled kit at a loud noise was not the way a member of the Fanged God's pride-circle behaved.

He returned to the creature, half afraid his display

of cowardice would result in the revocation of his newfound honors. Instead the demon simply picked up the weapon, handed it back to him, and went over it again, more slowly this time. Swift-Son paid close attention to the details.

The demon touched a protuberance on the side of the weapon and pointed to a blue light on the back of the handle.

"Armed. Being ready to fire," said the Jotok. He touched the protuberance again and the light turned yellow.

"Disarmed. Being unready to fire."

It indicated another part of the weapon. "Trigger. Being firing."

Once again Swift-Son raised the weapon to his shoulder and pointed it at the same boulder. He touched the first stud and the light obediently turned blue. He firmed his grip and his resolve together and pressed the second one. Again the ravening fire split the sky. The bolt came nowhere near his intended target, but at least he didn't turn and run.

The demon patiently took the weapon again and demonstrated the aiming arrangements. It took a while for Swift-Son to figure them out, but once he did his accuracy improved markedly. Soon he was at home with the magical weapon, able to aim and fire with a reasonable chance of hitting somewhere in the vicinity of his intended target. Still he scared himself several times and, though he didn't know it, his mentor as well. Joyaselatak was afraid its overexuberant student would, despite all admonitions and the overwatching AI, pump a plasma bolt into the side of its spyship and strand it forever.

Once Swift-Son could hit a target more often than not, they moved on to more sophisticated skills, taking the weapon apart and putting it together properly, reloading and solving various problems that might occur. Swift-Son found himself enjoying the challenge of putting all the pieces together just so. One little mistake at the beginning meant something wouldn't fit properly later on.

Joyaselatak was pleased as it watched the kzin strip and assemble the weapon and perform jam clearance drills. Its student was progressing rapidly. It and its kind were clearly born warriors, needing only weapons. True, a great deal of risky work remained to be done before the primitive kzin were in a position to strike their advanced brethren. After much discussion between its self sections, it had decided on a cadre approach. The smartest, most aggressive primitives would be taken to the nearest base-star. There they would be trained into the core of an elite force while forced growth techniques raised an army for them to lead. Jotoki bioengineering was the best in the galaxy.

That idea had already been explored, unsuccessfully, using DNA from kzin prisoners. The problem was that kzinti died quickly in captivity and the force-grown youngsters failed to develop properly without parents, a concept alien to the Jotok. Experimentation proved that adult kzin would often adopt a cloned juvenile and the relationship thus formed would help both to survive. There was a cost, though. The revitalized kzin became even more aggressive and proved themselves adept escape artists, invariably doing a great deal of damage before being brought down. Eventually the warclone clanpod despaired of its task. The essential parental bond ensured that the juveniles grew up viewing their Jotok masters with undiminished enmity.

But if the Jotok made common cause with this retrograde culture against their high-technology oppressors, the equation would change. They would be allies by virtue of a common enemy. The Trade

Council would provide the weapons and the primitives would supply the bodies. Containment costs would be extremely low, and conversion from enemy to Trade Council membership would be rapid.

Jotok and kzin continued to practice with the plasma gun throughout the afternoon. In between sessions the Jotok outlined a careful subset of its plans to its protégé. Swift-Son's responses were encouraging. The kzin was eager to cooperate and was sure that its family-group would as well. At that point Joyaselatak decided to return Swift-Son to his point of origin. He had mastered all the basic weapon drills and the Jotok was anxious to get its plans underway.

Joyaselatak's gravlifter was designed for two passengers, as long as both were Jotok. Swift-Son was cramped even riding in the cargo compartment, but the view through the transparent clamshell doors was awe-inspiring. This, he knew, must be a skyship. One day he'd learn to sail it.

He'd spent his time before departure running over the pertinent verses of the pride-ballad as he tried to identify mast, sails, windlasses, and rigging. It wasn't easy. The craft was gracefully curved just as the ballad said it should be, but none of its few features seemed to correspond to the references in the verse. Eventually he had to be satisfied with the strangely musical Jotoki referents the demon gave him.

He stopped asking questions once they were airborne. The whole world was spread out beneath him! There was no limit on how far he could see. Often he'd lain on his watch-rock, idly following the graceful maneuvers of the soaring scavengers overhead, and wondered what it would be like to fly as they did. Now he knew, and it was exhilarating beyond expression. And the speed was incredible. He recognized a waterhole that he'd stopped at for four days while probing his way west. Before he'd finished wondering at the sight of it, the next waterhole was already sliding underneath. A day's journey in a single leap!

Soon they had followed a series of waterholes back to the savannah, and Joyaselatak began to ask its passenger for directions. It took quite some time and many landings for the kzin to get its bearings. Clearly the feral hunter was quite disoriented. Time and again Swift-Son would insist that a certain hill or watercourse was a landmark. The Jotok would bring the gravlifter down and the kzin would examine the terrain, sniff the air, then admit its mistake. Nevertheless it always knew which direction to set off in and they were making progress. At least Joyaselatak *hoped* they were making progress.

The sun was on the horizon when they set down by a small crest overlooking a pool in a rivulet. It looked no different from any other place they'd landed, but the kzin insisted that this was home. It hit itself on the nose again, an odd gesture that Joyaselatak had yet to figure out, and promised to return in five days with the best males and females of its family group.

The Jotok was glad that it had remembered to specify both sexes. The warclone clanpod would have flayed it alive if it'd brought only males. It gave its student a few last-minute reminders about the weapon as the kzin clambered out. Then it tabbed the navigation panel to mark the coordinates, looked to make sure that its passenger was clear, lifted out and turned west, keeping low just to be on the safe side.

As the skyship rose into the air, Swift-Son leapt onto the familiar surface of his watch-rock and settled down. His eyes followed the magical craft as it shrank to a dot over the horizon and disappeared into the setting sun. He kept watching after it was gone, until the sun was gone too and the purple skyglow faded to star-dappled black. Then he slid into the shadows, making his way homeward down familiar trails, carrying the magic weapon slung on his back.

That night took him better than halfway home. He stopped before daybreak and found a well-hidden hunt-blind to lay up in. He could have pushed on and been back while the sun was up, but what he had in mind would have to wait for evening and the gathering at the pride-circle. He slept soundly, dreaming of demons and fire magic and flying and stars. When the sun slipped below the horizon, he was up and moving, more carefully now. For the last thousand-twenty-four paces he approached the pride-circle as if it were prey alert for the watchers he knew were waiting in the darkness. Finally he gained a vantage point that looked onto the hillock beneath the bluff, where the pride gathered in the open den.

Surroundings changed as the pride moved, but the spirit was always the same. There was Pkrr-Rritt, lying in his place of honor on the rock by the fire and old Ktirr-Smithmaster himself was silhouetted against the flames, conjuring up the shapes of another story as the youngsters crowded close. Further back the adults reclined against rocks, listening or talking quietly. New mothers would be there nursing kits, while other kzinrett supervised older newlings as they tussled in the sand. And somewhere out in the dark, four-or-eight of the young adults were hidden in the shadows, silently watching to protect the pride. Swift-Son had stood such watches himself, missing the comradeship of the fire but proud of the trust the pride put in him. The whole cycle of life was represented in the pride circle, each generation playing its role, then passing it to the next. Here mothers presented their newborn kits to the pride, here the young learned traditions from the old. Here the challenge duels were fought and the stories told. Here the dead were mourned and, so said the legends, here their spirits returned every year on their Name-day.

For a moment he paused, caught up in his fate. He was a legend now, a legend that had just begun to unfold—a fated warrior of Chraz-Mtell, and his yet-to-be saga would be heard at tale-tellings forever. He, Swift-Son, who was content to watch his brother claim a double-name; he, Silent Prowler, who preferred only the Hunter's Moon for company; he would be Patriarch! Patriarch not only of Rritt-Pride but of the Great-Pride of the broad savannah, Patriarch of all the countless lands beyond that. He raked claws across the sky. Patriarch of the very stars!

A faint click of rock on rock twitched his ears to the sides to pinpoint the sound's source. It was not repeated, but he had already recognized the heavy tread of Iron-Claw. He must be one of the watchers tonight. Swift-Son could hardly wait to relate the news of his adventure. Soon they would be together again, joking and sparring like old times. It was good to be *home*.

But first he must claim a Name. He rippled his ears and stood up, then strode boldly toward the pride-circle. Behind him a rustle of paws on grass warned that Iron-Claw was crouching for the kill should he prove unworthy. Elder Brother had never been stealthy enough to surprise Swift-Son. Let him crouch, he would not leap.

As he entered the circle of light, Pkrr-Rritt rose from his place of honor in the center of the gathering. "Rritt-Pride welcomes this stranger to our pride-circle and asks for news of Swift-Son." The Patriarch intoned the tradition.

Swift-Son raised the alien weapon to his shoulder and fired over their heads, splitting the darkened sky with his thunder. The startled pride fled, even Iron-Claw and Pkrr-Rritt, leaving gratifying fear scents behind. He leapt to the center of the circle and screamed in triumph as a few of the braver ones took cover behind rocks and peeped out at him.

"Swift-Son is dead," he scream-snarled the tradition into the night. "I am Chraz-Rritt!"

SLOWBOAT
NIGHTMARE

•

Warren W. James

Stark white cold. That was the first thing I noticed. That and the quiet sounds you learn to ignore while in space; the whisper of the air circulators, the hum from the electronic systems and the subsonic rumble of the drive. But there was something wrong with those sounds, like a chord with one note off-key.

The glassine shell of the autodoc was frosted over. I blinked my eyes wide open and saw nothing but milky whiteness and someone moving haltingly outside the 'doc. I blinked some more and the milky shapelessness became individual strips of brightness on the ceiling.

My labored breathing puffed thin white clouds into the cold air as I felt a warm dry breeze start to blow into the autodoc. I became aware of the clean antiseptic smell of the autodoc's interior, layered over with a stale metallic tang and a scent like that of sweaty grass mixed with ginger. My arms and legs were tingling, as if they had fallen asleep, while their muscles pulsed with the rhythmic contractions of electronically induced isometric exercises. I felt a sharp jerk and looked over to see a set of intravenous needles withdrawing themselves from my arm. How long had they been feeding me? Where was I? Sick or recovering from some accident? In some organlegger's chop shop? My thoughts came as a jumble of memories and dreams. And then I remembered. The anticipation, the hopes, the dreamless sleep. I was on a starship bound for a colony world.

Would we find a world as perverse as the others the ramrobots had found? Like Mt. Lookitthat on Tau Ceti II, a sliver of inhabitable land on an otherwise uninhabitable world. Or a world where conditions were clement, but only for a few days out of the year, like what the Crashlanders found on Procyon IV.

For several hundred years humans had been sending unmanned interstellar probes, ramrobots, to find habitable environments in other star systems. And that they did. But showing true machine literal-mindedness, they couldn't tell the difference between a habitable environment and a habitable world. As often as not, the worlds they found bore as much resemblance to their reports as the typical vacation destination resembled its tridee advertisements. Who knows how many colony ships finished their long interstellar trip with no way to return to Earth and only a marginal world to carve into a home. Would our voyage end differently?

Observations of Vega from the multi-kilometer fresnel lens telescopes at Persephone Station had indicated the existence of planets along with a large and densely populated disk of post-accretion debris. Those rocks had interested the Belt Science Commission enough to make them cough up half the UN Marks needed to send an unmanned probe to investigate further.

Ramrobot #124 had found that Vega's fourth planet, a gas giant slightly larger than Jupiter, had a moon that was larger than Mars with a thicker atmosphere. The scientists thought it would be inhabitable, although a bit cold and dry. But being a young planetary system, the gas giant was still glowing brightly in the IR and that would make the sub-primary parts of the moon quite bearable, if not downright comfortable. (Who cares that in a million years or so that gas giant would have cooled to the point to where it could no longer help keep the moon warm. Let the people of 1,957,811 AD worry about that problem.)

But what interested us Belters wasn't that moon, but the extensive family of rocks circling Vega. Analysis of the ramrobot's data showed that they were a rich combination of ice, rock, metal and carbon compounds. The stuff of life. Let the Flatlanders have what was at the bottom of that moon's well; we Belters would have no problem carving out a civilization from the rich rocks surrounding Vega.

Well, at least that was the plan. But something seemed wrong and I didn't think it was just the imaginings of my coldsleep-addled brain. If we had really arrived at Vega IVb, then the Med-Center should have been filled with glassine coffins being thawed out by the ship's autodocs. I couldn't see clearly, but I could tell that my coffin was the only one in the room.

With a click the restraints that had been holding my arms and legs in place retracted and I held my hands in front of my face. Their nails were long and clean. The pale pinkness of my skin surprised me, but then coldsleep wasn't meant to be like dozing under a tropical sun. My face and scalp were itching and I touched my hand to my face to scratch but pulled it away in shock. Hair. On my face. On the side of my head. I had always worn my Belter's crest trimmed short, but now it was lost in the confusion of fresh hair covering my head. How could this be? Hair doesn't grow when your body is a corpsicle held at liquid nitrogen temperatures. When did my head have the time to become covered by a ragged stubble of hair?

By now the glassine cover of the autodoc had become clear of its condensation and I recognized the familiar equipment of the Med-Center with Tom McCavity standing over me, watching the autodoc's readouts. Tom was an n-th generation Lunie with ancestors going back to the founding of Hovestraydt City, but he had emigrated to the Belt because he thought cis-lunar space was too crowded. He kept his Belter's crest of black hair cropped short so as to not accentuate his almost seven foot height. (But then he was always a bit self-conscious about being short by Lunie standards.) But now his hair was thickly laced with gray and his movements were slow and deliberate. My god, he was so old. As a crew member he would have spent much of the voyage standing watch. Einstein might let us slow time, but we couldn't stop it. Tom had grown old slowly while I had agelessly slept my way to the stars.

The cover of the autodoc began to slide out of the way, the sounds and scents of the Med-Center washed over me unfiltered. What was it that smelled like sweaty grass? I tried to get up, but Tom put his hand on my chest.

"Take it easy, Ib. Your body isn't up to the demands your head is making." Tom's bedside manner was firm but reasonable. Even without his restraining hand I would have found it difficult to get up at that moment.

"There's lots we have to talk about and not much time." Tom's blue-gray eyes focused on me briefly and then darted around the room nervously. I tried to speak but couldn't.

"Drink this," Tom said. "It's got stimulants and electrolytes. You'll need it." He lifted a squeeze bottle of juice and held it to my mouth while I sucked the fluid through the tube. The moisture helped free my throat.

"What happened? The others . . . where . . ."

"Still in coldsleep. There's been a problem." Tom tried to continue but a sound at the door stopped him and focused all of my attention on the other side of the room. The source of the sweaty grass and ginger scent was now obvious. Coming through the door was a creature that walked upright but looked like a cross between a tiger and a gorilla. (I remembered seeing both at the holozoo at Confinement Asteroid when I took my sister there in '57.) It must have been close to eight feet tall with long arms that ended in hands with four digits and a naked rat-tail twitching behind it. The creature was wearing rough-hewn clothing that looked like leather. Metal shapes with handles, ugly but vaguely familiar and sized for overly large hands, hung from a belt at its waist. As it looked at me I had the distinct impression that I knew what a frozen meal felt like when it got popped out of a microwave cooker.

A second creature came through the door and then a third. This last one was different. Smaller and unkempt. The others walked, no, make that *strode,* with an upright posture that bespoke an unquestioned belief in their authority. But this one? He (she? it?) walked slowly, hesitatingly, and with a slumped posture that screamed fear. The others had long orange-brown fur with variegated patterns of stripes that showed the obvious effects of frequent grooming. This one, his fur looked as unkempt as the unwelcome hair that covered my head. And his eyes. They were—sleepy? No, maybe not sleepy, but definitely strange.

The large one that had entered the Med-Center first turned to the others and snarled something that sounded like a group of gravel-throated cats having a fight. The others made hissing and spitting cat sounds back and damned if they somehow didn't make them come out sounding deferential as they surrounded the autodoc. Tom was pressed against the side of the 'doc, trembling.

The second creature, whose face had distinctive asymmetric stripes and dark markings around his eyes, looked down at me and then did the one thing I would have never expected. He spoke, in hard to understand and heavily accented Standard.

"This one knows how? Yesss? He must work."

I almost passed out from the shock. Here we were between the stars, twenty-plus ship-years from the Belt, and aliens from who-knows-where just waltz into the Med-Center. And they speak Standard. No one ever told me that our first contact with outsiders would be like this.

Then I looked closer at the biggest outsider—the one who was eyeing me closely. And I saw them. Hanging from his belt. At least a half dozen, maybe more. Strung together on some kind of cord.

Ears.

Human ears.

That's when I passed out.

When I woke up again I wasn't in the autodoc, but lying on a waterbed in an empty room. From its size, about as large as a small walk-in closet back on Earth, I guessed it was the Captain's quarters. I wondered what had happened to Jennifer, but I remembered those ears hanging from that outsider's belt and decided I didn't really want to know.

The image of a hungry tiger that walked like a gorilla made me want to fade back into black oblivion, but my fear of what might happen to me while unconscious kept me awake. I tried to sit up, but the room turned gray and started spinning around. Lying down seemed like a better idea. On the wall next to the bed the ready light of the intercom softly glowed green.

"Hey! What's going on? Where is everybody?" I wasn't sure who (or what) was going to answer.

Tom's voice crackled over the intercom, "Relax. I'll be right there."

A few minutes later the door of the cabin slid open and Tom limped in carrying a medkit. "Take it easy. You're weak and you've got a lot to catch up on."

"What happened?" I asked.

Tom ignored my question as he rustled through his medkit and removed drinking bags, drug hypos and bottles of medicine. "Here, drink this and don't interrupt."

I swallowed the chalky pink juice from the drinking bag. It tasted worse than it looked. The burning sensation from a hypo pressed against my arm distracted me from further thoughts about Tom's bartending skills. He tapped a touchpad near the bed and a memory plastic chair extruded itself from the adjacent wall. Tom sat down, composed his thoughts and began talking.

"Those aliens call themselves 'kzinti,' though I don't know if they're talking about their race or some socio-political subgrouping."

"But what are they?" I asked. "Explorers? Scientists? What?"

Tom blinked at my question. "Not quite. They're warriors."

"That's impossible! Who are they fighting?"

"Us," Tom replied. "As near as I can tell, we're at war with them."

War.

There hadn't been a war on Earth in dozens of generations. The last historically verifiable intergovernmental conflict had been before the time of Galileo. There were stories about misunderstandings and UN police actions, like the apocryphal stories about a global conflict involving genocide and nuclear weapons during the twentieth century. But even children knew that those were just fictions used to teach moral philosophy. Every child in the ARM sponsored school system learned that war was impossible for any advanced culture. Any civilization that lasted long enough to develop interstellar flight must have lasted long enough to outgrow their aggressive behavior. If they hadn't, they would have killed themselves with their technology.

"I don't believe you," I said as I tried to think of some other explanation.

"You can believe me or not, but that doesn't change the way the kzinti act."

Silence filled the room until Tom continued. "Look, Ib, maybe we're at war, maybe we're not. Maybe these creatures are psychopaths escaped from a mental institute and they're living out their delusional fantasies using stolen technology."

Now that, I thought, made sense.

"But what matters is what's happening here and now. They act like we're at war, and they don't take prisoners."

I just stared. My mind didn't want to accept star-traveling warriors. "But what do they want with us?"

Tom looked away as if in shame. "To them we're just potential slaves." Silence filled the room until Tom continued with his story.

"It happened a couple of weeks ago. We were six months out of Vega when we detected the approach of an unknown vessel at outrageous speeds and accelerations. We shut down the ramscoop so its magnetic field wouldn't be a danger to the alien ship's crew. Then we waited. The kzinti ship rendezvoused with us and just hung a few hundred kilometers off our nose, doing nothing at all."

I interrupted, "How did they come across us? Random chance?"

"No," Tom replied, "they were reconnoitering Vega when they detected our approach and came out to intercept us."

I interrupted him again. "You're telling me they were able to accelerate out to our position, come to a dead stop and then match our velocity for a rendezvous. Man, what kind of technology do they have?"

"I don't know anything about their technology. Jennifer thought it might be some kind of field drive, something where the drive forces operate on the entire ship and its contents equally. That way they could accelerate at hundreds of gravities and not feel anything."

I was still having trouble believing this. First, hostile outsiders. No, make that hostile slave-taking outsiders. And now I find out that they have technologies that made our best ramships look like cloth and wood biplanes in an era of hypersonic jets. This really wasn't the way that first contact was supposed to happen. Tom continued his story.

"The crew tried every communication scheme you could imagine. The kzinti never responded to any of them. Maybe they misunderstood us, but it sure seemed like they were just ignoring us. I wish that's all they had done."

Tom paused, remembering. I tried to imagine the hopes and anticipations of the crew. Lightyears from Earth, lightdays from a new star, and then they make first contact with the outsiders—the often imagined, more often imaginary, intelligent creatures from another world. Everyone knew this would be an epochal moment in human history. The fulfillment of many lifetimes of dreaming and imagining. Tom's voice threatened to break as he told me the rest of the story.

"Then the kzinti sent over a couple of small craft and forced their way onto our ship. There was a fight, but we were outmatched. Most of the crew were killed in a matter of minutes. I was in the Med-Center and didn't even have time to get to anyone who needed me."

Tom's eyes took on a distant, haunted, look. I didn't want to think about the things he must have seen.

"Jennifer tried to restart the drive. I guess she hoped its magnetic field would kill the kzinti who were still on their ship. Maybe she wanted to use the drive's exhaust as a weapon. Who knows? The kzinti broke into the control deck and killed her and the remainder of the crew. In the fighting our drive got damaged and it executed an auto-shutdown. But not before its magnetic field had destroyed the drive and most of the electronics on the kzinti warship as well as killing all its occupants."

Warship. A word from our past. In school they had taught us that the last human warships were boats that plied the oceans with sails. The idea of a warship that could sail between the stars was almost unimaginable.

"Our ramscoop destroyed the drive on the kzinti ship?" I couldn't bring myself to call it a warship. "How's that possible?"

"Don't ask me. I'm not an engineer."

"Well, how badly was our drive damaged?"

"Ib, I keep telling you, I'm not an engineer. I can't answer that question. That's where you come in. We need someone who can repair the drive system and pilot us into orbit around Vega IVb."

"Me? I'm just a singleship jockey, not a ramship pilot."

"That may be, but you're our best hope. The crew's dead. I had to thaw out someone. There were . . . complications."

"Complications?" I interrupted.

"You don't want to know," replied Tom. "You had to spend almost two weeks in the autodoc. Of all the people available you had the most . . . qualifications."

"What qualifications?" I demanded.

"You're the only Belter with an advanced degree in astroengineering."

Tom was holding something back. What was it? "You can't be serious. It's been ages since I did any engineering. And all that was design work, not fixing stuff. That can't be enough."

"It better be enough." He hesitated then continued. "I know you singleship pilots. You brag about being able to fix anything with nothing. If you can't, we're dead meat."

I interrupted, "But . . ."

"But nothing. Our only chance for life is if you can fix the ship." Tom's eyes pleaded with me as we stared at each other. I'm not sure if I believed him. Finagle, I'm not sure he believed himself. I thought of something else.

"How many kzinti are on our ship?"

"Not many. Just the boarding party that was behind our shields when Jennifer started the drive."

I interrupted, "But then can't we reason with them or . . ."

"You can't reason with them," Tom interrupted. "They don't think like we do." Depressed silence filled the room, until it was broken by Tom getting up to leave.

"I'm going to go and let you get some rest. Twenty years of coldsleep can really mess up your endocrine balance. I'd like to have you spend a couple more days in the 'doc to let it sort out your biochemistry. But the kzinti won't let me do that. Hell, they didn't even want to let me check in on you today."

Tom handed me a small vial filled with orange pills. "Here's some medicine that the autodoc made up for you. Take two every eight hours. They should help you get back to normal."

His eyes tried to tell me more than his words could convey, but I couldn't understand him. "Take your medicine and rest. It's important. I've convinced the kzinti that you won't be able to do anything for a day or so. I don't know how long I can stall them."

Tom turned and headed for the door. As he did I

noticed he had a pronounced limp that I didn't remember from when we'd left the solar system.

"Tom, what happened to your leg?"

Tom grimaced as he slowly turned to face me. He leaned against the wall and lifted the leg of his pants. Where there should have been a sock covered leg was a gleaming titanium stump that disappeared into his shoe and up his pants leg.

"The kzinti have short tempers," he said. "Don't get them upset."

I spent the rest of the day resting, eating and sleeping. I set a timer to go off every eight hours and when it chimed I took my medicine. Those pills must have been strong because taking them made my head feel light and put my whole body on edge. I would have been worried, but all my life I'd been taught to trust the ministrations of the autodocs. In any case, I spent a lot of time dozing off, waking up only when my nightmares of overgrown cats and the forgotten art of war caused me to jerk upright screaming.

The next morning came too soon. Was it morning? My time sense was really out of kilter. I woke without assistance and found that there was a small autochef in the room, though many of its meat items were logged as being unavailable. (Should I blame that on the kzinti also?) I had just finished eating a breakfast of eggs, toast and coffee without sausage when the door to my quarters slid open and two of the kzinti walked in. The larger of the two had to duck his head down to get through the doorway, but the smaller, disheveled one was slumped down so far that he didn't need to duck. I recognized the larger of the two kzinti as the one who could speak Standard. He started talking without preamble.

"I am 'Slave Master.' I will speak slave language until

you learn Hero's Tongue. First, prove your worth. Solve ship problem. Then we treat you as worthy slave."

"And how would you do that?" I asked.

"You will live."

I didn't have any response to that comment and the big cat stayed silent for a moment. I looked into his face, but his emotions—did he have any emotions, I wondered?—were a complete mystery to me. What was the meaning of his twitching ears? And should I be worried that he was showing me his teeth, or was that just his idea of a smile?

The rat-cat (that was all I could think of while I watched his naked tail flick back and forth) snarled something to the smaller, disheveled kzinti who shivered and seemed to pull into himself. He reached down into a bag he was carrying and took out a syringe with a gleaming silver needle. His stare went from the syringe to the larger kzinti and finally to me. The larger kzinti snarled at him again, I'd swear I could sense disgust in his snarl, and the small kzinti plunged the needle deep into his forearm. He shuddered and seemed to pull into himself even more, almost as if he was going into a trance, and then he looked at me.

It was like he was looking straight into my soul. His eyes sparkled with a life that I hadn't seen before but his body still shivered and shook. I heard a low moaning growl come from deep in his throat. I felt a pressure building in my head. It might have been nervous anxiety from my fear of the upcoming interrogation.

"Now talk." Slave Master stared at me. Somehow I didn't think this was the time or place for the quick rejoinder or smartass remark.

"Okay. We'll talk. About what?"

"No. Not 'we talk.' You talk. Can you fix ship?"

I started to frame an evasive answer, when my head exploded in pain and disorientation. It felt like I was falling down an infinitely deep hole while being hurled up toward an ever unreachable sky. I felt like I was spinning rapidly while being completely immobile. If not for decades of freefall reflexes I would have spewed my breakfast all over the kzinti and the four walls of the tiny room. (I didn't think that would be a good career move.) Slowly the sensation diminished but never completely went away.

The disheveled kzinti sat in a corner of the room. Glowering at me. His eyes boring through me, while his body shivered almost uncontrollably. He haltingly growled something to Slave Master.

The larger kzinti stared at me and I watched in horror as thick black claws sprang from his four fingertips. He raised his clawed hand above my head, as if ready to bring it down in one swift killing move.

"Truth only. No lies. I will know." He paused. "Understand?"

It was clear as a bell.

"Yes sir."

He raised his hand higher. His fur was pulled back and lying flat across his face.

"Use proper form of address. Not *Sthondat* form. I am Slave Master. Not sir." He lowered his face close to mine. I could watch each whisker on his muzzle twitch. I could smell the fetid odor of dead meat on his breath. One wrong answer and my scent would be added to his breath.

"Yes si—Yes. Slave Master." I tried to make it sound respectful. Fear for your life can do that.

Slave Master slowly lowered his arms. His fur began to fluff out, his claws retracting slowly as he lowered his arms. "Now tell of your ship knowledge and repair skills."

And so I tried to tell them what I hoped they wanted to know. If I promised more than I could deliver I knew

I would die, but if I didn't promise enough I knew I'd never get the chance to be proven wrong. I let them know that I'd have to make an inspection of the ship's systems before I could decide on a course of action. That I might need to thaw out someone else from coldsleep to help me. (They didn't like this idea.)

Although Slave Master knew some Standard there were big lapses in his technical vocabulary and at times we had to stop and work out language problems. He had me visualize things and describe them until finally he understood me. And all through this the disheveled kzinti sat there staring at me while my head felt like it was going to explode at any minute. By the time we were finished I was totally exhausted. (I think they knew this, but they didn't care.) Luckily for me they seemed to have gotten what they needed. I hoped I had bought myself a few days of looking for options. Time to find hope in a hopeless situation.

Slave Master looked me in the eye. "We go now. Discuss. Churl-Captain will decide. Inspection and repairs later. Rest now. Eat. Prepare." With that the two kzinti turned and left the room. The only thing remaining from their visit was the scent of sweaty grass and ginger and my fear of what would happen next.

I thought of staying up and planning, of plotting how I might work against them. But my head still ached. I thought it might have been from tension, but if it was, it was unlike any tension headaches I'd ever had before. It was nothing like that time when I was smuggling a shipment of luxury foodstuffs to a Flatlander science station on Enceladus and tried dodging a Goldskin patrol by hiding my ship in the braided ring of Saturn. By comparison that was a relaxed afternoon at Heisenberg's Pub back at Ceres Base.

I stretched out on the waterbed to organize my thoughts and only ended up organizing my dreams.

Except that those dreams kept getting interrupted by nightmares where I was a mouse being chased by a tiger.

I woke up with my mind filled with half-formed imaginings and leftover nightmares. In my sleep I had imagined that our slowboat had been overrun by ferocious outsiders that looked like a fantasy image from an old flat film. (The kinds of films that the ARM thought they had suppressed, but which were popular humor among Belters in their singleships far from the patronizing protection of the ARM.) And then it hit me. This was no dream. These outsiders were real. And they weren't a Saganesque fantasy of wise and peaceful creatures who wanted to guide us on the path to enlightenment. These were killers who thought of humans as nothing more than another race to be subjugated. I wanted to go back to sleep, to dream my way out of this nightmare, but I'd been sleeping too much the last couple of days. (Why should I be so tired after spending twenty plus ship-years in coldsleep?)

I didn't know how much time had passed since my last meeting with the kzinti, but I expected they'd be coming soon. Either to use me to repair the ship, or to dispose of me as a useless implement. In either case I needed to prepare myself. Breakfast was another meatless exercise in frustration but standing under the shower did more to refresh me than all of my sleeping from the last few days. I stared at my face as I dried off and thought about shaving off my beard and retrimming my hair into its Belter's crest, but didn't have the energy or inclination.

I didn't have to wait long for my captors to come and fetch me. The door opened without warning and in walked Slave Master followed by the small disheveled kzinti. Slave Master growled at the smaller kzinti, who reached into his pouch without making a sound, pulled out his syringe and pressed it into his arm while staring at me. The look on his face made me want to take pity on him, but when I thought of what he and his kind had done to the crew of our ship, I hoped that whatever he was going to do was going to hurt him. Badly.

For a moment nothing happened. Then my head exploded in pain and disorientation. Slave Master looked at me without any concern for my condition and spoke without preamble. "You come now. Fix ship."

"I need to go to the Command Deck so I can check out the ship first."

The disheveled kzinti . . . I was going to have to come up with a name for him. Fritz. That would do. Fritz moaned a few sounds to Slave Master and then went back to glaring at me.

"We go. Obey or die."

We went.

The ship's curving corridors were empty as we made our way to the Command Deck. I hadn't seen any other kzinti since the first day, but I knew they were around. I could smell them. And sometimes I heard their caterwauling sounds echoing down the air ducts as we walked through empty passageways scarred by burn marks and ragged holes.

The Command Deck was deserted, and its condition made it painfully obvious just how desperate our situation was. All around me was a scene of death and destruction. I remembered my friends who should be here, but who weren't. I tried not to feel the pain of their absence. I didn't do a good job of it.

The empty captain's couch had a broken headrest, with long tears going down the sides of the couch with cushioning material hanging out in tatters. I didn't want to bring myself to recognize the stains on the couch and the surrounding floor.

Many of the command and control displays were dark or showed digital static. Ragged holes in the control panels gave evidence that weapons of some kind had mindlessly destroyed the ship's equipment. Rusty stains having little to do with iron oxide covered many of the panels. A few flickering lights on the consoles were the only sign that power and life still flowed through the controls. The kzinti paid no attention to any of this, but just stared at me. Waiting for me to do something. Slave Master growled something and I sat down at the Engineer's station and went to work.

A few of the flat panel displays still functioned and I used them to bring up colored charts and rows of numbers showing the status of the ship's systems. But the picture they gave me was simultaneously confusing, incomplete and over detailed. All I could access was raw data, with vast amounts missing, with no easy way to synthesize it into concise information about the ship's status. If other people had been here we could have worked together to make sense out of this patchwork of data. But that wasn't an option the kzinti would make available to me. I'd need to use the VR system to try and make sense of the jumbled data.

The data gloves and head mounted displays for the VR system were in a storage locker at the rear of the Command Deck. The kzinti didn't do anything but watch as I got up and went to get them. They stiffened as I reached for the locker and Slave Master growled.

"I'm just getting some equipment I need." I hoped they didn't misinterpret my nervousness.

Slave Master growled over at Fritz, who stared at me. And my head wrenched in a fresh wave of pain. Fritz muttered something to Slave Master that sounded like a cat having a fit and the large kzinti appeared to relax.

I pulled out a set of data gloves and a head mounted

display from the locker and carried them back to the Engineer's station where I adjusted them to fit my hands and head. My custom gear would have fit better, but considering the situation these would do just fine. After I plugged them in they went through their diagnostics and beeped their readiness. I adjusted the audio volume to a level that would let me hear Slave Master if he spoke and the video display so it would leave a transparent image of the Command Deck overlaid behind the immersive VR display. I knew I couldn't concentrate on the ship if the VR system left me wondering what the kzinti were up to.

Slave Master and Fritz were watching me intently. I don't know if they had anything like VR. Maybe they did, maybe they didn't, but in any case, they didn't move to stop me as I slid my hands into the data gloves and nestled the display unit over my head.

The audiophones were a warm softness on my ears. I could hear the empty echoes of silence and the ocean wave sound of the blood flowing through my ears. The data gloves fit my hands like, well, like gloves. They provided a tight pressure on my hand and I could feel the resistance of the force feedback sensors as I flexed my fingers. The watching kzinti became pale ghosts as I lowered the half-silvered visors of the head-mounted display and activated the VR program.

Windows filled with data appeared and floated in the virtual space in front of my face, superimposed on the scene of destruction in the Command Deck with the two kzinti watching me. This two-for-one visual display was disorienting and it would get even worse when I went full immersive. Hopefully, my freefall reflexes would help keep the conflicting visual cues from getting me too confused.

I moved my hands and brought up a window filled with display options. I selected a synthesized view of the ship along with overlaid options for displaying the status of various systems. It was time to go for a virtual walk and check things out. As the VR system executed my commands, the image of the Command Deck faded and a "god's-eye" exterior view of our ship came into focus.

The view I saw might have been synthesized, but that didn't make it any less impressive. Our ship, *Obler's Paradox,* with its eight-hundred-foot trusswork spine and assorted modules, was hanging motionless in space surrounded by millions of stars with a small orange craft attached to its side like a sinister parasite. A larger spherical ship hovered menacingly nearby.

Our ship appeared to be in surprisingly good shape, other than the obvious damage caused by the kzinti and the normal discolorations caused by solar radiation and thruster firings. At the rear was the fusion engine that could push us up to a good fraction of the speed of light and the magnetic field generators for the Bussard ramscoop. Directly ahead of them were a set of spherical tanks, used to hold hydrogen for use when we were moving at merely interplanetary speeds. Near the middle of the ship was the cylindrical pressurized module used to store the coldsleep tanks, as well as the equipment and supplies needed by the crew, along with a hydroponic garden that provided fresh vegetables and air. A rotating toroidal module provided a living space for the crew. Finally, at the front of the ship were the vacuum storage areas where we kept our singleships and other vacuum-safe equipment behind the flat micrometeoroid/thermal control panels. Covering everything were the smooth superconducting panels that protected the equipment and people from the effects of the drive's intense magnetic fields.

As I studied the damage to our ship, I had the computer bring up data blocks and display them over the image of the ship. Gradually I built up my assessment of the ship. I zoomed in my view until I was staring at the field generators.

It looked like something heavy had smashed into them. Perhaps a small kzinti ship had been drawn into the field generators when Jennifer had activated our drive. Those field generators developed magnetic fields that were strong enough to draw in ionized hydrogen from hundreds of miles away when we were moving at a good fraction of the velocity of light. Careful tuning of the fields shunted aside anything that wasn't interstellar hydrogen, but I doubt the designers had considered having to deflect something as large or as close as one of those kzinti spacecraft. If they contained anything remotely susceptible to magnetic fields they would have been grabbed and pulled directly into the field generators.

I had the ship's computer apply an overlay showing the field strength of the drive and the flux density contours of the surrounding hydrogen. Instantly, the ship was surrounded by glowing neon yellow and blue contour lines. I reached out with my hands and felt the field lines. I pressed on them and gauged their strength with my fingers, the force feedback sensors pressing against my fingertips. Data displayed in overlaid windows showed the numerical data that confirmed the qualitative impressions formed by the force feedback system.

The asymmetries of the field showed that some, but not all, of the field generators were off-line. The ones that were on-line were only operating at the level needed to provide us with radiation protection by deflecting the interstellar medium away from the ship. They couldn't feed hydrogen to the engine fast enough to slow us from our Einsteinian rush through space.

Things looked bad, but not unsaveable. There were

some spare parts in the ship's stores, but more importantly there was a lot of redundancy in the design of the drive. For the first time since I had been brought out of coldsleep I started to feel optimistic. Here was a problem I could deal with.

That thought focused my mind back on the kzinti. There they were, like ghosts at a funeral. There was a problem that I wasn't sure I could fix.

My hands made motions in the air—I wondered what the kzinti thought of that—and the image of the ship and the stars vanished, only to be replaced by the image of the Command Deck and the waiting kzinti. With the flip of a switch the display went blank and I pushed the display lenses up away from my eyes.

Fritz was still staring at me as I tensed with anticipation of the head-splitting pain from his juju eyes but it never came, just a dull ache like the pain from a broken tooth before an autodoc could implant a fresh bud. Unpleasant, but I could live with it.

I looked Slave Master straight in the eyes. "The Bussard field generators are really munged. It's going to take a lot of work to fix them."

"You can fix?" The look in Slave Master's eyes only allowed one answer.

"Yes. Given time and resources."

"Do so."

"How long will it take for your crew to get their equipment transferred from your ship to ours and how much mass will they be bringing?" I didn't like the idea of the kzinti occupying our ship, but knowing how long it would take them to get their things moved over would give me an idea about how long I'd have to get the field generators back on-line.

"Heroes do not abandon their ship. You will transport *Screaming-Hunter-Who-Leaps-From-Tall-Grass* with your ship."

I didn't think he was joking, but I knew he couldn't have any idea about the magnitude of the problem he was creating. We couldn't just throw a rope to them and tow them. There was no place to attach their ship with the over-long name to *Obler's Paradox* and even if there were, their ship might be compact, but I suspected it was massive. That ignorant overgrown excuse for a housecat had just over-constrained the problem. We'd be lucky if my jury-rigged repairs worked well enough to get just *Obler's Paradox* to Vega. I was about to tell him that in just those tones when that familiar head-bursting feeling came back with a vengeance and I rethought the phrasing of my words.

Slave Master came and towered over me. "You cannot do?" His fur was flat against his face, the claws at the ends of his fingers were sliding out.

And then I noticed his ears. They had extended out like a pair of bat wings or small parasols. The image was almost—almost—funny. I would have laughed at the sight of those delicate ears on that huge orange tiger-gorilla, except I knew he didn't have a sense of humor. And the pain in my head had become so great it was all I could do to grunt an answer.

"You ask too much. There's no way to do what you ask. We'll be unbalanced. Uncontrollable. And our drive is damaged. We don't have the power to handle both ships." I hoped he was reasonable.

He wasn't.

"Heroes order, not ask. Worthy slaves obey, others die." He paused for a moment then continued. "You can do?" His lips had pulled away from his teeth showing a set of impressive canines. Back on the other side of the room Fritz was pulling himself into a little orange ball. I knew there was only one answer.

"I'll tr—" I reconsidered my answer. "I can do the job."

Slave Master looked over to Fritz and growled something. Fritz growled back deferentially and the pain in my head subsided. Slave Master loomed over me as his fur relaxed and his claws retracted.

"Do so."

I did.

There were several problems to be solved. First, reconfigure the Bussard field so I could get the drive working at partial power. I'd already given up on getting enough field generators up to run the engine at full power. Second, figure out how to attach that kzinti ship to the *Paradox* without making us so unbalanced that we'd be uncontrollable. Third, get the ship's computer busy investigating the trajectory space available to us with a munged engine and find a way to get us safely into orbit around Vega IVb while carrying that kzinti ship. And fourth, figure out what to do about the kzinti. But this last problem was moot if I failed to solve the first three, so I put the kzinti out of my mind. Or at least as much as I could.

Actually, the third problem was the easiest because it wouldn't take my full concentration. Just set up the problem on the ship's computer and let it cogitate.

But first I'd have to get the kzinti to tell me how much their ship massed. This was a challenge to my descriptive skills but after an hour or so of working with Slave Master and Fritz I was able to get them to understand what I needed. Afterwards it felt like my head was going to fall apart but they had an answer for me a few minutes later. I was right. Their ship was massive. Carrying it was going to come close to doubling our mass.

I called up the trajectory programs and entered in everything I could think of. The program refused to take my inputs, interpreting the new ship mass as a user error. I overrode its objections and made it continue the process. I looked at the trajectory options it would investigate and made it open the option space even more. After a few hours of setting things up I turned the computer loose on the problem. The estimated time to solve the problem was not promising.

We might well fly right by Vega at point something *c* before the ship's brain solved the problem. But that was something I could worry about later. Right now there were more pressing problems facing me. Two of them in fact, on the other side of the room.

Slave Master had an uncanny ability to stand motionless, watching me with intent hungry eyes, that reminded me of the way most Belters could hang motionless for hours on end. (That was a self protection reflex developed from living in the cramped quarters of a singleship, where one false arm movement could create chaos.) Or maybe he was just stupid and not easily bored. In any case, working must have been good for me because the juju headache that Fritz gave me was becoming just a dull ache, and a fading one at that.

I don't know what I looked like, but Fritz looked like a wreck. He was shivering and shaking. His head was lolling from side to side. I wasn't sure how to read Slave Master's body language but he didn't look like he enjoyed being next to Fritz. Maybe that disheveled kzinti had a case of big kitty bad breath. Or something.

It had been over eight hours since they had come to get me and they hadn't let me have a chance to eat. I wondered what their physical limits were. I knew they didn't care about mine, but I did. I looked directly at Slave Master.

"Slave Master. I have finished this part of the task. We must wait for the ship to answer my questions. It will take some time. May I eat before doing more work?"

Fritz saw the way I looked at Slave Master, cringed and moved away from the larger kzinti like he was afraid of what his response would be. What? Was it something I said? Slave Master looked me square in the eyes. "Slaves do not ask, they obey."

I looked him back, square in his orange tinged brown eyes. "Well this slave won't be able to obey much longer if he doesn't get food."

Angry ripples rolled through Slave Master's thick muscles, but when it came to the kzinti everything they did looked angry. He growled something at Fritz who mewled something back. Now Fritz didn't just look bedraggled, he looked positively frightened. And all the while he mewled at Slave Master his eyes were looking down, away from his superior's face. I wonder what he said to Slave Master? The large kzinti eyed me hungrily. I hope he knew I was asking to be a diner, not dinner. Then it occurred to me, maybe my body language was saying things to contradict my words. I took a page from Fritz's book, I averted my eyes to the floor.

"Slave Master. I could eat here. The autochef behind you could provide me with fruits and vegetables. I could serve you better if I could eat before working more." I counted the red scuff marks on the decking while I waited for his answer.

I raised my eyes slightly when Slave Master starting talking and saw that both kzinti were shuddering, perhaps in revulsion. The large kzinti glared at me. "Heroes do not watch slaves debase themselves with slave food. Return to your den. You eat roots only there."

Who was I to argue? We left.

The click of the door's lock let me know that the kzinti didn't trust me. So what? I didn't trust them either. I walked over to the autochef and checked to see what it could make. It looked like it was going to be another meatless dinner so I made the best of it by ordering up spicy Bombay potatoes, ghobi sag, and a meatless vindaloo curry topped off by garlic naan bread, raita and chutney. I was glad the Flatlander company that had built this ramship had subsidiary offices in Newer Delhi. Flatlander food was the best there was and this, with the exception of the missing meat, was better than most shipfood.

In a few minutes the autochef beeped and I removed steaming trays of food from its interior. The scents made it easy to forget that the raw stock for this meal had been recycled through the crew innumerable times while *Obler's Paradox* had flung itself through space toward Vega. I wanted to work while I ate so I tapped on a keypad and a memory plastic desk extruded itself from the wall.

The data display unit was buried in the wall above the freshly extruded desk. I sat down in front of it and started tapping on its keyboard. It was soon clear that I didn't have the command passwords needed to use this device to control the ship's systems from here, but I could use it to access the data records held in the ship's computer. A few more minutes of work had the system pulling off archival records going back to our first encounter with the kzinti, including video feeds from various autocams.

I keyed a few more commands and was able to tell the computer to do a continuous scan of the current autocam outputs and store that information for later retrieval. I might not be able to do anything about the kzinti just yet, but now I'd know where they were and what they were doing.

That done, I started eating while the data display unit showed the archival records of humanity's first contact with outsiders. The images played out just like Tom had described while the scent of garlic and garam masala wafted up from my plates.

The kzinti ship approached *Obler's Paradox* at a high fraction of *c* and demonstrated unbelievable maneuvering capabilities. The numeric detail on the window next to the video feed looked like something from a tridee fiction. Accelerations like that should have flattened anything living and most things not. Surprisingly small, the ship was a compact orange sphere, with bumps, indentations and ugly cylindrical protrusions covering its surface. There weren't any obvious exhaust ports for the drive, but then with something as advanced as they had, perhaps they didn't need any. Covering much of its surface was writing that looked like a combination of scratches, commas and dashes that I imagined was the ship's name.

I reviewed the hurried message that the crew had lasered back to Earth, knowing that it would not be read for several decades. Long after our problem was resolved, one way or the other. I ate the last of my spicy vindaloo—damn those mother-auditing kzinti for their theft of the meat from our storage lockers; I loved shrimp vindaloo—while I read the crew's speculations about benevolent aliens and their hope for possible trade in knowledge and art. All of these said more about the crew than they would ever know. I paused the display while I finished my dinner, the image of the kzinti ship frozen against the stars while the minty yogurt of the raita cooled the spicy tingle of the vindaloo from my mouth. Then I restarted the program.

The images were from horrors long banished from human experience. Two small craft separated from the kzinti warship and moved at breathtaking speed to *Obler's Paradox*. One attached itself to the side of our ship. Clouds of white vapor streamed into space when it blew holes in the outer hull and then internal cameras showed a crowd of vacuum-suited kzinti flooding into the ship. They rushed into the ship with their weapons raised—weapons designed to kill people; there hadn't been anything like that outside of pornographic fiction in hundreds of years, maybe thousands—and went on a rampage.

Now I remembered why those things the kzinti wore from their belts looked so familiar. A few subjective years ago I had been desperate for cash and shipped out with a partner I didn't know very well. Things went well until one day I stumbled onto his cache of pornographic vids filled with weapons and scenes of killing. He never figured out why I cut our mining trip short or why I never worked with him again. Those things on the kzinti's belts were handheld weapons. Though those kzinti handguns would have looked like a rifle, yet another almost forgotten obscenity, if carried by a human.

One member of the kzinti boarding party ran into Jack Smithie near Emergency Airlock Three. He was slipping on his skinsuit and pulling on his biopack. The first kzinti to reach him didn't ask any questions or slow down but just shot Jack where he stood, blowing a hole in his chest the size of a Belter's helmet. Tanj, I didn't know a human body contained so much blood.

That scene of death and destruction was repeated every time the kzinti encountered a human. They never even tried to communicate but just killed anyone that moved and blew open closed doors. On the tape I could hear the sound of the alarms wailing in the background. The intercom was alive with frantic confused messages. I toggled the display from camera to camera, randomly sampling the images of carnage, hoping that it was all a mistake. A confusion caused by our mutual alienness. But I knew it wasn't.

The "prepare for freefall" klaxon sounded followed by the "acceleration stations" warning. I knew the kzinti couldn't understand the alarms, so they were taken unawares a few minutes later when they lost their footing as the rotating section spun down and the centrifugal force that simulated gravity vanished. It was almost funny watching them slip and slide as their weight vanished. When the ring section went weightless the kzinti bounced off all the walls and flailed helplessly against the air. Whatever technology they had didn't help them in freefall. They looked like a bunch of Flatlander honeymooners having their first experience in space. Some of the kzinti got violently sick in their suits and I hoped they choked on their own purple vomit. But as disoriented as they were, they just kept coming.

The display flashed to an image of the Command Deck. There was Jennifer in the Captain's chair, her Flatlander hair exploding out around her head like an organic nebula. She was hammering at the controls as if her fervor could make the systems activate faster. Next to her, Nathan Long with his close-cropped red hair and short beard was racing his hands over the command console, reconfiguring systems, bringing things on-line and doing everything he could to give Jennifer what she wanted. Chi Lin, a Belter with whom I'd shared more than a few drinks back at Heisenberg's, was at the Engineer's station running the systems check faster than was right for any normal human. Joel Peltron worked the navigation console flying through displays, entering data, calculating the maneuvers to accomplish whatever Jennifer had ordered. Such fervored activity was seldom seen in space. In any emergency you were either dead or you had plenty of time to work the problem. This was one of the rare exceptions to that rule.

Then suddenly the door to the Command Deck blew inward with a cloud of smoke and debris. Orange-suited kzinti rushed in, their weapons drawn and pointing forward. Some of the kzinti were still disoriented by the freefall and they tumbled in rather than dove in, but there were too many of them and they were too determined. Their weapons spewed fire and smoke. Jennifer's head exploded, coating her command chair with sickly red blood and masses of organic matter. Nathan tried to rise from his seat to fight back. Who knows what he was thinking, who among us had ever raised a fist in anger? (Answer: no one who could be cured by the autodocs. The ones who couldn't were in the freezer banks back on Earth waiting for the psychists to come up with a cure for them.) Nathan never had a chance. He was cut in two by a long flat weapon wielded by one of the kzinti that went through him like a cutting laser goes through a fractured carbonaceous rock. The blood and ichor from the crew in the Command Deck filled the air with throbbing red spheres and quivering chunks of pink meat that only moments before had been my friends.

I couldn't take any more. I slammed my fist down on the display's off button. I wanted to rush out and kill the kzinti. I wanted to feel their bones break under my hands. I wanted to watch as I ran a cutting laser through their assembled masses, to divide them and divide them again into smaller and smaller pieces. I wanted . . . I wanted . . .

I wanted to be sick. I almost made it to the 'fresher.

I woke up sometime later. I didn't remember getting myself into bed, but I must have somehow. I felt weak and chilled. The sour taste of my sickness coated my mouth and the scent of my vomit laced the smell of the room. It was an odor that the life support system could not easily get rid of. And by Goddard's ghost, the ship designers had been working that problem for a long time. I rose and went to clean up. The 'fresher looked like it would need more cleaning than I would.

But that could wait. For now, cold water on my face and mouthwash was what I needed.

The timer chimed and I knew it was time for my medicine. I picked up the vial of pills that Tom had left for me and took a couple. I think I missed my earlier dose so I took another couple to compensate. The remnants of my dinner that were splashed over the 'fresher reminded me that dinner hadn't done me much good. But I didn't feel like eating, so I set about cleaning up the mess I made.

I was ashamed of myself, for the thoughts I'd been feeling and for my desires to strike out and kill. Surely there had to be another way. All my life I'd been taught there was always an alternative to violence. I felt disappointment at myself for my inability to see any nonviolent ways to solve our problem. And my sadness for the friends I'd lost made me feel guilty for even being alive. By the time I'd finished cleaning up things I was past guilt and shame and was working myself well into self-pity. As I tossed the last of the soiled wash cloths into the clothing recycler I saw myself in the mirror. My head covered by a tangled mass of dirty brown hair, my Belter's crest a mere patch of slightly longer and thicker hair. A ragged and unkempt beard covered my face. I looked a mess, but I didn't care. Not now. Not after witnessing the senseless deaths of so many friends.

There was a knock on the door. I knew it wasn't the kzinti. They didn't bother to knock. The door opened to show Tom standing outside holding his portable medkit with a kzinti I didn't recognize standing behind him.

"Ib, you okay?" said Tom. "I tried to get you over the intercom but you wouldn't answer. It took me a while to convince Slave Master to let me check in on you."

"No. No, I'm not okay." Tom came in, the kzinti stayed out, and I told him the short version of what happened and about my shame.

"Don't hold that against yourself. Your reaction to what happened was normal. I . . . I keep thinking there must have been something we could have done to prevent it." Tom's voice trembled, "We shouldn't have let our hopes color our actions."

"They always do." I paused. "Why the medkit?"

He hesitated for a moment as if he was afraid of what to say next. "The medicine you're taking can have some powerful side effects. You really shouldn't take it without being in the autodoc, but Slave Master won't let me do that. How about letting me check you out?"

I didn't complain as he attached the sensors from the medkit to my body. He watched closely as the medkit began its diagnosis of my condition and then spoke softly. "Have you formed any conclusions about that disheveled kzinti?"

"You mean the one who looks like a programmer?" Tom grimaced at my comment. Then I remembered his wife had been a programmer and a member of our crew. I didn't want to think about what had happened to her. I answered his question. "I think Fritz is a telepath."

"Fritz?" Tom was taken aback for a moment then realized who I meant. "Oh, that's what you're calling him. I think of him as Argus, the creature from Greek mythology with a hundred eyes who saw everything. But yes, that was my conclusion also."

"I don't think he's always telepathic. It's only after he takes a drug of some kind. I get a hell of a headache when he's reading my mind but in a few hours it goes away and he can't read my mind any more."

"Those headaches near tore my head apart." Tom watched the display of his medkit as it ran its diagnostics.

"Then they stopped. I haven't had that kind of headache in two weeks."

"Fritz stopped reading your mind?"

"I think so. It's not likely he does it for fun, is it? They probably think of me as harmless. Just a doctor. Couldn't make a weapon even if I knew what it looked like. Then again, that telepath probably feels crippled when he's inside my head. Those kzinti look like they could be quadrupeds as easily as bipeds. Being inside me must feel like he's always off balance—"

He appeared startled when the medkit started beeping, then he hit a few buttons and the beeping stopped. "Have you thought about what it means to deal with a telepath?" he said, looking up from the medkit.

"No. That's not a problem I've ever had before," I answered.

"When Argus reads your mind he can tell what you're planning to do."

"Tanj! You're right." I paused to take that thought in, then continued. "Maybe I could get away from them. Hide out somewhere in the ship. They don't know it as well as I do. Then I might be able to do something about our predicament."

"That wouldn't work," Tom continued. "Argus could read your mind, see the things you were seeing in real time and deduce where you were."

"Are you sure he could do that?"

"I'm sure of it," said Tom emphatically. "That's how Slave Master learned our language. He had me look at things and Argus told him what I was thinking. It was a slow process but it worked. I'm just not sure how deep into our subconscious he can read or if he can only read the things we actively think about."

"It doesn't matter," I pointed out. "Ever try and not think about something? You can't do it. The act of trying to not think about something makes you think about it."

"You've got a point there," agreed Tom.

"I'll have to act without planning and let Heisenberg take the consequences," I concluded.

"Don't try that. You're outclassed physically and numerically. If you do anything, you're going to have to out think them." The medkit beeped and Tom silently stared at the display. Thinking.

His silence bothered me. "Well, am I okay?"

Tom picked his words carefully. "You're not really recovered from the effects of coldsleep, but you're getting better."

"Are you sure?" I asked. "Those drugs you gave me leave me feeling . . . I don't know . . . strange. Like I've never felt before." I was more than a little worried. No one ever willingly endured the effects of drugs and medical treatment without the constant attention of an autodoc. I wouldn't have felt less secure if Tom had been treating me by chanting and throwing powders into an open fire.

"Trust me. You'll soon be as normal as two million years of evolution can make you. But just to be sure, I want you to start taking three pills every eight hours."

If he thought that comment was going to make me feel better he was wrong. But I decided to just let it go. Tom looked at his wristchrono. "Slave Master doesn't trust us. I've stayed here longer than I was supposed to. I can't stay any longer." He packed up his medkit and prepared to leave. "Ib, just keep taking your medicine. You'll be back to normal soon."

I smiled weakly as the door opened and there was the kzinti guard standing outside. Tom smiled at me and then turned to leave. The kzinti guard hardly looked at me before he closed the door.

❖   ❖   ❖

The next day started with my dual failure to find either the energy for personal grooming or a satisfactory meatless breakfast. There was nothing to do except wait for the inevitable arrival of Slave Master and Fritz.

The wait gave me time to think about our captors. They were a curious mixture of advanced technology and primitive values. So much for the idea that scientific advances lead directly to advances in ethics. And it was obvious that they were completely unfamiliar with things that every Belter and Lunie understood instinctively. Perhaps the kzinti had been using their advanced technologies for such a long time that they'd forgotten about the nuances of living on a spacecraft like the *Paradox*.

My thinking about our captors was interrupted when Slave Master arrived alone at my room. Had something happened to Fritz? One could only hope. Slave Master stood towering in the open doorway looking at me.

"Continue ship work," he said. It was not a question.

"Sure. Where's your little friend?"

Slave Master said nothing, but just lifted a small chrome box to his mouth and growled into it. Scratchy growls answered him from the box and then the now-familiar feeling of Fritz splitting my head apart returned. Damn that mother-auditing Fritz! If I ever got my hands on him . . . The chrome box in Slave Master's hand growled again and the large kzinti looked at me and made another cat sound into the box before he put it back into a pouch on his belt.

"You work now."

You had to give him credit. He was a cat of few words.

"I work yes. Today we start repairs."

Slave Master interrupted. "Not 'we.' You. Heroes do not do slave work."

Who was I to argue with him? I went to work.

The most important problem to solve was fixing the

damage to the Bussard field generators because the thrust of the engine would depend on the size and power of the magnetic field feeding it ionized hydrogen. If I couldn't get enough field generators back on line, then we wouldn't have the thrust to carry the kzinti ship to Vega and then, I was sure, Slave Master, or more likely his captain, would make sure that I didn't have to worry about anything else. Everything depended on my actually getting outside and fixing those field generators. If possible.

I headed for the non-spinning section of the ship. Slave Master didn't say anything, he just followed me, his eyes boring holes in the back of my head. When we reached the transition lock he hesitated before getting in with me. The ladder "up" to the non-spinning section of the ship stretched above our head. We could have used the lift, but why make it easy for the kzinti? And anyway, I needed the exercise. I indicated that we had to go up the ladder and he followed me.

The rungs on the ladder were spaced conveniently for humans, but the kzinti's long arms were constantly faced with the choice of making tiny little reaches or making big stretches. I hoped this was making his arms and legs get cramped. As we rose "up" the ladder I could feel our weight decreasing and I glanced below me to watch the kzinti climbing behind me. His face was tight and his eyes focused on me like I was to blame for centrifugal force and its disorienting cousin, coriolis force. Tough.

By the time we had reached the rotational axis of the spinning section we were floating in a good approximation of freefall. The transfer hub connected to the non-spinning part of the ship was ringed by the four tubeways that formed the spokes going to the toroidal crew section and shared the slow rotation of that part of the ship. A large hatchway opened into the freefall parts of the ship, but the view was a bit disorienting, since the transfer hub was slowly rotating and the freefall section wasn't.

I grabbed a handhold on the wall and watched Slave Master get his bearings. I might not be able to read his body language exactly, but I could tell he was uncomfortable. Great. Serves him right for being where he wasn't wanted. I indicated a corridor through the open hatchway.

"We've got to go to the Telepresence Operations Center. It's this way. Next to the cargo lock." Slave Master said nothing. Looked like freefall had gotten the cat's tongue.

We floated down the corridor until we went past one of the coldsleep chambers where fifty of our two hundred colonists floated in cryogenic stasis. I looked in through the frost covered window in the air-tight door. The individual coldsleep coffins were filled with liquid nitrogen and all the insulation in the world could not keep that cold from leaking out into the chamber. The lights in there were dim but I could see the banked rows of coffins. One on top of another, in neat rows and columns like an exercise in matrix math.

Then I noticed holes in the array of coffins. Several were missing. No wait, over a dozen were missing. A thought tickled the back of my mind, but it was too outrageous to consider. Then I looked back at Slave Master who was looking into the coldsleep chamber longingly. Hungrily. Just as if the coldsleep vault held nothing more than a bunch of frozen dinners.

I could learn to dislike the kzinti without much effort.

The cargo lock was down the corridor and up a passageway. We drifted into the Cargo Lock Ready Room. The Telepresence Operations Center occupied one corner of the large and cluttered room, and Slave Master scanned the area with wary eyes as if he expected a trap. How he expected something like that was beyond me. My head was splitting from Fritz's mind reading so he had to know I wasn't planning anything. Maybe Slave Master was just naturally paranoid.

Several different types of telepresence 'bots were racked on the wall of the ready room. I went over to an EVA workbot and tapped a self-diagnostic command into its keypad. While it ran through its self check I floated over to a locker and pulled out a full body VR suit. Slave Master never took his eyes off me and all the while one of his hands rested on the gun hanging from his belt and his other hand held the chrome communicator near his face. I tried to concentrate on what I was doing while growling sounds from the communicator reminded me that Fritz was telling Slave Master everything I saw and thought.

The 'bot beeped its readiness as I finished putting on the VR bodysuit and pulled myself over to a VR workstation. A harness assembly provided straps to hold my body in place while leaving me complete freedom to twist my torso or move my arms and legs without having to worry about bumping into anything or swimming myself out into the airlock. The straps of the harness were a warm reassuring pressure around me as I slipped on the data gloves, the helmet and the foot sensors.

Tapping the controls on the VR workstation I lowered the visor of my helmet without waiting to see if Slave Master had any comments and went full immersive with the 'bot. There was a moment of disorientation as my visual perspective changed. The view was so real that it was easy to forget that it was coming from the sensors of a telepresence 'bot and not directly from my own senses.

My eyes were now close to the ground and I could see the 'bot's spider-like legs stretching out in front of me. My legs felt the springiness of the 'bot's legs as the force feedback loop activated the solenoids in my suit. I selected a walk cycle for the 'bot and moved my legs to control it, the eight legs of the 'bot moving in synchronization with each swing of my legs. I could feel the sticky sensation of the 'bot's foot magnets sequentially activating and then releasing when its legs were raised. It was a strange yet reassuringly familiar sensation.

I could see Slave Master off in the corner of the Cargo Lock Ready Room and my own body strapped to the VR workstation, its legs moving in a strange mimicry of the motion of the 'bot's legs. I moved my hand and keyed a control for the cargo lock. The inner door swung open and the 'bot walked into the lock. The outer door cycled open as soon as the inner door closed and I was finally, in a virtual sense anyway, free of the ship.

Seeing the stars from the outside of a ship never fails to fill me with awe and wonder. So many actinic points of light spread out between expanses of black nothingness. So many things waiting to be discovered. And then I remembered the kzinti. Tanj!

The 'bot moved easily outside the ship; after all, that was what it was designed to do. It only took a few minutes for me to walk the 'bot from the side of the ship's freefall module where the cargo lock was located to its base where the ship's main truss was attached. Once there I grappled onto a transport dolly that could carry the 'bot all the way to the rear of the ship.

As the dolly moved down the length of the ship's truss I could stretch my legs and just enjoy the view. The gold foil-covered hydrogen tanks loomed large over my head as the crew section grew small behind me. In a few minutes the dolly pulled up to the rear of the ship where the Bussard field generators and fusion drive were located. After the dolly stopped I released the 'bot from its anchor fittings and walked it over to the field generator assembly and started my detailed inspection.

Fortunately, the damage was not as bad as it had appeared from my first VR inspection. Several of the generators were badly damaged and wouldn't be repairable, but the others looked like they could be repaired or operated using redundant systems. This was good news. I could reprogram the ship's computer to stop looking at some of the more pessimistic trajectory options.

The repair work on the salvageable units was tedious but not, as it turned out, terribly difficult. I had to determine what components were damaged, check the ship's spares inventory to see if replacements were available, then get them from storage and install them. If replacements were unavailable, then I had to see if I could circumvent the damage by using redundant systems or by reconfiguring the field.

I could have speeded up the process by activating several 'bots and letting them bring the spare parts out from the stores locker using their self-guidance systems while I worked on the field generators. But for some reason I didn't want to do that. Whenever I needed a spare part I walked the 'bot I was using back to the dolly, rode back to the crew section, walked the 'bot back to the cargo lock, went inside to the spares locker to get the parts and then reversed the process to get back to the rear of the ship to continue the repairs. I enjoyed the chance to relax when the 'bot was making its trek up the ship's spine.

And it wasn't like Slave Master was from the Spacejack's Guild; he couldn't fine me for slacking or featherbedding.

The work went on for hours. I don't know how many. I was able to almost forget about the kzinti and what they represented until my headache started to fade. I knew what that meant. Fritz was losing his ability to read my mind. I wondered if Slave Master would have me keep working once Fritz became blind to my thoughts.

My juju headache was almost completely gone as I piloted the 'bot in through the cargo lock to get more repair parts. Slave Master quickly floated over to the 'bot like it was a long lost friend, or a big piece of catnip. He stared down at the 'bot and addressed it as if somehow I was "in" the 'bot and not hanging weightless over at the VR workstation.

"End work. Continue later. Leave now."

Who was I to argue? We left.

Back at the transfer hub, I let Slave Master go "down" the ladder to the spinning section before me. If I got lucky and he slipped and fell I wanted him below me, not above me. But no such luck. We entered the spinning section of the ship without incident.

I felt heavy and weighed down by the centrifugal force of the spinning section, but Slave Master seemed buoyed up by the surrogate gravity. I guess his people don't have any equivalent to Belters. Slave Master escorted me back to my cabin and left with his daily admonition to eat and rest. Like I needed the encouragement.

I decided I needed a shower before I resigned myself to another meatless meal. For some strange reason I felt good about how the day had gone and about myself. I still didn't have a solution to the kzinti problem, but I had made real progress on solving a problem I could deal with. I'd just take things one step at a time and deal with each problem in its turn. The kzinti would have their own turn before too long.

Looking at myself in the mirror of the 'fresher I felt disgust over my appearance. My image wasn't that of a Belter, it was a Flatlander wirehead or maybe VR addict. Enough was enough. What was I? Could there be any question?

I pulled a hair trimmer out from a drawer in the 'fresher and ran it over my face and head, being careful to leave a belt of close cropped hair running across the top of my head. That done I used a bottle of depilatory cream to finish the job and before long my unruly tangle of hair was replaced by a neatly trimmed Belter's crest. This was the best I'd felt since coming out of coldsleep or maybe even longer. Now if I could just do something about those censored kzinti.

The timer for my medicine chimed and I reached for the vial containing my pills. If three were good, maybe more were better. I'd start taking four each time.

I'd have to ask Tom to bring me more soon. At this rate I'd be running out of them in a few days. As I stepped into the shower I reflected on a job that had started well and on other jobs waiting to be done.

The next few days went by in a haze of routine. Each day consisted of taking my medicine, eating meatless meals and working. Each day Fritz would attach himself to my mind and read my thoughts while I worked on the Bussard field generators without thinking about anything else. And each evening when Fritz had gotten out of my head I would look for information that would help me do something about the kzinti, by reviewing the data files from our first contact with them along with any new information the autocams had picked up— though this information was sketchy because many of the autocams had been damaged when the kzinti had attacked the *Paradox*. Many times I had to guess where the kzinti were by knowing where they weren't.

I became able to recognize each of the kzinti occupying our ship and even gave more of them names as I learned their habits. Like Snaggle Tail, who spent a lot of time examining the Command Deck and other engineering areas. Or Shit Head, with the distinctive brown patch at the top of his head, who seemed to draw guard duty more often than the other rat-cats and who spent more time prowling the corridor in front of my quarters than any of the other guards. The kzinti seldom ventured into the freefall areas of the ship and when they did they didn't stay long. What they were doing there was always a mystery to me. All told, there were about two dozen kzinti occupying our ship though most of them spent as little time here as possible, flitting over in one of their small ships when they had something to do and then rushing back to their orange warship at the first opportunity.

Slave Master and Fritz were different. They had moved into a pair of unused crew quarters and seemed to have taken up permanent residence on *Obler's Paradox*. Fritz spent most of his time in his quarters, only occasionally venturing out to roam the empty halls. Slave Master spent his nights in his quarters and his days watching me work. A couple of guards always prowled the ship, or stood watch as I worked, but they were rotated back to their own ship every few days to be replaced by two new guards.

Some nights I used the autocams to prowl the ship, reminding myself of what it was the kzinti were threatening. I looked at the empty crew spaces and tried not to think about my friends who should have been laughing and working as we approached Vega. Scanning the coldsleep lockers I thought of each of the two hundred colonists who shared the ship with me and tried to make them come alive in my memory. Jeff, with his love of old books and music; Louis, with his passion for chess; and Carol, with her love for practical jokes and puns. They and all the rest lived in my dreams, when they weren't interrupted by nightmares of kzinti on a killing spree. I looked longingly into the vacuum hangar at the singleships that we planned to use to explore a new asteroid belt. My ship, *Trojan Rover*, was as bright and shiny as the day I had watched the cargo loaders latch it into position in the hanger bay twenty three ship-years ago back at Juno. Would I ever get to fly it under the light of a new sun?

The kzinti and I had established a working rhythm. A way of accommodating ourselves to our situation. And each day my resentment for Slave Master and Fritz and Shit Head and all the other named and unnamed kzinti grew larger. Each time I reviewed the data files my reaction became stronger and more focused on striking back at the kzinti. I no longer ran retching to the 'fresher when I watched the scenes of death and destruction, but thought of ever more imaginative ways to pay them back for what they had done.

Each day it became harder to accept our fate, to not make my imagined payback real and strike out in revenge. But whenever I had those thoughts I remembered how easily the kzinti had overpowered the crew of our ship. And so I focused on the problems I could solve, the field generators, and tried—unsuccessfully—not to think about the problem that seemed to have no answer. But each day I grew more curt with the kzinti, less afraid that I'd offend them and incur their wrath. I should have been afraid of them. I knew the danger they represented, but I just didn't worry about that any longer. They could kill me but that was all they could do. And I'm sure they knew that doing that would destroy their only hope of getting off this cosmic *Flying Dutchman*.

Fritz must have sensed my growing hatred for the kzinti, but if those rat-cats had done things like this before, then they must be used to being hated by now.

◊   ◊   ◊

After almost a week of work, most done in freefall at the Telepresence Operations Center, I finished the last of the repairs to the field generators. I had them back up so that they should be able to feed hydrogen to the drive at seventy-eight percent of its maximum rated fuel flow rate. This was better than I had hoped for but I didn't expect Slave Master to praise me for this accomplishment. I wasn't disappointed. He took this information with a low growl and then asked about the remaining work. I explained that now I would have to finish reprogramming the field generators to make sure they could provide a stable ramscoop field. He seemed pleased when he learned that this could be done from the Command Deck and that he would have a reprieve from freefall for a few days.

We had arrived back at my quarters when the remnants of today's juju headache let me know that I should tell him everything about the upcoming tests. So I reminded him that all of the kzinti would have to be onboard *Obler's Paradox* when I did the tests since their ship couldn't shield them from the deadly effects of the magnetic field generated by the Bussard field generators. He looked at me closely when I told him this; perhaps he thought I might have tried to hold back such information. But why bother? Fritz would have just read it from my thoughts when I was getting ready to run the tests. Still, there was something strange about the way he looked at me, like maybe I was more than just a potential meal on the hoof.

"You are becoming a worthy slave. The Patriarchy will reward you."

I looked straight into his eyes and could read his irritation at my arrogance in his body language. But I didn't care. "Yas shu, massa. Serving yous what ah likes doing best." I wondered if he, or Fritz, could catch the insult in my words. I guess not. He let me live.

The door clicked shut and my medicine timer chimed before Slave Master could respond to my arrogance and insult. Time for my pills and food, followed by more time spent reviewing the data files. Worthy slave indeed, I snorted as I dry swallowed five of Tom's pills. Whatever they were, they were working. I felt better, or at least different, than I had ever felt before. But Fritz had hit me hard today with his mind reading tricks and I was really tired. I thought I'd lie down and rest for a few minutes before eating. Before I spent more time thinking about my hatred for the kzinti.

I awoke hours later unrefreshed and more tired than when I had laid down. But at least my headache had faded away. I knew there were things I should do, but I couldn't remember them. I knew I had to prepare for something, but I couldn't think of what it was. I wanted . . . I wanted this to be over. Hell, I wanted to be anywhere but here; even the bottom of a hole looked good from here. I punched an order into the autochef while I walked over to the 'fresher to throw some water on my face in hopes that that would help clear the fuzz from my mind. It didn't.

The autochef chimed and a handmeal popped out of the dispenser. But more important, a mug of steaming coffee accompanied it. I was ravenous as I bit into the handmeal. Then I stopped. A bacon, lettuce and tomato handmeal without the bacon? I had expected this but was still annoyed.

The meal took the edge off my discomfort but I was frustrated because right after eating was when I most missed my pipe. It had always helped me to relax and focus my thoughts. But the limited medical resources of a colony world could not be spared for the preventive doctoring that such a nonessential vice required. I had been forced either to give up my pipe or give up the stars. I chose the stars.

Then I remembered just what it was we had found out in the stars. Not our dreams but nightmares from our violent past. Contact with the kzinti had taken all the dreams of my youth, all the hopes of what we might find out in the stars, and made them a bitter taste in my mouth. What was the value of dreams, if reality was nothing but a nightmare?

I wanted to lash out and give back to the kzinti some of the pain that they had given me when they stole my dreams. But I couldn't. Generations of socialization and chemical adjustment by psychists and autodocs had removed the violent streak from humanity. So I did the one thing I could do. I reviewed the data file from our first meeting with the kzinti. Feeding my anger, feeding my hate and looking for a way to solve our problem.

As I reached for the "on" button of the data display unit I noticed my vial of medicine. I couldn't remember if I had taken them the last time my timer had chimed. What the hell, they were making me feel good. Taking more couldn't hurt. I swallowed five of the pills with a coffee chaser while the memory plastic desk and chair extruded themselves from the wall, then I settled down to study the kzinti and the forgotten art of war.

I watched in numb horror as the now familiar images ran before my eyes. I fast forwarded through the initial confusion of the arrival of the kzinti, then slowed the pace of the images to focus on what they did and how they had done it. I studied how they aimed their weapons, carefully, not indiscriminately, making sure that each shot killed its target. I saw how they were confused by freefall. Some quickly learned to brace themselves when firing their weapons, while others never learned and went tumbling away in dramatic proof of Newton's law of action and reaction.

I carefully studied their actions when the kzinti entered the Command Deck of the *Paradox*. I could recognize each and every one of their ugly faces. It was the largest one, Churl-Captain, who was first into the Command Deck. He was the one who had killed Jennifer. And just behind him came Slave Master, who disemboweled Chi Lin and then shot Joel Peltron through the face as his hands danced over the navigation board.

No matter what form my revenge took, I knew I would find something special for Slave Master. For the fear he had made me live under for the past week and for what he had done to my friends on that fateful day. I would be sure that whatever I did to him would be painful and very final. I trembled—either from fear or anticipation, I didn't know which—as I envisioned killing that tiger that dared to walk like a man.

The violence of my thoughts frightened me. I knew if I got in an autodoc now I'd be out cold for weeks as its systems filled my blood with chemical agents designed to bring my violent impulses under control, to make me a safe and well balanced member of society. But right now I didn't want to be balanced, well or otherwise. I didn't want to be nonviolent. Right now I wanted to take back my ship and my future from those star-stalking tigers. By any means necessary.

I didn't want to watch the aftermath of the slaughter on the Command Deck, so I switched to an exterior view of our ship on that fateful day. There was the kzinti boarding craft, sticking to *Obler's Paradox* like an obscene growth. Hovering a few hundred feet away was another similar craft. I watched in delight as the magnetic fields from the Bussard generators grabbed that second ship and flung it away from the crew section. I knew that the kzinti craft was being drawn into our field generators but I didn't care. I knew that the magnetic fields were killing the rat-cat crew of that ship and watched in perverse fascination as that ship slammed into the Bussard field generators at the rear of *Obler's Paradox*. The destruction to a part of our ship was a small price to pay for the death of those damned invaders. The kzinti in that ship were dead and the damage of their passing was already fixed. Yes, it was a small price to pay.

Watching these images reinforced the unfamiliar feelings of anger and revenge that were racing through my mind. My body quivered with the unspent energy of my desire to strike back at the kzinti. I had never experienced anything like these feelings. I was surprised by my lack of fear over my unchecked desire to strike out at the kzinti. My mind knew that the smallest kzinti outweighed me by over two hundred fifty pounds. But my body didn't care.

I felt myself tremble with frustration because try as I might I couldn't think of any way to strike back at the kzinti without dying instantly. I felt desperation and depression because I knew there wasn't anything I could do to change our fate. We were the product of millions of years of evolution and thousands of years of civilization and yet it all came down to this. Outsiders with technology far beyond ours could take away our future and there was nothing we could do about it. In frustration I turned back to the data display console and had it show me the latest images of what the kzinti had been doing.

It was easy to have the computer find the images of the kzinti using the frame-differencing algorithms used for data compression. In places where no kzinti had ventured, the successive frames showed no differences and the computer ignored them. But let a kzinti come into the scene, then the image matrices changed and the computer recorded the sequential pictures. It was trivial to keep a log of where the kzinti were. I found Slave Master and Fritz had gone to their quarters, though I wasn't sure what they were doing there, since there weren't any autocams in the private spaces. Shit Head was patrolling the corridor outside my room, but it looked like he was walking away to check out other parts of the ship. Good. I didn't like him lurking around outside my cabin. One Ear—how did he lose his left ear?—was patrolling the corridors outside the transfer lock to the freefall section of the ship.

I didn't expect to find any other kzinti on the ship at this time, since they kept to a roughly human diurnal cycle and most of them spent their "nights" back on their own ship. I guess it smelled better to them or maybe it was because our doors and other equipment were too small for their comfort. The normal complement of kzinti during the evening was just Slave Master, Fritz and two guards. Very seldom did I find other kzinti on the *Paradox* after the day's work had been completed. But the computer was flashing an indication that one of the autocams in the freefall section was detecting a change in its image matrix. I tapped a key and the autocam from inside Coldsleep Chamber Number Three showed me its picture, a pair of kzinti floating weightlessly and inspecting the coldsleep coffins.

They stopped in front of one coffin and stared intently through its cloudy glassine cover. Then they did the unimaginable. They slid the coffin out of its place in the carefully designed arrangement of cryogenic storage units, started the pumps to remove the liquid nitrogen from the coffin and afterwards forced open its cover.

I tried to see who it was, to make out the identity of the person in the coffin. And then I saw the thick shock of flaming red hair cut in a Belter's crest, the tall slender frame with improbably large breasts. It was Sara d'Lambert, a Belter with whom I'd spent several months in a three-person ship prospecting the Saturnian Trojan points for volatiles, rare earth elements and monopoles. I remembered the excitement of the discoveries we'd made, the friendship and camaraderie, the disagreements and reconciliations. I imagined the things we might have done but were now forever impossible.

No!!! Those mother-raping kzinti were making no pretense of trying to activate the thawing mechanism! They ripped away the restraints that had held Sara in place and stripped away the gold-foil mylar blankets that were wrapped around her. Flecks of ice and shredded gold mylar went tumbling into the frosty air of the coldsleep chamber.

The kzinti were reaching into Sara's coffin and removing her from it. Clouds of fog formed around Sara's liquid nitrogen temperature body as the remains of the restraining straps waved in the breeze of the air circulators like mindless snakes. Her nude form was obscenely stiff as the kzinti floated her weightless corpse toward the door of the coldsleep locker.

As they were about to reach the door of the coldsleep chamber One Ear entered the room. He eyed Sara's body like she was nothing more than a piece of meat. The three kzinti's mouths moved but I didn't have the audio feed activated so I couldn't hear what they were saying. (Like I could understand that growling spitting excuse for a language that they spoke.) One of the two kzinti who had pulled Sara from coldsleep turned and grabbed a bag that was floating near the door and pushed it over to One Ear who opened it like it was a Winter Solstice present.

From within the bag One Ear extracted something that horrified me more than anything I'd seen since coming out of coldsleep. It was a human leg, raggedly cut off at the thigh with a stump of bone projecting out from the raw red wound. One Ear eyed his gift hungrily and then put it back into its bag before pushing off into the corridor carrying it off for purposes my mind did not want to imagine.

I watched in horrified disbelief as the other two kzinti made their way with Sara toward one of the cargo locks where they had attached a docking collar for their boarding craft. I was thankful for the freefall since it would keep them from dropping Sara. At liquid nitrogen temperatures things don't break when they fall, they shatter into millions of pieces. No matter what horrors might be in store for her, at least she would be spared the indignity of becoming a snapsicle. I watched in stunned silence as the two kzinti guided Sara's body through the docking collar into their ship and then vanished through the hatch behind her.

The computer chirped and switched the display to an external camera. A small kzinti boarding craft undocked from *Obler's Paradox*, slowly withdrew a few hundred meters and then pointed itself toward the kzinti warship and moved off without any trace of flame or exhaust. In minutes it was just another star lost in the darkness.

No!

This couldn't be happening!

I screamed out in rage and fear. I threw my 'cafe mug against the wall and watched the green intercom light wink out as my cup shattered against it. I gripped the plate that held the remnants of my meatless handmeal—damn those kzinti for forcing me to be a vegetarian—and threw it against the mirror over the 'fresher. The mirror shattered into thousands of unsafe pieces with two large fragments hanging from the wall reflecting my image. My eyes were wide and my mouth pulled back in a rictus of anger. Sweat beaded on my forehead and my body quivered with the energy of unrequited hatred.

I screamed and leapt at the door of my room and pounded on its unmoving metal surface. I felt my hands pulling into the unfamiliar shape of fists and beat on the door with them like they were organic mallets. The door rattled under my fists but stayed closed in locked mockery of my anger.

I turned and looked around the room, trying to find something to use for a weapon. My back curled into an angry arch, the muscles of my arms bunched up in tension. I'll teach those rat-cats the danger of fighting with humans over who's at the top of the food chain! My eyes darted around the room but our oh-so non-violent culture had made sure there weren't any weapons.

I searched the room, tearing things apart in my search for something I could use to force the door open so I could get at those future-stealing kzinti. Something that I could use to put paid to the debt of pain the kzinti had laid upon us. Just give me a weapon and I'd teach those rat-cats to fear us. Give me the chance and I'd introduce the kzinti to the extinct Sabertooth Cat, African Lion and Bengal Tiger. I'm sure they could explain just how dangerous humans were.

My search for a weapon took me into the 'fresher where my shoes crunched the broken glass from the mirror as I looked for anything that could be turned against the kzinti. The prick of a bit of glass through my soft ship shoe made me think of using the broken mirror as a weapon. Most of the pieces were too small but those two large pieces . . . They had potential.

I set about freeing those two large pieces of silvered glass from the wall and in a moment had two large sharp shards in my hands, ready to use on my enemies.

The sharp edges of the mirror fragments had cut my fingers, causing rivulets of blood to stain the arms of my flight suit, but I felt no pain. The feel of these weapons made me dizzy and delirious. I was the embodiment of Man the Hunter. The killing rage flowed through my veins and I knew the primal blood lust that our innumerable animal ancestors must have felt. And it felt good. Now all I had to do was find a way to get past the locked door.

"Ib! What's the matter? I heard your screaming. The intercom's broken. I didn't know what to think. I had to tell Slave Master there was a medical emergency before he let me check in on you." The words tumbled from Tom's throat as he rushed up behind me and stood in the door of the 'fresher. I turned to face him with those large shards of the mirror held in my hand. It took a moment of concentration for me to bring him into focus, to not lash out at this new sound source.

"Tom! Those kzinti are taking people out of coldsleep. Killing them and eating them. I've got to stop them. Get out of my way." I pushed forward to get past Tom but he blocked my way.

"Don't try it that way, Ib. You'll just get killed and accomplish nothing."

"Get out of my way," I barked again, harshly this time. "I should have done this a long time ago. I don't know why I didn't."

"You couldn't. No one could. Until now." Tom looked at me with guilt in his eyes. Or was it fear?

"No one on this ship had the mindset needed to confront the kzinti," he continued. "That type of person would have been labeled a schitz and kept back on Earth where they could be treated by the psychists."

"What? You're saying I'm schitz? Can't be. I feel fine. Better than ever."

"You weren't schitz. Maybe you're not even one now. I'm not sure. But you were almost borderline. Nothing serious. But close enough."

"Close enough? For what?"

"Close enough that the right medicines could alter the chemical balance of your neural system. The techniques that cure a schitz can also be used to push the right person the other way. It took some careful reprogramming of the autodoc, but you'd be amazed at what a determined practitioner can do."

"What? You made me schitz?"

"No. I keep telling you, not schitz. Just unbalanced. At least by the standards of our age. By the standards of any other time, you'd probably be considered perfectly normal. It's our situation that's abnormal, not you."

"But why?"

"Because the rest of us are too conditioned, too well-balanced. We can't even consider the possibility of using violence to accomplish anything. You were the only person who was borderline enough to be pushed over the edge. Pushed into becoming a warrior." Tom looked away. He knew what he had done to me. He'd done it for the best of reasons. But now, like Doctor Frankenstein, he was afraid of his creation.

"But Ib, you can't go off unprepared like this," Tom continued. "You'll be killed. Maybe your body has been pushed into being aggressive, but you don't have any training as a fighter. You've got to fight with your brain, not your emotions."

"Tom, if I think too much then Fritz will see what I'm planning and I'll get killed just the same."

"Well, at least take a minute and try to think of something you might use against them. Something you might have picked up in the last week. Some weakness or maybe some blind spot they have, something they don't notice. I don't know . . . Something. Just think before you act." Tom stared at my bloody hands for a minute. "And put down those glass shards. They'll just get you killed."

His suggestion was reasonable. I dropped the pieces

of the broken mirror to the floor and thought about what he had just said. There had to be some blind spot in the kzinti's behavior. Something that I had seen during my nightly sessions reviewing what they had done. An idea tickled the back of my mind while Tom got out his medkit and went to work on my hands.

"First thing we've got to do is get out of here," I said as Tom finished working on my hands. "Find some place where they'll have trouble finding us." I walked past Tom, out of the 'fresher and into my room. "But how do we get past that?" I said motioning to the locked door.

Tom looked at my bloody flight suit. "You're doing a convincing imitation of a hurt crewmember. I can probably get them to let me take you down to the autodoc. After that," he paused, "it'll be up to you."

A plan had begun to acquire form and substance in my imagination. Maybe not a great plan, but at least it was something. "Then let's do it," I answered, before my higher brain functions could kick in and convince me of the insanity of my plan.

Tom went to the door and rapped twice on it. The locked door slid open and Shit Head stared in at us. Tom pantomimed something and pointed at me as I tried to do my best imitation of a person in pain. The kzinti guard stared at me and growled as he removed the communications device from his belt and handed it to Tom. I caught snippets of his conversation with Slave Master, comments about an accident and my needing the attentions of the autodoc if I was going to be ready for tomorrow's test of our drive system. Tom must have convinced him because more spitting growling sounds came from the communications device and Shit Head motioned us into the corridor.

I made a show of leaning on Tom as we walked in the down spin direction toward the Med-Center. Dead light strips, broken down doors and burn marks on the walls spoke silent volumes about the nature of the kzinti. It didn't take long before we were passing an emergency equipment locker set into the wall.

This one seemed unused, its door closed and latched, but most importantly—it looked undamaged.

I counted my halting footsteps as we went past it. Turning my head I could see that Shit Head was still a couple of paces behind us. And then with what I hoped was a convincing cry of pain I fell to the floor taking Tom with me. Our kzinti guard couldn't stop in time, his feet tangling with our rolling bodies—my flailing arms didn't help his balance—and went tumbling to the floor.

Performing the fastest recovery in medical history, I leapt to my feet and dashed to the emergency equipment locker and twisted open its door. The locker contained a full set of tools for dealing with emergency situations, but nothing had been included for the problem facing us right now. I'd have to improvise.

Shit Head was rising from the floor as I pulled out a three-person vac-raft. This was nothing more than a fabric sphere that was large enough to hold three people in a pressurized environment while they waited for someone else to come and get them. But in its unpressurized condition it was just a limp hunk of Beta cloth fabric. I unzipped the vac-raft and threw it at Shit Head. I got lucky. His arms got entangled in the vac-raft's open end and multiple hand holds.

His claws tore at the vac-raft and ripped long tears in it as ropes of fabric became entangled with his arms. I looked back into the locker and found a breathing mask with an oxygen bottle. I threw them at Shit Head but he batted them aside, though the reaction made him slip back onto the floor.

The oxygen bottle rolled down the corridor and Tom

hurled it back at our guard's head, which it hit with a satisfying thump. The kzinti lashed out with one free arm, leaving deep gashes in Tom's chest and sending him tumbling down the corridor.

In a moment Shit Head would be free of the vac-raft. I was pulling out another one when I saw a heavy pry bar that was designed to open sealed doors during power failures. It was over a meter long and had a bulging torqueless ratchet on one end.

Turning back to Shit Head I saw that he was pulling out his communications device. This was not the time to let him call for reinforcements. I grabbed the pry bar and swung it with both hands. It connected with our guard's arm with a weird snap like glass breaking under water, and the communications device went sliding down the corridor. Tom stepped on it, smashing it into a star of electronic debris.

I tried to bring the pry bar back down on our guard's head, but he was rising from the floor and coming toward me with his injured arm dangling limply by his side. There wasn't room to swing the pry bar again so I stabbed at him with it. The impact against his chest knocked the air out of his lungs and almost made me fall backwards. Shit Head swung his good arm against the metal tool and sent it flying out of my hands.

I snatched the weapon I'd dropped, turned and ran, hoping that Shit Head would ignore Tom and follow me. He did.

Running up-spin I could feel my synthetic weight increase slightly as my running speed added to the rotational velocity of the spinning crew section. It was a small effect and I could easily compensate for it. I didn't think the kzinti chasing me was familiar enough with centripetal acceleration to do the same.

Shit Head lowered his body toward the floor as he chased me. At any moment I expected him to drop down and run on all fours. He was inhumanly fast and gaining on me.

I was holding the second vac-raft. My weapon. I did the only thing I could. I pulled the inflation tab on the vac-raft and tossed it behind me. It expanded to a size that almost filled the corridor. Shit Head ran into the inflated vac-raft and it bounded in front of him like a demented beach ball. He swung the claws of his uninjured hand and the vac-raft exploded with a loud pop. Again he lowered his body toward the floor and closed the gap between us. The raft clung to his claw and dragged behind him until he shook it loose. And then he screamed and leapt with his uninjured arm stretched out before him.

But he hadn't counted on the effect running would have on his centripetal acceleration or on the fact the floor was gently curved, not flat. Those two small but significant differences between our ship and a planetary surface made him hit the deck sooner than he expected. He went sprawling behind me. That kzinti was ignorant but not stupid; I didn't think he'd make that same mistake a second time. I had to think of something.

The entrance to one of the cargo transfer tubeways loomed ahead of us. I ran in. The tubeway was a hollow cylinder over six meters in diameter that stretched a hundred meters from the rim of the spinning part of the ship to the weightless transfer hub. A ladder surrounded by a safety cage made of wide spaced metal frames ran up the length of the tubeway and ended in the zero-g area. The lift was parked in the zero-g part of the ship and I didn't have time to wait for it to come down to me. I ran over to the ladder and started climbing as if my life depended on it.

I had never gone up a ladder as fast as I did just then as I raced for the weightless part of the ship. I only hoped that One Ear had not heard the commotion and come to investigate. The thought of being trapped between two angry kzinti was the stuff of nightmares.

As I rose up the ladder I could feel my weight dropping as I got closer to the rotational axis of the spinning section and the centrifugal force was correspondingly lowered. The effective gravity had fallen to almost half of its normal value when I heard Shit Head enter the tubeway.

I hazarded a look below but did not slow my hurried journey upward. Shit Head saw me with his upraised eyes. In a moment he was on the ladder and following me upward. He was using his injured arm to help maintain his balance on the ladder. I hoped it hurt him. A lot.

Nearing the end of the ladder my effective weight had been reduced to almost nothing and I pulled myself upward in a continuous motion. A lifetime of zero-g reflexes helped me increase the distance between myself and the hungry carnivore that was chasing me. I thought about the times I had played weightless tag with my friends while growing up in orbital habitats in the Belt. Those games had seemed so important to us children, but the stakes were never as high as the game I was playing right now.

Then I thought of something. Spin diving. A Belter child's game of chicken to see who could jump the farthest down the tubeway of a spinning habitat. If you played it safe you didn't win, but if you tried to go too far you ran the risk of falling all the way down to the full gravity section of the habitat. The newsnet had carried occasional stories of spin dive games that had ended in deadly tragedy. It had been one of my favorite games while growing up.

As I popped out from the safety cage surrounding the ladder I glanced back down at Shit Head. He was rising rapidly but the lowered gravity was causing problems for his coordination. His pace was no better than it had been back at the lower, and much higher gravity, part of the climb. I chanced a look over at the large hatch leading out of the transfer hub and was relieved to find that One Ear was nowhere to be seen. Finagle must be a Belter because he was surely working on my side right now.

Shit Head was nearing the top of the ladder and his concentration was torn between me and the ladder that he gripped as if he was under full gravity.

I positioned my almost weightless body against the top of the tubeway and compressed my legs while I gauged my upcoming jump. I made a quick double check of the safety placards on the wall and reassured myself that I would be jumping spinward. Shit Head was reaching the top of the ladder when my legs exploded under me and I dove headfirst down the tubeway toward the spinning part of the ship.

A look of surprise raced across Shit Head's face as I flashed through the air rapidly falling toward the other end of the hundred meter tube. He watched with focused concentration while my body followed a compound curve made up of the linear motion of my jump and the rotational motion of the tubeway.

I slammed into the safety cage just a bit below where I had wanted to land and held on tightly against the forces now pulling on me. Damn! I guess I wasn't the spin diver I was in my youth. An effective gravity of over half-a-g tugged on my arms as I swung myself inside the safety cage and over to the ladder. I turned my head up to look at Shit Head. He had emerged from the safety cage and was watching me intently, trying to decide what to do next.

I slid down the smooth aluminum ladder so rapidly my hands were burning from the friction and my feet were tingling from tapping them against the rungs of the ladder as I controlled my fall. I felt my weight increase with every second. By now I was almost two-thirds of the way down the tubeway.

Shit Head must have known he couldn't climb down the ladder fast enough to catch me. So he did what must have been the natural thing to do. He imitated my actions. But he hadn't played spin dive as a kitten.

Shit Head dove from the top of the tubeway aiming directly for me. He didn't have zero-g reflexes, so his jump imparted a spin to his body and he did a slow tumble as he arced downward. But, more importantly, he didn't know how to compensate for the ship's spin. He was jumping in the spinward direction and so as his body was moving downward and toward the ladder, the ship's rotation was moving the ladder away from him. The result was that he followed a graceful curve downward and not towards the point he had aimed for. He quickly realized he was in trouble, though I'm sure he didn't know why. His arms and legs started flailing, but they couldn't help him.

He slammed backward against the safety cage just below me and the force of his impact made him rebound back into the empty air of the tubeway. He tumbled until he hit on the far side of the tubeway less than twenty meters above the floor. He plummeted downward like Galileo's proverbial cannon ball. The fluctuating forces must have been confusing but he was trying to get his feet underneath him. Everything he did just made things worse.

In a matter of seconds it was over. The thrashing kzinti hit the floor of the tubeway head first with the sickening crack of breaking bones. He collapsed into a motionless heap as a pool of purple-red blood formed around him.

Silently I lowered myself down the last few meters of the ladder and went over to my silent tormentor. The scent of wet ginger and copper-scented blood, mixed with the foul smell from when his sphincter muscles had released, filled the air. I glanced up the tubeway and remembered One Ear. I better get Shit Head out of sight in case One Ear had heard anything and came looking to see what was the matter.

I grabbed the dead kzinti by the arms and started pulling him out of sight, leaving behind a trail of drying kzinti blood. Once clear of the tubeway I released his arms and they fell limply to the deck, his long fur sticking to me with the glue of his drying blood. I stared down at his lifeless body and thought about what I had just done.

I felt like some sort of obscenity. I wanted to run and hide. To never be seen by anyone ever again. Perhaps I hadn't killed another human, but that was splitting a fine philosophical line. That kzinti had been an intelligent creature with his own hopes, dreams and aspirations. What right did I have to take his future away from him? I was ashamed because Tom could bear witness to what I had done.

And then I realized just what I had done. I had gone up against a creature much larger than myself, who saw humans as nothing more than slaves or quick meals, and beaten it. Those damn rat-cats weren't invincible. They could be defeated. One down and how many to go? It didn't matter. There was one less kzinti on our ship than there had been a few minutes ago and soon there'd be even fewer.

I removed anything from Shit Head that looked useful, like his long sharp knife and his handgun. The knife looked like a short sword in my hand. I remembered seeing films of athletes using swords for touching competitions, the sharp blade of this knife made it obvious that the touching of swordplay could have a meaning far beyond points and medals. The handgun was a mystery. I didn't have a good idea about how to use it, though I'd seen just how devastating it could be. I'd take it and hope I could figure out how to use it when the need arose.

Tom came stumbling down the corridor carrying the medkit, his shirt hanging in bloody tatters while he pressed one hand against the ragged cuts that raked across his chest. I had thought Shit Head chased me half-way round the ship but I guess in the excitement I hadn't realized how short the chase had been.

"Is he . . . dead?" Tom's question came out haltingly as he slid down to the floor of the corridor.

I just nodded. "How are you doing?" I asked afraid of the answer.

"The cuts are painful, but not deep," Tom said slowly. "Ib, go on without me. I'm just going to slow you down."

"No way. We're in this together. What do you need to keep going?"

"Just give me a painkiller and put something on these cuts to stop the bleeding. But make it quick, we've got to get away from here before the kzinti figure out what happened."

"Okay, but you've got to give me a hand. I don't know how to use any of this stuff," I said as I sat down next to him and opened the medkit. Tom blinked at me in pain as he started to point to things in the medkit.

Following his directions I pulled out an analgesic hypo and gave it to him. I spread a coagulant accelerator over the ragged cuts and then pulled bandages over his wounds. I didn't have time to shave the hair from his chest and didn't want to think about how much it would hurt when the bandages ripped out those hairs later. If we survived until later.

I put an arm under Tom to support his weight and we turned spinward and headed for the Command Deck. Disgusted with myself, I said, "I can't believe I did what I did. I feel so . . . unclean."

"You did what you had to do, not what you wanted to. Don't ever forget that."

We walked in silence, as quickly as we could manage, down the empty corridors. Our hearts were pounding in our chests as we expected at any minute to run into our remaining kzinti guard. We were moving away from the rooms where Slave Master and Fritz were staying. One Ear was in another part of the ship. But still, every unexpected sound or shadow made us jerk in fear. In a few minutes we were going through the wrecked door of the Command Deck. Tom looked at it wistfully, "I guess we can't use that to keep them out."

"It didn't work the first time," I replied. "Now quick, I'm going to set you up here at the Captain's position and have you monitor our friends." I helped Tom lower himself into the tattered chair. The grimace on his face might have been from pain or might have been from knowledge of what had happened to the last occupant of this seat. I tapped a few commands to the computer and the displays brought up the autocam images, searching for the kzinti. Slave Master and Fritz couldn't be seen. They must be in their rooms. One Ear was still down by the coldsleep chambers carrying the bag those two kzinti had given him. Its shape did not reveal the horror of its contents. Maybe One Ear was picking out tomorrow's dinner or perhaps he was just following today's security route.

I sat down at the Engineer's station, every minute expecting my head to erupt with the head splitting pain of Fritz's mind reading but it never came. Maybe that meant we still had the element of surprise. My hands danced over the controls activating the Bussard field generators. The computer kept trying to run diagnostics but I kept overriding it. Time was of the essence. Everything would have to work. If it didn't we would be dead. There wasn't time to make sure the equipment was ready. I'd have to trust my jury-rigged repairs.

"No one's moved. I think they don't know what's happened."

"Good. Just keep watching. We're almost ready. But once things start happening, we're going to have to move fast."

I reached for the VR helmet and data gloves as the computer finished its final checks on the field generators. It thought everything was ready, but what else could it think? I'd forced it to step over every safety check. If there was a problem we might not know about it until our ship turned into a small nova. I slipped on the data gloves and helmet, plugged them in the VR console and then slapped down the display lenses as I activated the VR system.

Suddenly my perspective changed. I was a disembodied entity floating in space, seeing *Obler's Paradox* hanging motionless against the stars. A few quick commands and data windows came up surrounding it. A few more quick selections and I saw the ship surrounded by the neon blue electromagnetic flux lines from the field generators. They were dim and held close against the ship, which is as it should be since they were only operating at flight idle. The electric yellow hydrogen flux density contours appeared, but I ignored them. Right now I wasn't interested in propulsion.

I increased the power to the field generators. The neon blue flux lines brightened but didn't move. So far, so good. I moved my hands and shaped the field. It got larger and brighter. Better. My repairs had worked. There were some asymmetries in the field but they'd be controllable. I shrank the scale of the display until the *Paradox* was just a thin pencil outlined in blue hanging in space with the kzinti warship a small orange dot hanging silently a short distance away.

My hands moved controlling the magnetic field from the Bussard generators. The blue outline around the *Paradox* grew. I shaped it and molded it, growing it as fast as I dared. At one point a safety override beeped, but I forced the computer to ignore it and keep up the power to the Bussard field generators.

The neon blue magnetic field lines grew larger and brighter. I forced their shape into an asymmetrical ellipsoid pointed at the kzinti warship. I grew the field larger and larger until it was almost to the warship and then with a quick sweep of my hands the field encompassed the kzinti warship. I ramped up the strength of the drive until it was as powerful as the generators could make it. I constrained the field so it didn't spread across hundreds of kilometers of space, but stayed focused on the kzinti ship, concentrating the killing strength of the magnetic field there.

I didn't know how long it would take that field to kill the kzinti in their ship. Humans would have died almost instantly, but who knew about the kzinti? I made the field strength fluctuate within lethal limits while keeping the flux lines focused on the kzinti ship. That changing magnetic field should be inducing electrical currents in every conductor on that ship. I hoped it would destroy their remaining electrical equipment and keep them from sending a warning. Who knows, I might even get lucky, it might induce killing electrical fields in the conductive blood of the kzinti.

I felt as if I were a god, reaching out to kill the kzinti with the force of my will and the motions of my hands. I made the magnetic field fluctuate faster and wilder, from almost nothing to the largest field the generators could create in seconds. The induced electric fields made the kzinti ship glow with the stuttering light of electrical discharges. I forced the magnetic field to its maximum value and held it there.

And then the computer flashed an alert that I couldn't ignore. My manhandling of the Bussard generators had overstressed a couple. I was going to have to shut down the field or risk destroying them completely. As I did so I hoped that our ship's magnetic fields had been as lethal to the kzinti as they would have been to unprotected humans. Silently the neon blue flux lines collapsed back to a dim outline pressed tightly against our ship. The kzinti warship floated dark and motionless against the stars. I toggled off the VR system and pushed the lenses of the display helmet away from my eyes.

"There, that should have killed any kzinti that were on their ship," I exclaimed more hopeful than certain. "If it didn't, then I don't know what we can do."

"Uh oh," Tom breathed nervously. "The guard is moving. I think they've gotten some warning."

"Then it's too late to be subtle," I replied as I hit the emergency despin button on the Engineer's command console. At once the shrieking sound of mechanical brakes and nutation dampers echoed through the ship and things lurched and tumbled as the rotating crew section quickly slowed to a stop. In a moment the familiar feeling of freefall enveloped us like a soothing warm bath. "How's that for equalizing the playing field?" I said as I unplugged the VR devices. I didn't waste time taking them off as I pushed over to get Tom.

"Come on! We've got to get out of here. It's the first place they'll look." I glanced at the displays looking for One Ear. He was going toward one of the tubeways from the freefall section and headed our way. We had to hurry. I didn't give Tom a chance to argue as I rushed him out into the corridor.

We traveled in long fast dives, pushing off from anything convenient and guiding ourselves with nudges from walls and ceilings. Tom's missing leg wasn't an impediment to his motion in freefall and soon we were approaching a tubeway to the weightless part of the ship. I motioned for Tom to stay back as I pulled out the gun I had taken from Shit Head.

In a swift move I pushed myself into the transfer lock and looked up the tubeway. There was One Ear fumbling in freefall. His eyes were focused on the ladder of the tubeway as he slowly pulled himself downward. He hadn't noticed me. I raised the large kzinti gun and then remembered how unbraced kzinti had rebounded when they fired their guns.

I lodged myself against the "floor" of the transfer lock looking up the tubeway. One Ear was coming closer. Soon he'd look down and see me. I had to act quickly. I rested the gun against my stomach, pointing it up the tubeway and pulled the trigger.

Nothing happened.

I held the gun in front of my face and stared at it wondering what I was doing wrong. There were a couple of small levers on the side of the gun. I moved them both and retook my aim just as One Ear looked down the tubeway toward me.

His eyes grew large, I don't think he was expecting to see a human holding a kzinti gun down at the bottom of the tubeway. He started turning himself to face me, his arms tensing on the ladder. I knew he was going to come flying my way in an instant. I braced myself against the floor and wall of the transfer lock with the gun resting against my belly. I pulled the trigger.

All hell broke loose. A cacophony of noise exploded from the gun as a succession of explosions echoed in the transfer lock making my ears ring painfully. Thick clouds of acrid smoke quickly filled the tubeway. The gun fired rapidly without stopping, there was nothing I could do to control it, much less aim it. I tried to keep it pointed up the tubeway and hoped I'd hit One

Ear. The gun bucked and thrust against my stomach, almost making me throw up from the pain and the pressure. High ringing ricochets echoed though the tubeway accompanied by the screaming sound of One Ear. But I couldn't tell if his screams meant he'd been hit or if he was diving for me in a murderous rage. And then the gun stopped firing, though an empty clicking kept coming from it, and silence echoed through the transfer lock.

One Ear came flying toward me out of the haze of smoke that filled the tubeway. I pushed off from the floor just as he collided with me. I expected to be ripped apart by his claws, but his body just limply pressed mine into the floor of the passageway and then rebounded back up the tubeway. He was dead. It was luck, not my skill, that had done it, but I didn't care. Another kzinti down and two more to go. I looked for One Ear's gun but it wasn't on him. I didn't have time to go hunting for it.

Ducking back into the corridor I grabbed Tom. "Come on. We've got to keep moving. Got to get to a part of the ship they're not familiar with." I pushed Tom ahead of me into the tubeway and gave him a shove that got him floating up toward the freefall section of the ship. He didn't need any further encouragement. He pulled himself up the ladder with quick strokes, making it hard for me to catch up to him. In a moment we were floating in the transfer hub to the freefall section of the ship.

"I'm going to stash you in safe place," I said as I guided Tom down one of the corridors lit with red emergency lights. "Have you get in an emergency transfer suit and hide in an airlock with the outer door open. At least that way they won't be able to get to you for a while."

"But what about you?" Tom asked with ragged breath as we hurried.

"I'm not going to tell you. Fritz can't read what you don't know." Our hurried motion brought us to Emergency Airlock Two. I pulled open one of the lockers and dragged out an emergency transfer suit made to Lunie proportions and pushed it over to Tom. "Put this on. Quick."

The suit was designed to fit a wide range of individuals and provide minimum level of life support and mobility, not comfort. Tom spoke as I helped him get into the suit and adjust it. "Speaking of Argus. Why haven't we felt his presence?" Tom grimaced as he wiggled into the emergency suit.

"I don't know," I answered. "He doesn't seem able to read my mind for more than a few hours at a stretch and then he can't read it, or least he never has, till the next day. Maybe it has something to do with that drug he takes. Maybe he's in no shape to read our minds right now."

Tom nodded, "He might be able to use an extra dosage of his drug to shorten his down time. Maybe he only reads you once a day to avoid overtaxing himself. Don't bet on his not being able to read you now." I nodded back to him as I grabbed the integrated helmet/biopack and slipped it over his shoulders and dogged the vacuum seals.

"Don't worry. I'm counting on it." Tom looked perplexed as I pushed him into the airlock but if he said any more I couldn't hear him through the glassine shell of his suit helmet. I watched as the lights showed he was depressurizing the airlock and opening the outer door. Then I pushed off from the wall and went rushing away from the airlock.

The Telepresence Operations Center where I'd spent most of the last week was just a short distance down a cross corridor. As I went sailing through the corridor my whole body was tingling with nervous anticipation.

At any moment I expected a huge wall of orange fur to explode in front of me filled with angry claws and teeth. Each time I came to an intersection of corridors I expected to find Slave Master coming at me from the other direction. I had lost track of where he was once we had left the Command Deck and now I imagined him everywhere. I wondered how much longer I'd have before Fritz would be invading my head, finding out where I was and signing my death warrant. Only in the case of the kzinti, I was most likely to end up inside a kzinti and not inside an organ bank.

I sailed into the ready room outside the cargo lock. There was the familiar wall of racked telepresence 'bots. Floating past them I slowed to hit their emergency activation buttons, watching as the wall of 'bots came alive with blinking status lights and legs and manipulators moving in short test sequences. I grabbed one of the 'bots and carried it over to the VR workstation while it activated itself. I jury-rigged an attachment for it, making sure its eyes were where my head would normally be. Silver tape and some ingenuity quickly had the 'bot attached to the workstation with its legs and manipulators restrained and out of sight.

I was almost done but I forced myself to move faster. If Fritz invaded my mind now my actions would all be for nothing. I had to finish my preparations quickly. I picked up a pair of 'bots and floated them over to near the door and pressed them against the wall, letting their magnetic feet hold them in place. I grabbed two more 'bots, turned them upside down and gently pushed them toward the ceiling. They hit the ceiling and their magnetic grapples held them in place. The other 'bots would have to wait. I grabbed two more 'bots and hurried out the door with them. I almost forgot the VR console but I ducked back inside to grab one of the portable units that was sitting loosely on an air suction workbench.

That done I went back to my two 'bots and dove down the corridor clutching them in my hands. If Fritz would just stay out of my mind for a few more minutes. If Slave Master would not show up too soon. If . . . If . . . If . . .

I opened my eyes and looked around the Cargo Lock Ready Room and could not believe my good fortune. I had managed to complete all my preparations without Fritz getting into my head. The chrono on the wall showed that less than fifteen minutes had passed since I had stopped the rotation of the crew section, plunging everything into freefall, and clearly announcing that I was free and coming after the kzinti.

Obler's Paradox was a large ship and we had hidden in a part that was not familiar to the kzinti, but how much longer did they need to find us? How much longer before Fritz could take his drug and read my mind and see with my eyes and figure out where I was hiding? Hopefully soon. I didn't want to wait anymore. I wanted this confrontation to be over. One way or the other. A shiver ran up my back and I told myself it was from anticipation, not chilly temperatures.

I brought up a display window showing me the outputs from the autocams. If they couldn't find me maybe I'd give them some help. The computer quickly found Slave Master and Fritz in the Command Deck. The large kzinti looked angry, which for him was normal, but Fritz . . . He looked miserable. Normally he was disheveled but now he looked like death warmed over. No, I take that back. I'd seem corpses pulled out of vacuum that looked better than he did.

Fritz's fur was matted and stuck out at strange angles, his eyes had purple tinged circles around them and his limp body floated listlessly. He looked like he was going to die, or at least fall asleep, at any moment.

The two kzinti were trying to make sense out of our ship's displays and the silence from their ship. Maybe they needed some help. I selected an option from a virtual display and brought the intercom on-line with it set up so my voice would come out of every speaker on the ship.

"What's the matter, Slave Master? Can't figure out what happened?" My words echoed through the ship, even down here. It sounded like an angry god was everywhere. It was disconcerting. It was exactly what I wanted. "They're dead. I killed them all. Just like I'm going to kill you."

Slave Master let out a terrifying growl and his arms swung round in angry defiance of me. Fritz was cowering in a corner, trying to get away from his angry superior and from my voice. Slave Master ripped a display unit off its stand and threw it against the wall. It didn't change anything.

"Slave of Humans. That's what they'll call you now. All of you kzinti together couldn't beat two humans, and one of them was a cripple. How's it feel to be defeated by a crippled eater of fruits and vegetables?"

Slave Master raged around the Command Deck. His anger didn't make him any more adept at getting around in freefall. He turned to Fritz and growled something. Fritz whimpered something back and Slave Master hit him backhanded sending him tumbling across the room. "Soon, Human," Slave Master roared. "Soon you shall die. I will let you watch as I kill everyone on this ship and then you shall watch as I consume you, one limb at a time until you are dead."

"Fat chance, coward. The only thing you'll get to eat will be my shit. You'll like it. It's made from roots and vegetables."

Slave Master roared in frustration and anger as he grabbed anything he could tear free and hurled it against the walls. Several times Fritz had to duck to avoid getting struck by flying equipment. Slave Master turned back to Fritz and growled at him, Fritz whimpered something but when Slave Master made a move toward him Fritz dug into his pouch and pulled out his syringe. He plunged it into his arm. His body language showed he was afraid of what it would do, but it was clear he was more afraid of what Slave Master would do if he didn't use his drug. I watched in anticipation of the headache that would announce Fritz's presence in my head. But nothing happened.

"Slave of Humans. I grow tired waiting for you. Why not kill your telepath? He can't read my mind. Must I tell you where to find me?"

Slave Master glared at Fritz who was shaking and shivering as he made erratic spitting sounds. I heard loud growls from Slave Master and could read the anger in his body language. Fritz hesitated. Slave Master rushed over to him and reached into his pouch and pulled out another syringe. Fritz was writhing beneath Slave Master, who forced another dose of the drug into Fritz.

And then there it was. The pain was diffuse and not as great as before, but I could feel it. Fritz was getting into my mind. Great. Now for the last part of the plan. I shut down all the virtual displays except one that showed me what the two kzinti were doing and concentrated on staring out at the ready room of the cargo lock and the Telepresence Operations Center. I made sure I looked at equipment and hardware we had been working with all week. Familiar items.

Things that would tell Fritz exactly where I was.

"Slave of Humans. You justly fear for your life. I will kill you and use your skin as a rug to warm my feet." I wanted to have him irrationally angry. I wanted him to be in a rush to attack me. I wanted to drive him over the edge. It wasn't a long trip.

Slave Master growled at Fritz who hissed something back to him. Slave Master pulled back his head and roared. He grabbed Fritz and pulled him out of the room. He knew where I was. He was coming to get me.

Good.

I watched in eager anticipation as the autocams tracked Slave Master and Fritz in their freefall rush through the ship. They gracelessly bounced off walls and ceilings as they made their way down the weightless corridors to the closest tubeway. They fumbled their way up the ladder, bumping into each other and knocking themselves away from the handholds. But graceless or not, clumsy or otherwise, you had to give them credit. They were on their way. Slave Master pulled ahead of Fritz and dove for the ready room of the cargo lock. I was waiting for him.

The large kzinti came into the room, roaring a challenge that I'd never understand, with his long knife drawn. Why he didn't have his gun out I'll never know.

Maybe it had something to do with honor, or maybe he just got excited and forgot. He flew toward the VR workstation with his eyes wide and mouth pulled open showing his long teeth.

I watched the expression on his face change from challenging anger to what I thought must have been confusion because he wasn't seeing me as he rushed toward the VR workstation. In my place was an EVA 'bot, strapped to the supports of the workstation.

Fritz might have known what I was seeing, but he didn't know where I was.

Slave Master collided with the workstation and ripped it apart. The display turned to static as he destroyed the 'bot. I toggled the display to another 'bot.

The room turned upside down. I checked to see which 'bot I had activated. It was one of the heavy duty EVA

maintenance 'bots that I had planted on the ceiling. I
scanned the room. There was Fritz cowering near the
doorway directly above the 'bot I was controlling with
Slave Master angrily sniffing the room in a fruitless
search for me. He'd get his turn soon.

I moved my legs and the 'bot exploded from the ceiling
hurtling upward toward Fritz and landed on his back.
I used a couple of manipulators to grab big chunks of
Fritz's fur. The telepath tried to shake me off, twisting
and turning as he tried to dislodge me. But all he really
succeeded in doing was getting himself separated from
the floor and anything he could react against. He became
a tumbling ball of matted orange fur floating in the
middle of the room, screaming in pain or fear or both.
And all the while my 'bot was latched firmly to his back.

Slave Master saw this and rushed over, but he wasn't
fast enough. The 'bot extended its laser cutting torch.
I sighted on the back of Fritz's head and set the torch
at its highest continuous power setting. One which could
have cut through aluminum like a flame goes through
dry ice. I pulled the trigger. Fritz didn't have a chance.

The laser was aimed at the base of his skull pointing
up toward his brain. A pencil width tunnel opened up
in Fritz's head with the light from the laser shining
incongruously through a hole in his forehead. The heat
from the laser cauterized the wound so there was little
blood to show for all the damage that was being done.
In an instant the headache that had bedeviled me all
week was gone, replaced by an unexpectedly sad
emptiness.

And then Slave Master reached what was left of Fritz
and ripped the 'bot off his back and dashed it against
the wall. The display filled with static. Scratch one more
'bot. I had plenty of 'bots.

I pulled up an option window and selected another
'bot that I'd planted on the wall next to the door. I

flipped off the intercom and routed my voice feed to the speakers on the 'bot. "Hey, Slave of Humans. Here I am." My voice echoed in the ready room. Slave Master jerked around at the sound and for a moment was confused.

I pushed off with my legs and the 'bot went flying toward Slave Master, who grabbed a workbench and pulled himself out of the way of the 'bot. I had to give him credit. He was learning quickly how to fight in freefall.

I jumped my presence to another 'bot, activated its magnetic grapples and sent it walking across the floor toward Slave Master using its autonomous navigation capabilities. Again I routed my voice feed to this new 'bot. "Here I am. Over here."

I jumped my presence to another 'bot. This one a small IVA model, used for doing repairs in out of the way places inside the ship, that was still racked in its storage cell on the wall. "Not there, here!" As Slave Master turned toward this new source for my voice I activated the 'bot's travel fans and made it zoom across the room toward him.

I jumped my presence back to the 'bot that was walking toward Slave Master. "Here I am. Catch me if you can, you vegetable-eating coward." Slave Master turned and roared at this insult, just as the IVA 'bot collided with his back. I jumped my presence back to that 'bot and grabbed onto his fur with its tiny manipulators. I increased the power to the 'bot's travel fans and pushed it hard against him so that his fur twisted into the fans. He shrieked as he twisted and turned, trying fruitlessly to reach around to his back to remove this aggravating attacker.

While he was distracted I jumped to a couple of more 'bots in turn and had them activate their magnetic grapples and self-navigate toward the roaring mountain of orange fur in the center of the room. I jumped to a third 'bot, another heavy duty EVA model like the one that had gotten Fritz. I activated its magnetic grapples and started it walking across the ceiling toward Slave Master.

I jumped to the light duty EVA 'bot that was closest to Slave Master. "Here I am, Slave of Humans." He turned to face the new attacker.

I jumped to a 'bot on the other side of him. "No! Here I am."

Jump again. "No, over here."

Slave Master was a whirling mass of confusion. He kept turning to face my voice, but whenever he did, I changed positions. And all the while, the crowd of 'bots was walking toward him on the floor and on the ceiling.

I jumped to the closest one, deactivated its magnetic grapples and with a twitch of my legs jumped the 'bot directly onto Slave Master's chest. I grabbed hold of his thick fur with the 'bot's manipulators.

I jumped over to the IVA 'bot that was riding his back. I selected a drilling tool and howled my blood lust as I pressed the spinning drill against Slave Master.

He screamed in pain as it penetrated his skin. The agonized sound was surprisingly human and sent shock waves through my mind.

My actions horrified me. What kind of monster had I become? Then my mind flashed a memory of the sounds the Command Deck crew had made when they died and my doubts and fears became unimportant. I thought of all the people the kzinti had killed and would kill if they got the chance. I knew that I had to do for them what they could not do for themselves. I knew my actions would be as horrifying to my friends as anything the kzinti had done, but I forced that thought from my head as I did what I had to do.

By now Slave Master was a mass of bloody fur. Balls

of his purple-red blood were drifting around the ready room looking like small purple planets. When those quivering spheres hit the walls they spread out like crimson amoebas. A thin film of kzinti blood that looked almost orange covered the walls of the ready room.

Slave Master twisted and squirmed as he fought his attackers but for every 'bot he removed from his body I got another one attached to him. I would have felt sorry for him, but I remembered Sara and Jennifer and Nathan and Joel and all the others. Pity was something that didn't apply to the kzinti. I activated more 'bots.

He never knew which 'bots were running autonomously and which ones were under my direction. He could kill individual 'bots but there were always more and he couldn't get to me. He screamed in anger or frustration or maybe pain. I know it wasn't fear. You had to give him credit for that.

The heavy duty 'bot had finished its trek across the ceiling and was standing directly above Slave Master. I jumped to this new 'bot and routed my voice feed to it. I activated its cutting laser, which could only be focused on objects a few meters in front of it. Any farther and the beam was automatically defocused.

Slave Master was a bit farther away than desirable, but close enough for what needed to be done. I centered the laser's aiming reticule on his forehead. Give it a second or two for the pattern recognition circuits to cut in and the laser would automatically stay focused on him as long as he stayed in range.

"Slave Master," my voice echoed from above him with what I realized was a parting gift for his dignity. He looked up. "This is for Sara and everyone else."

I fired the laser. A hole opened in his forehead and the light from the cutting laser passed through him, burning a smoldering hole in the floor. His body jerked and began a slow rigid tumble through the air of the

Cargo Lock Ready Room, now nothing more than a lifeless relic from mankind's first contact with outsiders.

I floated in an empty coffin in the chill air of the coldsleep chamber with wires and cables for my VR equipment running out through the partially closed hatch of the coffin. I wondered if Sara would appreciate the gesture.

Soon it would be time to recover Tom from the airlock. To let him know that the danger was gone and that he was safe. (But would he ever feel really safe having me around, knowing what he had turned me into?) And then it would be time to thaw the remaining people from coldsleep so we could make our way into a different future than the one we had been expecting.

But before I could feel safe I had to have another look at the kzinti warship. To make sure that it was really dead. I selected an exterior VR view and zoomed my perspective over to the kzinti ship. It was lifeless and dark. I knew that nothing alive could be found there anymore. Yes, the fight was really over and mankind had won this round.

But now that the nightmare was over I wondered what would become of us. Now that our dreams had been stolen by an enemy who wanted to rip our hearts out and have us for dinner. I knew what I had become and that the 'docs could fix me. Just as I knew they shouldn't.

I gazed at stars that were no longer pinpoints of light promising the joy of newly discovered knowledge. Each hid a potential enemy. I feared that some would make the kzinti look like docile house cats. In any case, this was the end of a peaceful and tame humanity. For some there still might be a measure of peace and tranquillity, but not for myself or the others like me. Not for the ones selected by nature to be the warriors protecting the rest of humanity.

Element by element I turned off the VR display. I watched as the neon blue electromagnetic field lines from the Bussard ramscoop and the yellow hydrogen flux density contours vanished. Then the synthesized image of *Obler's Paradox* and the kzinti warship disappeared, leaving only the stars. Staring at what was left of the VR display all I saw were the hard points of light from a million stars. And all I felt was stark white cold.